CHRIST

She has everythi ...
beauty . . . passion . . .
ality so exquisite it has made her a legend.
Men and women alike are easy victims to her
charms. Adventure and romance are part of
her daily life. What more could she possibly
need?

Love. Of course. Love has claimed the ever-
desirable, ever-desirous Christina. She who
has been with the world's most dazzling
men, who has taught and been taught by the
greatest lovers in every corner of the world,
is in love. There is only one small problem:
her love has vanished—and to find him
again our plucky, lickerish heroine must
journey to some of the most remote corners
of the world, where new erotic mysteries and
titillations await her. For Christina may be a
woman in love—but she is still a woman.
And what a woman . . .

*Also published in Arrow
by Blakely St James:*

CHRISTINA'S CONFESSIONS
CHRISTINA'S PARADISE

CHRISTINA'S NEED

Blakely St James

ARROW BOOKS

Arrow Books Limited
17-21 Conway Street, London W1P 6JD

An imprint of the Hutchinson Publishing Group

London Melbourne Sydney Auckland
Johannesburg and agencies throughout
the world

First published in Great Britain 1985

© Blakely St James 1983

Printed and bound in Great Britain by
Anchor Brendon Limited, Tiptree, Essex

ISBN 0 09 936470 0

CHAPTER ONE

There is something about Eastern mysticism that has always fascinated me. I'm a pushover, I guess, for anything ornate, anything baroque, anything that celebrates life in all its gaudy detail. So when Xavier called me from Los Angeles to invite me to the Hare Krishna Festival of the Chariots, I reacted as I might have to an obscene phone call from Roger Vadim: with a gush of sensual enthusiasm that I could not have hidden if I had wanted to.

"You really should come, Christina," Xavier's clear tenor voice cajoled me. "With your taste in male tonnage, a parade of bull elephants ought to be right up your alley."

"Besides," I said, ignoring the raunchy undertones that I had come to expect from Xavier, "it'll give the Krishnas a chance to atone for all that miserable pandering they do at major airports."

We both laughed—it's an old friendship, Xavier's and mine, one that dates back to the days when I was little more than a rich man's daughter.

"So you'll be there?" he said.

"With bells on."

1

"How appropriate," he said drily. "And don't forget your roller skates."

Two days later I was comfortably ensconced in Xavier's beachfront penthouse, with its marvelous view not only of the Pacific, but of the Marina del Rey channel and its seemingly endless parade of sailboats. Xavier had invited a few close friends, taking care as always to mix professions, backgrounds, and countries of origin the way a fine chef mixes spices. Dr. Silvia Carlsson of Goteborg, perhaps the world's foremost expert on industrial pollution and a Nobel Prize winner twice over, was there, and she was counterpointed by John Bel Geddes, President of Pantheon Oil; while Tai Kwan Do master Claudio Gallardo of Uruguay argued the fine points of his craft with Louisa Chen, producer of fifty-eight karate movies and demonstrably the most successful filmmaker in Hollywood.

I must admit we made a striking party as we strolled along the strip of asphalt which bordered the beach and which Xavier insisted on calling a "boardwalk." Louisa was wearing a traditional silk outfit that had been in her family for twelve generations, while Silvia and I had chosen hand-painted adaptations of tea dresses from the royal families of the Tsaidam Basin—hers had a dragon motif, and mine a floral pattern inspired by the gardens of Mang-yai. The fact that the Krishna festival was based on an Indian holiday that had nothing whatsoever to do with China mattered as little to us as the fact that all the women in our party were taller than all the men.

The festival itself turned out to be everything Xavier had promised. Several dozen elephants promenaded down the "boardwalk," dressed in mirrored trappings which seemed to reflect the gaudy banners under which they passed. Krishna riders with topknots streaming comically in the stiff ocean breeze guided the elephants to a grassy area, where tents and booths had been set up in imitation of the Feast of Ramadan. Brentwood lawyers in Sperry Topsiders mixed with the artists and sixties leftovers who are the main inhabitants of Venice Beach, and these two groups in turn vied for space in the free food lines with the bums and winos for whom the festival was a serious source of nutrition.

The Krishnas were feeding everyone. A few plates of their charity passed under my nose, and the aroma of holy poverty was enough to make me want to stop eating for a month. I was far more interested in the stage that had been set up in the middle of the park, and in the several dozen glassy-eyed Krishnas on it who were chanting and occasionally jumping up and down in unconscious imitation of Bessie Griffin and the Gospel Pearls. I had to admit it: The power of the chant was entirely real, and, though the Krishnas did not know it, their orgy of the spirit was being translated in my body into an undeniable and equally powerful desire for an orgy of the flesh.

I could *feel* the chant, feel it as a palpable pressure in my belly, as a spider with a thousand legs dancing down my spine. I had not made love in several days— Xavier prefers the attentions of men, while Gallardo and Bel Geddes were habitual abstainers, each for his own reasons—and now my body was responding to the chant as if it were a lover, taking the insistent sound inside me as if it were a strident, rock-hard penis, letting it ply my soft insides with the sweet massage of the paramour. My fingers lay resting along the outsides of my thighs, and it was only with the greatest effort that I kept them still, kept them from attacking the already tingling flanges of my overwrought pussy.

Unconsciously, I closed my eyes and groaned out my

desire. The chant, the bells, the mass of raw emotion in the voices of the singers, even the wind from the Pacific, were combining to become what amounted to a symphony of lust, and my body was being played like some exotic instrument, like a magic lute that a Hindu god might use to arouse his priestess to a fever of immaculate yearning. I floated in my imagination to the palaces of Panjim, where a swarthy prince brushed his practiced lips over the stiffening tips of my breasts; and then onto the caves of Malabar, where a bandit chieftain ravaged my aching cunt from behind.

Soon it would be too much, I knew. If I didn't escape the throbbing power of the chant I would in a matter of minutes be straddling some open-mouthed hippie while the matrons of Krishna went screaming for the police. I had to get away, to calm the swelling urges in my loins, and perhaps, if I were lucky, to find some real satisfaction in the arms of a man of bone and blood.

I practically ran from the festival, from the maddening echoes of the chant, knowing that Xavier would understand my sudden disappearance and even wish me well. Xavier knew me better than anyone in the world and would know the effect that such a powerful experience would have on me. In fact, many times it had been Xavier himself who had discreetly provided me with a lover to calm my raging body, to still the sensual trembling that even the slightest emotion could cause in me.

In my frustration and my desire for something immediate in the way of release, I rented a pair of roller skates and roared off at top speed down the boardwalk. I had been an excellent skater as a girl, and the soothing, graceful motion of speed skating came back to me almost instantly, so that I was able to power through the crowds without touching anyone with anything more than my passing breeze. The faster I went the cooler and more manageable became the flame in my burning body, so that by the time I reached the row of outdoor bistros at the far end of the boardwalk I was ready to relax and enjoy the interesting (though asexual) entertainments that Venice Beach has to offer.

Scarcely out of breath, I stopped at one of the sidewalk cafés and ordered tea and *beignets* while I watched a pair of satin-bedecked, bell-draped folk singers wailing in a language that could have been Iroquois but was probably some patois from an album of the Holy Modal Rounders. An eight-year-old girl rode by on a unicycle, nearly running over a withered Jewish lady who was talking to a roller skater dressed in a Batman costume. The spirit of festival inspired by the Krishnas had brought out the circus performer in everyone, it seemed, and now that my desires had been squelched—for the time being, at least—I was quite content simply to watch the impromptu parade and pretend that it was all being staged for my personal amusement.

After a time my eye began to drift down the boardwalk, scanning absently along the rows of proffered oil paintings and Balinese basketry until it lit on a spot some twenty yards away where a large crowd was beginning to gather. The wall of people that had been drawn to the spot prevented me from seeing what the attraction was, but my curiosity was piqued, and I could not have avoided becoming part of that crowd even if I had wanted to. I've thought about it many times since—how radically my life was changed by that purely chance attraction, how, had I been anywhere else among the infinite number of other places there were to be at that moment the warp of my existence would have taken on an entirely different texture and direction. But such speculations, charming and piquant though they may be, are in the end entirely useless. Things happen because they happen, that's all.

Go back far enough in time and kill a butterfly, and you change the entire history of the world.

I paid my check and walked slowly down the boardwalk to the spot where the crowd had gathered. The ring of people by this time stood about three deep, so at first all I could see was an occasional blur and flash of white in the center. As I sought a better vantage point by means of demure little stabs of my elbow, the crowd began to part for me, first grudgingly, then graciously. (It's hard not to notice the extra courtesy that physical attractiveness seems to inspire in people who are ordinarily quite surly.)

By the time I reached the inner row of watchers I could see what it was that had drawn them so inexorably. It—he, I should say, for the masculinity flared from his body like a firestorm from the surface of the sun—was a mime, a man dressed quite simply in a black dancer's body suit and with only the barest suggestion of the white facial makeup that creates the mime's artificial pallor.

I will never forget that first glimpse of Paul, even though my mind is now like a photo album replete with images of him in various past attitudes and arrangements. He was simply and without doubt the most alarmingly gorgeous man I had ever seen, and this despite the fact that my personal treasury of men holds some of the world's most dazzling heartbreakers. But none of the devastatingly good-looking men I had known up to then had Paul's magnificent *integration*, that smooth flow of physical unity that submerged the beauty of each individual part, each rippling muscle, into a whole so glorious that the body became a river, or a graceful ribbon of waterfall plunging from peak to pool.

But I must admit it—my thoughts at that first moment were anything but poetic. I was hypnotized, yes, by his sheer physical presence, but the part of me that was already under his spell was definitely located below the waist. The minute I saw Paul—and he was at that moment in repose, gathering his forces of concentration for the beginning of his next routine—a jolt of purely sexual energy tore through my body, and the insides of my thighs were almost instantly salved by the first creamy signs of my prurient interest. The only thing coherent in the way of thought that I could muster at the moment was "I'm going to come just looking at this man."

Then, to make matters worse, he started to move, although *move* is an entirely inadequate word to describe what Paul really did. He moved the way the hands of a watch move, or the way a flower opens: imperceptibly, as if his body had somehow learned how to slow down the currents of the brain, the very junctions between nerve and muscle. One would have needed time-lapse photography to prove that he had moved at all, and yet what he did left a suggestion in the brain of the viewer, a sort of slow-motion streak across the back of the eyes like a diaphanous trail left by a jet that crawls through the sky at 40,000 feet.

Paul's routine, it soon became apparent, had to do with nothing less than being born, with the silent majesty of life's first great *stretch*. It was at the end of that stretch, during which he made all of us believe that he had completed the growth of a lifetime in no more than about seven seconds, that our eyes met for the first time, and the randy energy that was still coursing through my body was obviously transmitted directly to him. I knew it happened; I could see his eyes register my unmistakable message of desire and transmit it in turn to wherever he filed such things for future reference, and yet he did not miss even the tiniest of beats in his routine. He continued with the slow-motion extension of his body that seemed to signify the growth of us all, stretched and literally grew before our eyes until we all could have sworn he was at least eight feet tall. At that point he suddenly switched to a high-speed motion, leaped into the air, and popped an imaginary basketball through an imaginary hoop with a strong and graceful slam dunk.

This move was equivalent to the hypnotist's snap of the finger, and the crowd awoke with a collective and delighted laugh. Paul swooped into a low bow amid the generous applause, bringing to my mind the image of a medieval master proudly faking an attitude of submission to the court.

When he finally raised his head again, his dark blue eyes caught mine for a fraction of an instant, and he in turn released what I now know was only a small sample of his own churning sexual energy. He allowed the corners of his mouth to rise slightly in an almost imperceptible smile, then quickly turned his attention back to the mass of his audience. But my eyes had seen, and my body had read the message in that smile, and a knot of anticipation began to form in my chest, which was heaving as if we had already made love for three days running.

Paul now asked for requests from the audience, eager to prove his ability in the highest practice of any art: improvisation. I could not have kept quiet under threat of injury.

"Spread yourself on a piece of toast," I said.

He knew, of course. He knew that I was asking him

to spread himself, not like butter on a piece of bread, but like a smooth, slick oil over the contours of my burning body. He understood instantly, and took up the challenge of my invitation with easy confidence. His body literally dissolved before my eyes (I was by then quite unaware of the presence of the crowd), spreading into a form that managed to be almost entirely amorphous yet throbbingly muscular at the same time. His "bread" (the ground) and my body became one—he was as aware of it as I—and I could almost feel him pouring himself over me, onto me, into me, suffusing me with the hot lotion of his glorious sex.

Almost.

By the time he had finished I would have gone with him anywhere. If he had no place to go, I would have made love to him there on the asphalt, in the very heart of the crowded festival. I would have offered my body as public testimony to his skill, as a sheath in which to place the sword of his essence, as an urn for the oil of his steamy masculinity.

Luckily, no such public display on my part was necessary. Paul used the butter-on-toast routine as an excuse to end his show (prematurely, no doubt, as his interest had obviously made him as impatient as I was), thanked the crowd politely for the donations that fell like rain into his hat, walked over to me, and without the slightest hesitation took my hand.

"Paul Bayard," he said simply. (As if I cared! His smile was already causing delightful little stirrings in my abdomen.)

"Christina van Bell," I managed.

"Uh-oh," he said, that wonderful smile vanishing momentarily.

"Can't even get past the introductions without problems these days," I said, recovering myself somewhat. "What's the matter?"

"Two-word last names make me uncomfortable," he said, beginning to look a little sheepish. "The 'van' probably translates as 'millionaire's daughter,' and the 'Bell' as 'hands off.' "

"You've already had your hand on me for at least thirty seconds," I said. "Do you hear me complaining?"

He looked down and raised his eyebrows as he realized that he had not yet let go of my hand. Embarrassed, he let it fall loosely from mine. I grabbed it back immediately.

"You can't get out of this now," I said, wondering if he would be the type to be scared off by an aggressive woman. But already I was finding myself unable to stand being out of physical contact with him, and I knew that caution was going to get me absolutely nowhere.

I was relieved to see his beautiful smile return. "I wonder if I'll ever want to," he said in a voice so low I could scarcely hear him.

But hear him I did, and it was all I needed. We both realized, I think, that all the pertinent decisions had been made during those first few meetings of our eyes, that now—for today, at least—there was very little left for us to do outside of pure consummation. The touch of his hand in mine was sending frantic little messages screaming through my nervous system, and that interlocking of hands, so innocent in appearance to any outsider, was quickly becoming a terribly exciting form of foreplay.

We turned, still holding hands, and began to walk up the boardwalk, our direction carrying us away from the main flow of the festival. I was not in the least concerned about Xavier and the rest of our party—he knew me well enough not to worry about such inconsequential items as sudden disappearances. Besides, the little strokings of Paul's sensitive fingertips along the palm of my hand were already driving me crazy with desire, and I knew that no mere social obligation was going to prevent my seeing this thing with Paul through to the finish.

"Where are we going?" I whispered, feeling the butterflies of sensation stirring ever more rapidly in my insides.

"To my place," he said simply. "To dance."

He didn't need to say much more. "His place" turned out to be a concrete-and-dry-wall studio on one of the charming little court streets off the boardwalk. It was immense, and brilliantly white, and absolutely unadorned, giving the impression that it served as some kind of temple to its tenant. And once we were well inside, I understood that that was precisely what the place was: a temple. Not so much to Paul himself, but to the beauty inside him, which he had the good grace to realize was his only inasmuch as he had the privilege of choosing how to express it. It was as if he had left his place as bare as possible so that his living space would not pose any sort of distraction to the great business of his life, which was to turn silent movement into its own form of music.

There was a bed in one corner of the enormous room, a box spring and mattress supported by an arrangement of pipes that was obviously homemade, that could have easily looked salvage-yard tacky, but that with Paul's touch could pass very easily for the state of the art in high-tech interior design. He led me over to it without a word, and we sat down on the edge. My heart was pounding like a jackhammer, and I could feel my pussy-lips rubbing softly against one another through the silky juices of my ever-growing excitement.

"Is this the dance floor?" I said, looking deeply into his eyes and placing one of his hands gently on my throbbing breast.

"This is a cage," he said. "If you want true release, you have to start in a cage."

With that he began to slowly unbutton my blouse, taking each button like a trophy, with sure, practiced hands and at a measured pace. His deliberateness was already driving me wild, and in my anxiousness I punctuated each little space between unbuttonings with delicate little nibbles at the nape of his neck. Our knees were touching as we sat facing each other on the edge of the bed, and I could feel a hot current of sensation arcing across them. I fought a growing urge to simply plaster myself against him, to grab his rock-hard cock in my fingers and plow it into my dilating cunt, to pounce on it and wring the juice from it and leave him there in his "cage," sapped and quiescent. I fought the urge because I knew that Paul's way was better, that his delicate teasings and careful probings would inspire in me a slow-growing chain reaction that would ultimately explode in a rapture of fusion, would ultimately drive me screaming to that place deep inside me that was the source of all sensation.

By now Paul had unbuttoned my blouse down to my waist, and the shock of cool air hitting the surface of my tingling breasts made it seem as though Paul himself had a thousand fingers. Yet he had still not actually touched me. With my bare breasts now exposed—I never wear a bra, and take all warnings about sagging breasts in middle age as a sign of jealousy from the bra-bound—he began to blow ever so gently on them, little circular breezes that circumscribed the two deep pink aureolae and that made my nipples spike and harden as if reaching out for the maddening touch of his fingertips.

"Oh, God!" I moaned, throwing my head back so as to expose the full length of my throat and chest to him, so as to invite him to further and ever more tantalizing meanderings. He responded by tracing a trail of cool breath along the river of my neck, down the valley between my pliant, heaving breasts. He finally made his breath climb the peaks of the breasts themselves, stirring them, making the nipples stand up like flags of conquest, alive now to the thrilling sensations created by the gentle windstorm of his breath.

"Oh, Paul! Sweet Paul!" I moaned again. "You're driving me crazy! I must have you, Paul!"

"You will," he murmured, pausing briefly as he trailed his breath down a scintillating path to my navel. "When we're both ready."

"I've been ready since the minute I saw you," I breathed. Inside I was screaming, *Fuck me! Please, oh God, please fuck me! Fill me with your wonderful cock! Let me turn on it, let me hide it, let me take it up inside me and polish it until it gleams!*

Somehow I controlled myself, even though the feelings raging through my overwrought body were rapidly becoming all but uncontrollable. It was as if I had swallowed the sea itself, and now the mad ebb and flow of its surging tide was making my breasts rise and fall in a symphony of longing, turning the distended pink nipples into the foaming crests of breaking waves, rushing to crush themselves against the hard male touch of the waiting shore.

But Paul continued to play me like a bamboo flute, his breath continuing to suggest what his fingers, and ultimately his cock, could do. I shrugged my blouse from my shoulders impatiently, almost petulantly, and

lay down across his gleaming bed. He did not follow
me down for the moment—again I screamed inside:
Oh, Paul! Surround me! Bathe me with your body!
—but simply bent over me, tracing and retracing with
his breath the route that already had my breasts and
belly on fire with yearning.

Then suddenly, in one deft move Paul reached up
behind my undulating ass and swiftly pulled my skirt
down below my knees. I kicked it off my ankles and
arched my back so as to give him ready access to my
panties. But instead of responding immediately to my
cue, he raised himself up off the bed, imitating the arc I
had already made of my body, and locked me in the
first real embrace we had yet had. His wiry strength
was somehow a surprise to me as he pulled me to him
(although I knew I should have expected it), and as I
ran my fingers through his thick blond hair, I felt as if
he were melding our bodies into one another with the
fiery pressure of his fingers on my back. We were a
twin rainbow, a set of perfect curves, and I felt that if
he did not make love to me soon I would tear myself
apart in an explosion of riotous color.

But as quickly as he had turned strong he turned
gentle again, letting me settle softly on my back against
the cool sheets. For an awful moment I was entirely out
of contact with him, a lack of contact that only served
to double my mounting desire and impatience.

"What's wrong?" I said, not daring to open my eyes
for fear of seeing him in the other corner of the room,
hastily putting on his clothes in an orgy of second
thoughts.

But his voice was soft in my ear. "Open your eyes,"
he whispered.

I did as he asked and saw to my pleasure that he was
now as naked as I, his glorious body hovering over me

like an angel of life. The combination of purity and sexual power that emanated from that body was something I shall never forget—and my mortal legs spread rapidly in sacred invitation to this god.

How I wanted him! I yearned inside to be plundered, skewered on the gorgeous rod of flesh that even now was thrusting forth from his belly! I wanted to feel the powerful ripple of his assault, feel the walls of my creamy pussy clench around him, feel him drive toward the completion that would mean an end to this sweet torture!

"Look at your body," he said softly.

I raised my head a bit and looked down, half expecting to see steam rising from the twin volcanoes of my breasts, or to find that he was somehow turning me to gold. I stared a straight line down my torso to the patch of curly hair that crowned my vagina, and my eyes became like fingers as they plunged through the hair and down to the spot where the ridge of my labia was turning oily with my lust.

"Look at the shadows," he said, a bit more urgently.

Startled, I looked down again and saw immediately what it was that had drawn his attention. There were reed shades covering the window above his bed, and in front of the shades he had hung a single palm frond. With the afternoon light thus filtered, the shadows which lay across my body were themselves a topography of sex, a system of peaks and canyons that conformed almost perfectly to the vibrant contours of my breasts, the flat valley of my stomach, and the broad delta that led inexorably to the cavern of my longing.

Without further hesitation Paul began to explore the shadow lines with his fingers, tracing a delicate, lacy path along the lines made by the palm frond to encircle my breasts, then down the middle of the frond shadow with his fingernail, passing over my rippling belly, through the indentation of my navel, and down—slowly, maddeningly down—through the thatch of pubic hair to finally dip his finger in the honey of my sex and make a passing stroke along the throbbing ridge of my clitoris.

"Yes, Paul! *Yes!*" I hissed, by now quite beside myself with the electric fury that his touch generated in me.

He raised his dampened finger to his mouth and gave it a languorous lick. "Wonderful," he murmured. "Like ambrosia."

He then turned back to me and duplicated the tantalizing stroke, once again tracing the shadow patterns on my body with his marvelous fingers, leaving a trail of tingling heat as he ignited my body once more, and driving me to desperate thrashing on the bed as he stroked my clitoris again.

I could barely stand it. I was grinding my buttocks furiously into the bed, writhing and thrashing and throwing my head from side to side as an outlet for the tumultuous sexual energy that was gathering force, gathering charge, turning me into a windmill gone mad in a storm of passion. If I did not have him soon, I knew, if I did not have him stirring and thundering inside me, I would come involuntarily from sheer need and frustration, leaving us both unsatisfied.

"Now, Paul!" I practically screamed. "Take me now! I want you inside me! I want your wonderful cock filling me! Please, darling—take me now!"

"You want me now?" he said, breathing heavily as he once again passed his fingers along the shadow lines of my body. This time he lingered over my breasts, pulling gently at the nipples and rolling one, then the other between his thumb and forefinger (God, what delicious torture!) before skipping lightly down my belly to run a finger along my hardened clitty.

"Yes, Paul!" I cried. "Now, Paul! Please, don't lose me!" I was beside myself at the thought that I might pour my sweet juices over his finger, that I might have a premature orgasm without ever feeling the truth of his hardened penis inside me. Under most circumstances I'm quite willing to take my orgasms as they come, knowing with some inner patience that I'll eventually have my sex every way I want it. But with Paul I was hungry for more than just the sensation itself—I wanted to feel *him*, to have *him*, to know that there was something more essential about our lovemaking than a simple exchange of sensations.

I suppose I was already in love with him, although I would not have admitted it to myself at that point. All I could tell was that he was already more than just another in a long series of lovers (almost all of them excellent, by the way), more than just an instrument of satisfaction. There was something timeless and indefatigable about his sexual beauty, something that promised a fusion so pure, so complete, and so thrilling that it would have been a silly shame to waste it by coming too soon.

I had to have him inside me, and that was all there was to it!

I reached out and encircled the shaft of his cock with my fingers, feeling the wonderful warmth of it, a warmth that seemed to radiate down my arm until it filled my body with a sort of suffused glow. I let my fingers dance along the surface of it, let them caress the shining head, while with the other hand I reached up to flick my fingernails lightly along the sensitive underskin of his scrotum.

With that he came alive, shifting from the languorous

tempo of his previous strokings to a more insistent, stronger touch. Whereas before he had simply been content to brush and fondle my nipples with his fingertips, he now sank his mouth onto them and sucked greedily, hungrily, pausing occasionally to roll them between tongue and teeth.

Now it was as if we were wired together in the same circuit, passing a sexual current that now belonged to both of us equally along inner channels that could no longer be identified as purely mine or purely his. Each pull of his mouth on my nipples made me tighten my clenching grip on his cock-shaft; each tiny bite brought another flick of my fingernails along the surface of his balls. We were playing each other now, a lustful duet that was steadily building up a rolling power as we teased and touched each other, fingered and bit, stirring our loins and our mutual desire until we had built each other to a boiling passion.

My hand began to pump madly up and down the hot flesh of his prick as my fingers kneaded and caressed his brimming testicles. At the same time, his finger rubbed ever more maddeningly along the sensitive edge of my clitty, driving me berserk with need for him. Already I could feel the first stirrings in the deep inner wellspring of my flesh, could feel the first sparks of my internal explosion dancing in the depths of my belly, and I knew there was no more time for this teasing foreplay.

I had to have his perfect cock inside me, deep inside me, plowing new furrows in the soft, yielding flesh of my cunt! I had to feel him filling me, pressing my pussy walls out, pushing, driving, searing me with the hot skin of his passion!

"Paul!" I yelled in desperation. "Fuck me! It's got

to be now, darling, before it's too late! I'm on fire for you, Paul! Please, fuck me now!''

This time I gave him no chance to respond, no chance to invent some new and artful way to tease me to distraction. With one hand firmly wrapped around the base of his cock, I reached around behind him, placed my other hand on the firm muscles of his ass, and pushed him toward me. I continued to push as I guided his cock with my other hand, until the soft purple flesh of the tip rested against the tingling skin of my outer labia. My pussy-lips seemed to come alive, parting slightly and nibbling at the flesh of his cock head as if they had a mind of their own, as the hot cream of my desire bathed him and invited him further.

By this time he needed no prompting. My desperate impatience had been transmitted to Paul, and after a first few exploratory thrusts, he drove his wonderful penis straight into the depths of my hungry vagina with a smooth, powerful stroke; pushing the full length of it up inside my hot channel, rippling the walls of flesh before it as it came.

I sucked in my breath, too overcome with the unspeakable pleasure of his entry to even let out so much as a gasp. I felt his strident cock come to rest with the head nearly touching my cervix, and groaned in ecstasy as the inner walls of my vagina closed tightly, maddeningly around it. When I finally let out my breath, the accompanying groan sounded like a chord played simultaneously by a cello and the deep bass end of a pipe organ, a sound that belonged more to a primitive animal of the Pleistocene than to a civilized and presumably sophisticated woman.

"My Paul," I finally managed to say. *"You feel so perfect inside me, darling."*

"You're so beautiful," he said in a voice that sounded

almost like a lament. "One hundred percent beautiful, right down to the core."

And it was at the very core of my being that Paul was continuing to play out the adagio of his song of passion. He now began to move the lovely rod of flesh that was imbedded in me, to move it back and forth in smooth, abbreviated strokes, stirring my insides as he moved with delicious confidence in the deep and mysterious *within* of my body. My pussy was on fire with his artful penetration, and the little stirrings in my belly were becoming more pronounced, more insistent, setting up a demanding rhythm that was a perfect counterpoint to Paul's unrelenting movement.

I spread my legs as wide as I possibly could and pulled my knees up under my chin to allow him unimpeded access to the plain of my vagina. With a groan, he immediately slid further inside me, until I could simultaneously feel his cock reach its maximum depth inside me and his abdomen make contact with the now fully exposed flanges of my aching cunt.

What a sensation! It was as if I had only been half a person up to then, and that now, with Paul's magnificent prick filling me and his smooth flesh pressing against my tingling clitoris, I was whole, a complete woman with all circuits connected and all voids filled. At the same time I was being driven mad with yearning for the only form of fulfillment more complete than that I was already experiencing.

"*Oh!*" I cried out as Paul began to move inside me with ever deeper strokes.

"*Oh!*" I cried again in rhythm with his plunging cock.

"*Oh!*" I groaned as the sparks in my belly rose higher, as my inner temperature continued to soar and my cunt flared in and out around his penis like a bellows gone mad.

"Oh!"

"Oh!"

"Oh!"

I had taken leave of myself. The colors of the day, the rich brightness of the festival, the magnificent flow of Paul's mime routine, the white heat of his attention, now merged with the incessant rhythm of his thundering body to transport me through a whirl of time, space, and sensation. The flame inside me roared ever higher as he plunged back and forth, the strength of his heaves matched by my own thrusting hips as they rushed to meet him.

And all the while the sensation in my burning belly continued to grow, from the nagging tickle it had been in the beginning to what now amounted to a soaring fountain, a cascade of pure feeling that threatened to silence me, drown me in the power of its release. I was beside myself with longing for that release, and as it finally washed over me I screamed out my gratitude:

"Oh! Oh my God! Yes, Paul, yes! Oh, my gorgeous lover!"

I had never experienced such a powerful climax. It seemed to drive my very being out through every pore in my body, until my soul turned to vapor and passed harmlessly out to mix with the steamy air of Paul's studio. At the same time, Paul was gasping out his own climax, an explosion of breath that seemed to bathe me in the glory of his exertion. I opened my eyes just in time to see the look of pure, transcendent ecstasy on his face, then closed them again as I welcomed his collapse into my open arms.

Later, when we awoke, the first thing I saw was the shadow of sunset lying across our bodies, the lines made by the window shades now highlighted by the deep red trails left on our bodies by the dying sun.

CHAPTER TWO

I was in love with Paul, of course. I say "of course" because that's how it felt to me: natural, honest, and so inevitable that it hardly seemed worth talking about. But my friends were nowhere near so matter of fact about it. They behaved as if some tiny, previously undetected flaw in my makeup had suddenly opened up to become an emotional chasm as deep and as dangerous as the San Andreas Fault.

"I can't believe it," was Xavier's first comment when I told him. "Have you gone batty?"

"No battier than usual," I said. "Besides, darling, everyone should fall in love once in a while."

"You've confused love with multiple orgasm," he said, shaking his head with a bitterness that I found quite surprising. "If three means love, then I suppose at five you get married and move to the suburbs."

"I have no such plans, and I haven't bothered to count the orgasms," I said, and walked out without another word.

Xavier's attitude—which was mirrored by that of the great majority of my friends—disturbed me at first, but only momentarily. I was quite simply too happy with my newborn love to have my bubble burst by something as trivial as other people's opinions.

And we *were* happy. I underline it now because it was a happiness so short lived as to make one wonder if it had ever existed at all. But it was real enough then, in those first few months, as we explored one another's spirits and minds and found them just as delightfully suited to each other as our bodies proved to be.

I left my apartment on Park Avenue in New York (this alone flabbergasted Xavier, who had been used to my complaints about the slack-jawed mindlessness of the typical southern Californian) and moved into a crow's-nest apartment overlooking the canals of Venice, an apartment that had once belonged to Isadora Duncan. Paul continued to maintain his studio, but we in effect lived together in the little white perch of an apartment with its serene view of the Linnie Canal bridges.

I painted a great deal during those months, the first time I had been able to discipline myself along these lines since I had ended my girlhood in Vermont. The results were encouraging enough to make me think I could make a career of my art if everything else in my life suddenly evaporated. In the meantime Paul continued to develop his own art, which I always saw—and still do see—as the most difficult, time-consuming, and individual in the world.

His dedication was astounding. He would spend hours, even days, perfecting the simplest of mime movements— running his hands along an invisible wall, for example, or descending a set of imaginary stairs into an imaginary cellar. He had an intensity and an ability to concentrate that positively unnerved me at times; as if he could turn his senses of sight and sound on and off at will, and simply plunge into the heart of himself where he could be neither disturbed nor distracted. There were times when I swore he had stopped breathing entirely, so still could he stand and so great a control could he exert over what are supposed to be involuntary functions. It even seemed that he could halt the processes of metabolism itself, could say "yes" or "no" to the messages sent from brain to muscle; could, in effect, hibernate on his feet.

But as impressive as Paul's raw talent and his mental discipline were to me, I was even more impressed by his unswerving integrity. Talent is not specialized; it's a crude, undifferentiated force that can be channeled in almost any direction. Paul could have been a wonderful actor, or dancer, or comedian, all potentially more lucrative than mime, which most people (most Americans, at any rate) saw as a curiosity, a sort of circus-y activity that belonged in the same category with tightrope walking—at which Paul also excelled—and pinktutued ladies doing toe dances on horseback.

Paul knew all this, of course. He knew that had he chosen an easier, broader route he could easily have been a major star—on television, if nothing else. (God forbid that this should have come to pass.) But he was convinced that he could educate the public, could show them through his own performance that mime was the deepest, most universal form of drama that the world of the stage had to offer.

"I *know* it," he would say suddenly, as we lay in each other's arms after a sweet afternoon's lovemaking. "I *know* I can do it."

"Do what, darling?" I would murmur, rolling my spent body against the hard muscles of his chest.

"Take mime with me," he would say. "Right to the top."

"Of course you can, darling."

"What?" he would say, startled out of his reverie.

At such times I think he truly forgot my existence, so feverish was he in his devotion to what he saw as his life's goal.

"Never mind," I would say, and slide my lips down the length of his gorgeous torso until I enveloped his freshly stirring cock in my soft lips.

It seemed I could never quite get enough of the man. As lush and as powerful and as ultimately satisfying as our lovemaking was, there was something about his body, about the essence of his maleness, that stirred my own sexuality as no one had before. We would screw each other until we nearly dissolved in a pool of sweat and cum, and still I could not keep my hands to myself—I *had* to be touching him, fondling him, fanning the flame in him until his proud cock stood ready once more to plunder my almost insatiable pussy.

There were times when something as simple and as seemingly innocent as a kiss, or even a slight brushing of the hands, would lead to a session of roaring sex that could last hours, days, in some instances. Some button had been pushed deep inside each of us, some central force had been activated, and it sometimes seemed that we were truly alive only when he was inside of me, when our bodies were melded in a fusion of the flesh, when we were screaming out our climaxes as inauguration to a deep new morning of love.

During those first few ecstatic months there was only this, only the lovemaking and the labor of love, the Siamese twins of art and romance joined at the belly. What little time remained was for the mandatory: eating, sleeping, and dealing with the nagging demands of the world at large. We saw few friends (my friends, it seemed, had, for the moment, deserted me entirely, while Paul was quite content to live almost entirely without friends of his own), went to few shows, took absolutely no vacations, wrote no letters home. We were an island, glad of our isolation, knowing it only served to increase the intensity of our feelings for one another. The rest of the world now seemed pallid, colorless, as if we were draining it of its sap to feed the hungry fibers of our love.

But in fact the world was still there, and Paul especially was forced to continue to deal with it. For me, of course, money from my ownership of *World* magazine continued to pile up automatically in my bank account, gathering dust and interest as I continued to simplify my economic needs. The truth was that I had little need for work, and less desire. But Paul still went out to auditions several times a week, concentrating purposely on the sort of small, arty club whose audience could appreciate his astounding skill in mime; he avoided agents, the Screen Actors Guild, anything that smacked of equity.

He got a few jobs that way, by answering small, self-conscious ads in *Dramalogue* and the *Casting News,* and occasionally by riding the coat tails of some better established acquaintance of his. These jobs—to Paul's everlasting credit, he never once called them "gigs"— were generally cameo appearances where a mime was needed for some idealistic little play in some struggling little playhouse, or for instructional showcases at one of the more arcane classes in the local drama schools. Paul was always genuinely happy to get these parts, and always touchingly earnest in his belief that each one was going to launch him on the path to stardom.

"Richard Lyon's going to be there," he would say, referring to the famous drama critic who had somehow been lassoed into attending a class called "The Unspoken Theatre" at UCLA. And when Richard Lyon was observed nodding off during the middle of Paul's performance, my lover would simply shrug it off as execrably bad taste on the critic's part and go buoyantly off to another audition.

I rarely went with him. Although I shared his unquenchable hope and his charming optimism, I had had too much close-hand experience of show business to want to expose myself to its heartlessness, especially when that heartlessness was directed at the man I loved. Rick Dempsey had been a lover of mine when I was eighteen, and through his eyes I had seen enough of the sordid cynicism of the star-making machine to last several lifetimes. Jason LaRue, the producer who still holds the record for money spent on an independent film—$45 million on *The War of the Roses*—was another of my paramours, and although he was extremely kind to me, I could see his personality take on a razor's edge as he slashed his way through the competition. Even Simonescu, the Rumanian ballet dancer who everyone hails as the new Nijinsky, had a hard and vicious streak that appeared simultaneously with each new promising understudy. So now I chose not to subject myself to the crushing indifference of a buying public that did not and could not understand the fierce power of Paul's art. I did not want to hear the "leave your phone number with Lydia"'s and the "we'll get back to you"'s that to Paul were hopeful signs of continued interest but to me were the kiss of death.

It was selfish of me, I suppose. I could have warned him, could have tried to make him realize how heartbreakingly difficult was the task he had taken on. I could even have used my influence, accomplished for him with a few quick phone calls (and perhaps a casual screw in some Malibu swimming pool) what he himself would never accomplish in two lifetimes of trying. But the reward would have been nothing more than a bit part for him in some yawning sitcom or perhaps some work as a mime-model in a service piece for *World*. And my help would have been particularly pointless because Paul would have refused the jobs anyway, and if he ever found out I raised even a finger on his behalf he would have been beside himself with fury.

So I held my peace, and tried to make up ever more creative excuses when he asked me to go with him to this audition or that showcase. I don't think he ever fully understood my reluctance—I made it a point never to tell him about my "exalted" past—but he seemed to explain it to himself as my wanting to stay out of his way, which was fine with me as long as it didn't trouble him too much.

One night, though, I simply ran out of excuses. He insisted, in his calm but steely way, that I go with him to a showcase at a famous improvisational club, the Whipping Boy. A number of unusually good, intelligent comedians had gotten a start there, and Paul was sure he had found a place where both the management and the audience would appreciate and understand him. He was so excited in his touchingly childlike way, so sure that his big break was staring him in the face, that I swallowed my well-founded reservations and went with him.

The room was too small, too dark, and too smoky, as such rooms tend to be, but I was glad of anything that would obscure my identity. I was mildly concerned about running into someone I knew ("God, Christina, what are *you* doing *here*?"), but I was much more worried that Paul would seek out my face at some unguarded moment during his performance and see the perhaps heartrending concern that I might well be unable to hide.

Luckily, neither of those things happened. Paul introduced me to the manager of the club, a thin, fey-looking man who had once taught at the Royal Academy of Drama. Despite myself, I was somewhat encouraged by his apparent devotion to classic art forms and by his air of rumpled pedagogy, and even found myself thinking, "Well, maybe this time there's really something to it."

Paul's performance was little short of magnificent. For once the audience seemed to sympathize with what he was doing, and it even appeared as if they understood what heroic effort it had taken Paul to perfect his routine. "Raise the level of your game," they say in tennis, and that's exactly what Paul did that night; he raised the level of his art until mime itself became something transcendent, and, with the urging of an appreciative audience, he nearly soared across the stage.

I was thrilled, not only with Paul himself and his performance, but with what seemed to be the genuine opportunity that was being afforded him. When I saw the manager beaming in my direction as Paul absorbed what must have been the first standing ovation of his career, I let my fears and my tempered cynicism slide away from me and exulted in Paul's momentary glory. "This just might be it," I kept thinking as I blew my lover little kisses from the darkness.

The illusion did not last long. I went to Paul's side as soon as he left the stage, and stood silently behind him as he accepted the congratulations of the crowd. Finally, the manager came over, his face split in an ear-to-ear grin.

"Well done, young man," he said in a gravelly voice as he took up a position next to me. "We should talk."

"I'd be glad to," Paul said. I could see he was

trying, without much success, to control his joy over what he had done.

It was just then, with the manager beaming and Paul nearly blushing with pride, that I realized it was all a sham. I felt the barest rustling at the top of my thigh, then the unmistakable sensation of a bony hand tentatively massaging my buttocks. Not wanting to embarrass Paul in his moment of apparent triumph, I looked surreptitiously behind me and traced the source of the hand up to its owner: the manager, of course.

So much for pedagogy. I brushed the hand lightly away and turned slightly, just in time to see him toss me a curious glance.

"When should we get together?" Paul asked him politely.

"Oh, soon, soon," the manager said. "Yes indeed. Very promising." All this time he was doing his best to knead the buttery flesh of my ass-cheeks with a hand that was surprisingly strong, as I continued to brush the hand away as quietly as I could. "We must have dinner some time. And bring the young lady." This last was said in an entirely different tone of voice, so that even Paul now understood what was going on.

I was amazed at his control. He simply said, "I understand," took my hand, and led me through the room and out of the club. He said absolutely nothing on the way home, although I knew he was burning with shame and indignation. But that night was a very quiet one in our bed, as Paul turned his face to the wall and tried to erase my existence. I understood, but at the same time I could not help feeling rather hurt. It had not been my fault, after all, yet here we were going through the first loveless night we had spent since the day we met.

Somehow it did not seem fair.

Happily, though, Paul's mood didn't last long. The next day he set to work on some secret project, banging away on a typewriter in the office he had made of poor Isadora's dining room, and when he stopped for the afternoon and came to me, it was with the same ardor and spirit as always. In fact, we had such a momumental screw that I completely forgot to ask him what the piece of work was that had inspired him so.

Whatever it was, he kept working at it for the next six weeks or so, slaving away in a fervor of intensity by day and letting off the excess emotion at night, with me. Finally he emerged from the dining room one afternoon, wiped his sweat-streaked face, smiled, and said, "It's done."

"What's done?" I asked innocently, knowing that six weeks of curiosity was about to be satisfied.

"My play," he said. "My vehicle."

So that was it. Apparently Paul had decided that his singular lack of success to that point had been due to the absence of a "vehicle," some piece of theater art that was custom-made for him and him alone, something that had value in itself, but that would also serve to spotlight his wonderful work in mime. The play, as he explained it to me, was set in New Orleans in the thirties, and involved a young mime who was obviously Paul himself.

"Would you like to help me with it?" he asked innocently.

In fact, I had done a bit of acting for fun (though modesty forbids me from going into too much detail here, the director I had worked with let me know in no uncertain terms that I had a star's career waiting for me if I chose to follow the profession, which I did not), and now I thought it might be a diversion to perform again in private, especially since I had my real-life lover as a leading man.

"All right," I said. "I'd love to, as a matter of fact."

"Good," Paul said. "Now, if you're going to help me, you must give me one hundred percent. You'll have to let your own personality just slide out of your body, and when you're completely empty let your body fill back up with the personality of Louisa."

He looked at me. His eyes were shining with the nearly vicious intensity that had attracted me to him in the first place. I felt that I could see behind his eyes, see his mind knotting up into a snarl. A feathery stirring began in my loins.

"Complete concentration," he said. "You ready?"

I nodded, closing my eyes as he began to speak, eager for this opportunity to take a psychic vacation, to become— even if only for a few moments—an entirely new person. Paul, I suspect, was feeling very much the same way.

"Think New Orleans," he began, his voice almost imperceptibly taking on the oily accent of that city. "The Vieux Carré. A little house on St. Peter Street."

Instantly the scene began to project itself on the screen of my mind. I saw the low, flat-topped buildings of the French Quarter, the lacy wrought-iron grillwork and the softening willow trees. I even imagined I could hear water lapping against the embankment along the quiet Mississippi.

"You're in the room on the second floor," Paul went on. "The shutters are open, but the curtains lie completely still. You feel the heat—it surrounds your body like an insistent lover. It *presses* on you; it's sultry and torpid and it touches you everywhere at once."

His voice now became the heat itself, and I could

feel it wrapping itself around me, caressing me, encouraging me by its sticky soft moistness. I began to rub my thighs together, smearing the insides of them with the perspiration that I knew was only a prelude to the flowing of my sex juices. I could feel the cartilage in my knees turning mushy with the power of my need. Unconsciously, I let out a low moan.

"That's it," Paul said, nodding his head gently, approvingly. "You feel the heat. It's beautiful, and it's unbearable. Your dress is a prison, but you know you can't escape it, at least not now."

"Why not?" I said playfully.

Paul frowned. "Because Lawrence is coming," he said.

I shifted restlessly in my dress, feeling the soft cotton jersey rub enticingly against my hardening nipples. Paul had done his job of scene-setting well—I *did* want to escape the confining garment. I wanted to let the heat come at me unimpeded, wanted to let it find the secret damp places of my desire. Most of all, I wanted Paul. I wanted to feel his hands roam over me, feel them defining the contours of my breasts, feel the soft palms sliding down over my sides to ride out along my hips. I wanted him to *touch* me, to probe and squeeze my aching body until it opened like a flower to the welcome invasion of his magnificent cock.

"You hear footsteps coming down the hall toward your room," Paul intoned. "Lawrence is here. You're glad he's come, but you're also terribly anxious about what will happen here this afternoon. After all, he has been behaving quite strangely lately, and you no longer feel as sure of him as you did before."

Paul went out of the room and opened the door without knocking. I stayed with my back to him, looking out the window and allowing my back to become stiff with the tension of the scene. I could almost feel his eyes boring into my body from behind.

"I hate that dress," Paul said softly. It was the first line of the scene, and it required nothing of me but to stand where I was and feel anxious.

He walked over to me, put his hand on my shoulder, and roughly spun me around to face him. The feel of his strong grip was like a heat massage to my already warm skin. His eyes were alive, almost fevered.

"I said I hate that dress," he said through clenched teeth. Immediately he reached out and grabbed the dress at the bodice, tearing it away from my breast with a violent motion. A fingernail scraped lightly along the side of my distended nipple, sending such a strong shock of delight running through my body that I could scarcely keep myself from tearing off the rest of the dress. My breast lay exposed through the tattered material, the nipple alive and stiff with excitement, pointing as if in invitation to his outstretched finger.

"Is that supposed to happen on stage?" I said mischievously, looking down at my torn dress and aching hard nipple. "You could get arrested, you know."

"Shut up," Paul muttered. "And stick with the script."

"But Paul," I said, "I don't have a line here."

He didn't answer. His eyes were glued to my protruding nipple, and I could see that a fine sweat had begun to break out along the sides of his nose. His finger was pointing straight at the rosy tip of my breast, which was still quivering with the aftereffects of his touch. It felt as if some sort of warm, spicy current was jumping the small arc from his fingertip to my nipple. My hand went up under my breast and pushed it out to him in offering, the little berry at the end of it fairly alive with the need to be flicked and caressed.

"It's your line, Paul," I murmured.

"Fuck it," he said. "Let's rewrite the play."

Immediately his finger moved the few inches through the charged air to land lightly on the head of my nipple. A hot, white thrill coursed through my aching body, and my overwrought pussy began at once to lubricate, spilling the warm, viscous fluid out over the cuntal lips to wash against the insides of my thighs. Paul moved his fingers around in tiny circles on the stiff bud of my nipple, occasionally teasing the underside of it with his fingernail. I was becoming so excited that my other nipple stiffened as if in sympathy, poking up from the end of my heaving breast like a small penis.

I looked down and saw a rising bulge in Paul's pants But like Louisa with her Lawrence, I was not sure enough of Paul's mood to indulge my impulse, which was to reach out immediately and cup my hand over the lovely tumescence of his cock. Instead I closed my eyes and parted my lips, thinking that I would have to go slowly, subtly, or I would scare him off.

How wrong I was, and how glad to be in error!

When he saw my other nipple stiffening of its own accord, Paul let out a low growl and clamped his mouth down on it. I could feel his soft lips moving up and down it, the tip of his tongue prodding it lightly and then withdrawing. I put both hands under my breasts, pushing the one against the palm of his hand and the other as far as it would go into his mouth. I *fed* him that breast, luxuriating in the sharp and delicious sensations provided by his lips, his teeth, his tongue; my mind and body now churned with the frenzy of my desire. My hips began to undulate of their own accord, moving in a suggestive little love dance as I took a step toward him. I had to have more contact, had to feel more of his gorgeous flesh rubbing up against me.

Unable to stand the continued separation of our bodies, I stepped into his arms. He let out another growl and encircled me, placing his hands on my weaving buttocks and pressing my lower body into his. The feel of his hardened cock against my belly made me want to forgo all further foreplay and stuff my burning hole full with his love-staff.

But I knew it would be in my best interests to stay within the boundaries of Paul's fantasy, so I encouraged him in the best Creole accent I could muster.

"Lawrence," I whispered, drawing the name out and letting my breath run cool along the edges of his ear. "I want you, Lawrence. I don't care about anything else. I want to feel you inside of me. I want to be full of you, I want your beautiful cock stirring in me." As I spoke I reached down between us and began to massage the palm of my hand up and down his thick staff.

He responded with a moan and a tightening of his hands on my buttocks. He began to knead them furiously, working his fingers up and down the nubile flesh, parting the cheeks and probing daintily with a finger. His breathing grew coarse and uneven, and the skin of his neck began to exude that randy smell that was like a clarion call to my excited nerves. He leaned back slightly so that the contact between his chest and my nipples became a light, teasing scraping as he moved his upper body from side to side. At the same time he began to flex his buttocks in and out, pushing his burgeoning cock that much more tightly up against my already throbbing mound of Venus.

"You want me, Louisa?" he whispered.

"I can't help myself," I groaned in return. "Help me, Lawrence! I'm on fire! Take me! Fuck me!"

"Yes," he breathed, panting hard. "I'm going to fuck you, Louisa. Just like all those other times. You're going to spread your legs, and I'm going to put my cock so far up inside your beautiful little cunt that you'll feel it tickle your ribs. Is that what you want, Louisa?''

"God, yes!" I moaned. His words stimulated me like so many fingers. I thrust my hips forward, beginning an up and down motion along the length of his wonderfully hard cock, feeling it part my willing vaginal lips through the material of my dress. Even through the barriers of our clothes my clitoris picked up the message, hardening and elongating as it rubbed up and down the full length of his massive rod.

Suddenly Paul broke the embrace. "More light," he muttered. "We've got to have more light. I've got to be able to *see* you." He went to each of the five windows in turn and rolled up the shades. The buttery afternoon light flooded into the room, and I could feel it bathe my aching body in its warm liquid glow. As with the sticky heat, I experienced the light as a series of hands exploring the soft topography of my breasts, my chest, my hot belly.

By this time I had entirely forsaken the personality of Christina. The light that was now caressing my body issued not from the Pacific but from the sun of the Gulf of Mexico; and I was Louisa, the errant Creole girl of New Orleans, now awash in the passion of my Lawrence. I looked at him. He had turned his back to the window and was standing facing me. His body was in shadow, the power of it mysteriously amplified by the vagueness of its features. The sun hit his hair from behind, illuminating it so that it became a fiery mantle. And all the while the heat poured in, the indolent, churning heat that now seemed to come from my lover.

Paul now began to take off his clothes, slowly unbuttoning his shirt and casting it to the floor. The muscles of his chest seemed to call to me from the soft shadow, and I longed to cross the room and place my hands on them. But where Laura would have done exactly that with no second thoughts, Louisa, the shy Southern girl, stayed exactly where she was, instinctively turning the control of the action over to her man.

Now he removed his pants, bending over slightly to step out of them one leg at a time. The doubling over of his torso in the shadow momentarily hid his cock from sight, but when he straightened up again it stood out proudly from his groin, so much so that the head of it escaped the shadow and gleamed in the rich light. So powerful was it, so full of his vital energy, that it actually seemed to fuck the very air in the room as he stood there. I ached to have it inside me.

"Come here, Louisa," he said softly.

I didn't need to be told twice. I crossed the room slowly, my head hanging slightly in a subservience that was entirely Louisa, a subservience that I myself would never have felt. But when I reached him and found myself staring down at the upraised head of his gorgeous prick, I suddenly lost all traces of recalcitrance.

I sank to my knees in front of him. His cock split the air before my eyes. My impulse was to sink it immediately into the very depths of my throat, to cup and pump at his balls until I squeezed him to orgasm. But I was Louisa, and I wanted to make the moment last. I stuck out my tongue an inch or so, letting the tip of it find and caress the little slit at the end of his cock. He immediately moaned and reached both hands down to stroke the sides of my face. I could feel his cock head twitching eagerly at the touch of my tongue.

"Yes, Louisa," he whispered. "Like that. I love to feel your tongue on me. Don't stop, darling."

Encouraged, I knelt down. I bit lower and ran my tongue from the very base of his cock slowly—oh, so slowly, lingering along the way to take tiny detours along the highways of purple veins—until I reached the head again. This time I didn't hesitate. I plunged my mouth onto it, feeling its rigid hardness slide past my soft lips, feeling the head of it lodge against the roof of my mouth. The sensation that rushed through me made me feel as if he had penetrated the entire length of my body, as if his cock had become a sort of second spine, an axis around which my body would gladly revolve.

I began to move my mouth up and down the length of his fleshy cock, feeling it throb in willing response. He moved his hands back from my face to tangle them in my hair, at the same time starting a slow pumping motion with his hips—not so much as to bruise the sensitive tissue of my mouth or to break the spell of softness cast by the golden sunlight and moist, erotic heat, but sweetly, gently, so that his cock became like a moving adjunct to my dampened mouth.

"That's it, Louisa," he panted. "Nice and slow. Nice and slow. I'm going to be inside you all afternoon, so there's no hurry. Mmm, yes. Yes, Louisa. I love to feel my cock in your sweet mouth."

As before, his words stimulated me to greater action. First I took his hands and cupped them lightly over my protruding breasts, moaning with delight as his palms made contact with the hard little berries of my nipples. Then I ran the tip of my middle finger along the seam of his scrotum, stopping at the end of the stroke to flick it playfully with my fingernail.

His response was unexpected. Instead of tightening his hands in my hair and urging me on to more and more delicious strokings, he seemed to freeze in his tracks. His hips stopped pumping and his grip on my hair loosened.

"Christina," he said, slipping out of character at the

same moment that his prick slipped out of my hungry mouth, "Christina, stop. There's someone watching us."

"Where?"

"In the apartment next door. He's got a pair of binoculars."

Under most circumstances my reaction would have been the same as Paul's. I would have stopped, not so much out of horror at being observed as an unwillingness to provide a snoopy neighbor with a free show. I have nothing in particular against voyeurism, having practiced it myself on many occasions, but I generally like the observing to be done only with the consent of the observed.

This time, however, I was too far gone to care. The heat, the hypnotic captivation of Paul's fantasy, and the delightful friction of his prick along my mouth and throat had dissolved what few scruples remained to me so far as voyeurism was concerned. In fact, I found the idea of being watched not only tolerable, but inexplicably stimulating.

"It's all right, darling," I murmured. "It's a play, isn't it? So now we've got our audience."

Apparently I had said exactly the right thing, either that or Paul himself was beginning to enjoy the idea of putting on a display for Mr. Binoculars. He grabbed me under my arms and lifted me to my feet. "Let's give him a real show," he whispered to me.

With one motion he neatly ripped away the rest of my dress, leaving me standing gloriously naked in the warm sunlight. I could imagine the hands holding the binoculars beginning to tremble as the rounded moons of my buttocks jumped into view, could imagine the peeper's prick beginning to throb and harden in his pants. This, in turn, excited me all the more, and I grabbed Paul's hand and placed it inside my dampened thighs so that two of his fingers rested against the entrance to my pussy. Immediately his fingers came alive, pressing and prodding at the lips to my pulsing vagina, finally parting them to run his index finger along the hardened ridge of my erect clitoris. My legs went weak with the thrill of his touch to my sensitive little node, and I shivered involuntarily. With Paul orchestrating my love-cord so beautifully, I felt like a violin in the hands of a Jascha Heifetz.

"Oh God, Paul," I moaned, no longer caring about Louisa and the fantasy, too ripe and excited to be anything but myself. *"I've got to have you! Take me, Paul! Fuck me, my beautiful lover!"*

I was too much in need to wait for his response. I began to climb up his body like a monkey on a vine, grasping his shoulders in a strong grip and throwing my legs around his waist. At the same time he bent his knees so that his wonderful cock dipped in under me, the head of it sliding along the creamy dampness surrounding my erect clitoris as it searched for the entrance to my aching love-channel. When I could feel it pressing against my secret doorway, I inched myself up a bit and then slid down the full length of his cock, feeling it part my swollen lips and drive relentlessly up inside the lubricated tunnel. His cock filled me perfectly, resting against the velvet walls of my vagina as if it had been grafted there.

Simultaneously I imagined our one-man audience holding onto his binoculars with one hand as his free hand crept down his abdomen to his groin. I imagined him unzipping his fly, imagined a gorgeous, slender prick escaping the confines of his pants. I imagined him pointing his throbbing meat directly at my anus as he began to stroke himself boldly. For a moment I could even see with his eyes, could see through the binoculars as my legs locked tightly around Paul's waist and my hips began to move slowly, enticingly up and down on his magnificent cock.

In effect, I had become my own voyeur. This was not the same sensation as watching oneself in a mirror, but something entirely new and different, something that was stimulating me beyond all imagination. I was two people, and as such I was enjoying two different sets of sexual stimuli at the same time. The mental picture of me sliding up and down Paul's cock effectively doubled the sensations of pleasure which were coursing through my hot body, and I knew that my orgasm was approaching.

When I opened my eyes to look at Paul, I could see that he was staring over my shoulder, staring, I assumed, directly into the twin barrels of our watcher's binoculars. Apparently my lover was feeling much the same way I was, for his eyes had a glassy, transfixed look, and the corner of his mouth had turned into an erotic little smile which only stimulated me that much more.

"Paul!" I gasped. *"Turn me around! Quick!"*

His hips still pumping into me at a leisurely pace, Paul did a slow 180-degree turn, which left me facing the sex spy in the opposite building. Although the window still bisected him neatly at the waist, I could see that his free hand had indeed gone down to his groin, and that the man—an older fellow, balding and somewhat paunchy—had begun to tremble. Seeing that only made me redouble my efforts, and I started to take long, lush strokes as I shimmied up Paul's marvelous pole and then let myself drop down on it, feeling it rack up into my burning vagina, feeling the crest of Paul's groin rub maddeningly at my clitoris.

Paul himself was now trembling, too, and I knew that somehow the three of us—Paul, myself, and our uninvited guest—had formed a sexual bond that was all the more powerfully exciting for being momentary and spontaneous. I knew I was about to climax, to spill my fragrant juices all over Paul's abdomen, and I knew that Paul would come with me. I wanted our watcher to come to orgasm too, right along with us, and I found myself almost regretting that he wasn't in the room with us to share in our erotic bounty.

The heavenly stimulation of Paul's skin on my clitoris finally took its toll. I opened my mouth and screamed out my orgasm. At the same time I felt Paul's cock balloon and then explode inside me, shooting its hot oily juices up into my burning quim. As my climax slammed through me with the force of a lightning bolt, I somehow managed to open my eyes to see how our neighbor was faring. I was just in time to see him buck and jerk furiously in the throes of his own handmade climax, all the time holding the binoculars trained on us.

I smiled over Paul's shoulder, knowing that our watcher could not help but see this sign of approval on my part. To my surprise, he averted his face, and I thought I could see a flush of embarrassment rising on his cheeks. He set down his binoculars, walked quickly over to the window and lowered the shade, just as Paul's strength gave out and we both collapsed in an exhausted heap on the floor.

"Did you see that?" I whispered in Paul's ear as we lay side by side. "He closed his window shade. I think he was embarrassed, poor thing."

"Sure he was embarrassed," Paul said, his face splitting into a wide grin. "His apartment's a *mess*."

I awoke later that evening to find Paul already inside me, moving back and forth in a gentle, rolling motion that reminded me of the night sea in the Bahamas. Somehow he had managed to fondle me into a state of high excitement while I was still asleep, and to wake up that way, with my beautiful man caressing me as if he were a clear blue wave and I the smooth sand of the shore, was an experience so lush, so dreamily erotic, that I know I shall never forget it.

He was smiling down at me as he moved his wonderful, soothing prick inside me, and in my half-conscious daze it was easy for me to convince myself that I was being straddled and mounted by one of the gentler gods. The soft moonlight backlit his hair much as the sun had done earlier that day, and as he bent over to kiss the tips of my breasts I swore I could smell the scent of hibiscus in his blond mane.

I could not imagine being any happier. I have been around the world so many times that I now grow bored in the counting. I have had the most exquisite lovers of every hue and persuasion. I have been propositioned by a large percentage of the richest men in the world, and I have been proposed to by kings. But never, anywhere, have I been cherished so ecstatically, stimulated so thoroughly, and overwhelmed so completely by the beauty of a man as I was that night and during those few months with my silent hero, my glorious prince of mime . . .

My Paul.

CHAPTER THREE

As I look back on it, I realize that that night marked a watershed in the history of my affair with Paul Bayard. I had a great deal of opportunity to analyze why things went wrong in the months that followed, as I much later walked the decks of foreign ships in unfamiliar oceans or waited to meet some new link in a chain of seeking that somehow seemed to grow longer with each new attempt on my part to reel it in. With the benefit of this cheap hindsight I came to know that our decline was inevitable, and had probably started the night that seedy club manager had tried to use Paul's talent to gain access to my body.

But during the period of decay itself, as things went from bad to worse between us, I was not able to see things quite so clearly. All I knew was that for some inexplicable reason, Paul had turned away from me. I think I would have been able to understand and handle it better had he turned argumentative, or irritable, or even vicious and violent. The coin of strong emotions has two sides, after all, and one expects a great love to breed great antagonisms as a sort of natural fallout.

Instead, Paul simply withdrew. He grew morose and

uncommunicative, and took to spending long periods away from our apartment. Although it was difficult for me to see him physically disappear in this way, it was even more tormenting to have him present in the house in body only, while the essence of him, the beautiful spirit that I loved so desperately, had obviously moved out.

I did not confront him at first, hoping as I did that his withdrawal was only a matter of some stray mood, or some necessary passage of the artist through the shadow of his own internal moon. At the time I had no other way to explain it, this mysterious and almost total absence, and I was not yet willing to admit that what I was seeing was nothing more unusual than another end to another love affair. I suppose I had ended so many of them this way myself—the sudden cooling of the flame, the awkward period afterwards when one tries to rekindle what has died forever, the petty arguments and the ultimate escape—that I refused to believe that it could happen to me in reverse.

Besides, I was convinced even then, even in my confusion and anxiety, that Paul had not stopped loving me. Something else was going on, I was sure, something that had to do with me only indirectly. Paul's withdrawal was not a sign of lack of love, but of some interior struggle that I could not understand without some kind of information from him, and he was simply not talking.

I think it was the long stays away from home that convinced me more than anything else that I had very little to do with what was happening to Paul. Within a very few weeks he was staying away for days at a time, and soon those days were stretching out to weeks. Although part of me knew there was a special, concrete explanation for this, another part of me was growing

wild with yearning for him, for the Paul I knew was
still alive inside this tough new shell.

Probably the worst aspect of this for me was the fact
that I no longer could count on any comfort whatsoever
from Paul's body. His withdrawal from me was absolute, total, so that even on the few nights when he
deigned to sleep with me in the apartment, he simply
flopped himself into bed and rolled over to face the
wall. Nothing I did could revive or encourage him in
any way; when I touched him, I could feel his body
turn to stone, a rigidity so complete as to be positively
frightening. After a few nights of this—interspersed
with those terrifying long absences—I even found myself wishing that he were the sort of man who could
simply objectify women, take advantage of them, use
them for their bodies alone, and that he would coldly
ravage me, impale me on the sword of his mysterious
anger.

Never have I come so dangerously close to losing my
integrity, the pride and confidence that have kept me
alive and triumphant even in life-and-death situations.
Never before had I been so willing to submit myself to
a man and his needs, never been so desperate to have a
man's interest and sexual reassurance. When I realized
this, realized how close I had come to total surrender,
some kind of alarm bell went off deep inside me, and I
knew that I would have to take the bull by the horns.

Finally I confronted him. He had come home from
one of his weeks away, had given me the same offhand
"hello" with the same unreadable expression that I had
now become accustomed to, and had brushed past me
to flop exhausted on the couch. I wondered briefly, as I
had wondered many times before, if Paul had simply
found some new woman to keep him happy and was

staying with me for reasons that neither of us could fathom. But as before, I again found that possibility unlikely, since absolutely none of the telltale signs of infidelity were there.

Still, I had reached the end of my rope. Something was going to get settled right then and there, or I would be on my way. I walked over to the couch and sat down next to him, feeling him stiffen as I did. But I was simply not going to be put off this time.

"Paul," I said, "let's stop this. Please tell me what's going on with you."

He turned to me with the face of an actor, as if he were trying to convince me that he was taken entirely by surprise by a bizarre and unreasonable question. "What are you talking about?" he said.

"Paul, don't do that to me," I said, honestly saddened by the childish weakness of his ploy. "Don't hide that way—it makes me feel ridiculous."

He didn't answer, only turned his face to the wall once more.

For some reason it infuriated me this time. I grabbed him by the shoulder and spun him around to face me. The look of surprise on his face was so comical that I could hardly keep from laughing.

But I managed to control myself. "Look, Paul," I said firmly, "if you want to go on staying with me, you're going to have to put a little effort into it. You're going to have to do some communicating."

His face, that marvelous, eternal face, now seemed to melt before my eyes, and his expression changed from one of surprise to one of sheer terror. The fear I saw nearly took my breath away, and I wanted to reach out to him, to hold his face between my hands and comfort him. If only he'd let me . . .

"First," he said, "I'm going to tell you what I can. It might not be the explanation you want, but it's all I can do right now."

Then he stopped. I waited for a moment, then said, "Well?"

He took a deep breath. "I'm under contract," he said.

"To whom?" I asked when he showed no signs of continuing. "For what?" This petty mystery was beginning to annoy me, and I could hardly keep the tone of irritation out of my voice.

"That's all I can say," he said. "Please don't ask me anything else." With that he turned on his heel and walked into the bedroom.

I could control myself no longer. My reaction to these months of neglect and sullenness poured out of me, and I could not have stopped myself even if I had wanted to. I screamed, "Paul! Stop this, dammit! What's happened to you? Can't you see what you're doing to us?"

When he didn't respond I followed him into the bedroom. To my great shock, he had a suitcase open on the bed and was packing. Furiously.

"Paul," I said, "what in the hell are you doing?"

"This isn't fair to you," he said, continuing to throw shirts into the open suitcase. "I've taken your life away from you, and I'm not giving you anything in return." He closed the suitcase and locked it. "And now I've told you too much."

"Too *much?*" I shouted. "You haven't told me anything, except that you're under contract for something. Well, I want to know. What contract? What something?"

"I'm sorry, Christina," he said, picking up the suitcase and brushing past me. "I just can't tell you."

"And now you're leaving?" I said. I could scarcely believe it myself. "Just like that?" I followed him into the living room and toward the front door.

"For you, Christina," he said over his shoulder. "I'm only doing it for you." With that he opened the door, walked through, then closed it ever so gently. But the slight click the door made in closing thundered through my nervous system like the clashing of cymbals.

I went cold and numb. As usual in tense situations, my emotions immediately receded, allowing my intelligence all the room it needed to make quick sense of things. It is probably a defense, this characteristic of mine, but it is one that has served me in good stead when life itself was on the line.

Instantly I began to think. I had little information to go on other than Paul's cryptic statement about being "under contract." Had he become a criminal, then? Had he signed a contract to undertake some menial job, or to donate his brain to science? I simply couldn't tell.

One thing I did know, though. That fear I had seen in his face was absolutely genuine. For some reason or another, Paul was in danger—either that, or afraid that some danger might befall me. Well, I decided, he was simply not going to leave me out of this. He was not going to walk out on me, on our love, and into this unknown danger and expect me to sit back and meekly accept it. That simply was not my style. I would do something about this, whatever it was, would get to the root of it and make it right no matter what the cost. And there was absolutely nothing anyone could do to stop me.

As usual, having made a decision made me feel better—for the moment at least. I walked toward the bedroom feeling somewhat relieved. But when I looked down at the bed, at the wrinkled bedspread where Paul had packed his clothes, some emotional sluice gate in me was raised, and all the feelings I had held back came out in a great, flowing gush.

I collapsed in tears on the bed, and for the first time since the death of my father I cried myself to sleep.

CHAPTER FOUR

The next morning I was awakened by what to me had become a strange sound: the ringing of the telephone. As I went to answer it I realized with a start to what extent Paul and I had isolated ourselves from the world around us. We had, in effect, completely cut ourselves off from friends and social life, at first out of happiness with the self-sustaining contentment of our relationship (God, how I hate that word!), but later out of some perverse desire to nurture our misery in private.

Now, as I heard Xavier's clear voice on the other end of the line, I sighed with gratitude. There was no one I would rather have talked to that morning. In fact, had he not called me I probably would have called him, as a natural place to begin looking for information about this "contract" of Paul's.

"Well," he said in an uncharacteristically jovial tone. "I hear you've been given the chance to climb back out from between your lovely buns."

I didn't even bother to wonder how he had found out, and found out so quickly. Somehow Xavier had always known instantly what was happening. It was positively uncanny. Had he not been born filthy rich, he would have made a superb gossip columnist.

"Delicately put, as usual," I said. "But it's good to hear your voice."

"What's even better," he countered, "is to hear that your Marcel Marceau has finally taken a walk."

"It's a bit more complicated than that," I shot back.

"Well, don't snap at *me*," he said. "I'm only trying to provide you with a little information."

"What are you talking about?"

I heard him sigh on the other end. "There's a screening tonight," he said. "I want you to come with me."

"Xavier, will you stop being so damned oblique?" I said. "What is going on here?"

"I'll pick you up at seven-thirty," was his only answer. "Wear your blackest dress."

My protest was interrupted by a click as he hung up the phone. I started to dial him back, but gave up in midnumber. It was useless trying to pry information out of Xavier when he was being mysterious, and I knew that I would only frustrate myself by trying. There was absolutely nothing I could do but wait until that evening and hope that he would be a little more loose tongued.

He arrived at seven-thirty on the dot—another shock: I had never known Xavier to arrive even within an hour of the alloted time—wearing A Bill Blass jump suit and a heartening smile. He handed me a bouquet of American beauty roses, and took my hand.

"You see?" he said. "I still love you, even in your terrible foolishness."

"The flowers are lovely," I said. "But I'd prefer an explanation."

"All in due time," he said, comically stroking a nonexistent mustache. "All in due time."

Xavier was full of surprises that evening. When we

went downstairs, the car that was waiting for us was not his Lamborghini Countach, but a studio limousine with black-tinted windows.

"So that's it," I said when I saw the car. "You've finally decided to go to work for a living. You've become a producer."

"Close, darling," he said, opening the door for me, "but no Tiparillo. Besides, there's no such animal as a producer who works for a living."

"True enough," I said. It felt wonderful to be bantering with Xavier again after so many months of leaden silence with Paul. We carried on a verbal fencing match punctuated with laughter all the way to the borders of Bel-Air, parrying and thrusting and giggling just as we had in the old days, so that the short ride with Xavier turned out to be better than a dozen hours with some somnolent psychiatrist.

The screening was a private affair in the home of Reese Jacklin, who, like Xavier, was one of those mysterious figures who never seem to do anything much but are always at the very center of movieland affairs. Reese's function was to be trusted friend, confidant, and harbinger of fresh news to the power elite of Hollywood, a job he performed with great relish and obvious natural ability. On the side he sold the juiciest tidbits about his friends' romantic failures to the *American Reader*, that scurrilous little rag that maintains the largest readership in the country by picking at the bones of the rich and famous.

Jacklin's home was magnificent, a twelve-bedroom old Spanish mansion designed by George Washington Smith, with fresh flowers in the courtyard fountain and an observatory with what Xavier described as "the world's only horizontal telescope." Jacklin was one of the few remaining Bel-Air–ites who maintained uniformed servants, and his kitchen, which occupied what must have been a full acre in the basement, was famous on both sides of both oceans.

Reese met us at the door, dressed as usual in a kimono and loafers with no socks. At his side was Wanda Pearl, the country singer whose popularity was much more a function of her elephantine breasts than her thin and rather irritating voice.

"Hello, my love," he said when he saw me, leaning over and giving me a peck on the cheek. "Wonderful to see you back in the pool."

We all exchanged greetings and stood at the door chatting for a moment, until Wanda said, "Reese, honey, don'tcha think we oughta get back? Mah throat's so *dry*."

"Cottonmouth," Reese explained to us with a wink. "Poor Wanda just can't smoke that Afghan boo without a bottle of Boone's Farm to wash it down."

"Now Reese honey, you apologize," she drawled, her voice rising half an octave in irritation. "You know I don't drink no Boone's Farm no more. Only mutton cadet."

"Mouton Cadet," Reese corrected, throwing us a weary look over his shoulder as he guided us down the first leg of his labyrinthine system of hallways.

After what seemed like an endless trek through art-bedecked passageways, we finally arrived at the screening room. Nowadays most private screening rooms in Bel-Air are simple affairs, comfortable and relaxing, but given more to function and less to pretention. Reese Jacklin, however, was not a simple man. He had disguised his screening room so that it looked like the book-lined study of an Oxford don (even though everyone knew that Reese never read anything but *Variety* and pornographic *fotonovelas* imported from Acapulco), full of leather easy chairs and crystal brandy decanters but with no screen or projection equipment in sight. When Jacklin pressed a button—usually with no warning whatsoever to the assembled guests—the entire *floor* descended, chairs, guests, and all, into a room one story down where all the screening equipment was kept. It was a dramatic enough experience the first time one underwent it, but by the second time it already seemed like nothing more than a boring and childish piece of ostentation.

Still, one was expected to ooh and ah, so I oohed and ahed dutifully as the floor carried us down to the screening room itself. The other guests—among them Bill and Dorothy Page of Roman a Clef, perhaps the best restaurant in America; perennial squash champion Haroun Ahmed, with an Egyptian boyfriend who I did not know; and neurosurgeon Miles O'Rourke with his wife Rhea—were all apparently making the descent for the first time, and neither Xavier nor I had the heart to make the withering comments that were so obviously appropriate.

Once the floor settled and the lights went dim, I completely forgot my surroundings and my companions. I have always been a pushover for the movies—as a little girl, they were my basic means of escape from my mundane Vermont childhood. I've been such a pushover, in fact, that I remain one of the most unreliable critics I know. I can find something I like in any film, even the cheapest and most grotesque, if nothing more than the saturated brightness of color itself or a single expression on the face of one ham actor. In addition, the dimming of the lights was also like a time machine to me, speeding me back to those careless Sundays at my father's side in a darkened theater.

Just before the screen came alive with the titles,

Reese Jacklin's voice cut through the darkness. "This film," he said, "is going to be the biggest grosser since *Star Wars*. They're pulling out all the stops on this one."

"Why?" I heard Xavier say.

"The male lead," Jacklin replied. "I talked with George D'Antonio over at Regal Studios, and he said this guy's going to be the hottest thing since free pussy. They're already billing him as the next Paul Newman."

"Hmm," I thought to myself, and promptly forgot everything Reese had said as the magic of the titles closed everything else out of my mind. The movie was called "Quicklime," and it starred Randall Stearns—who I assumed was the new heartthrob Reese had mentioned—Cindy Paxman, and Gloria Richards, an old favorite of mine. It was apparently one of those Grand Prix movies, which for me always manage to capture the glandular appeal and sheer speed of the sport while blithely ignoring the precision and unglamorous hard work that go into the making of even an average race driver, to say nothing of the freaks who rule the world of Formula I.

I knew that world well, and now the first roar of the sound track thrilled me as if I were one of the drivers once again. When the picture got to the point of putting me in the cockpit of an ice-blue Elf-Tyrell special, I forgot the calm maturity that had caused me to leave racing in the first place and wished that I could be plummeting once again down the long straight at Hockenheim, gearing the car to take that breathless leap over the *Flugplatz*.

I followed with pounding heart as the car in the movie finished its practice lap at what looked like the short course at Sebring, then I let out a long and probably audible sigh as it pulled into the pits. I smiled nostalgically as the driver stepped out of the car, remembering the inutterable and beautiful fatigue one felt after muscling a Formula I car around a circuit for two hours.

Then the driver pulled off his helmet, and I got the shock of a lifetime that had already had more than its share of shocks. I drew in my breath with a loud gasp and stared open-mouthed at the screen, hardly daring to believe what I was seeing.

For the driver, this "Randall Stearns" that Reese and the studios had been crowing about so loudly, was none other than my recently departed lover, Paul Bayard!

There is no way I can convey the paralyzing effect that the sight of Paul on the screen had on me. The impact of it was so stunning as to numb my senses almost entirely, and the only reason I now know what I did next was that Xavier recited it to me later in great and embarrassing detail.

The only thing I actually remember is running like a loon down the dark Bel-Air drive that led away from Reese Jacklin's house, running and sobbing and yelling, "No! No!" into the uncaring night. I must have run like that for miles, for the next thing I knew the street had merged with the serpentine main line of Sunset Boulevard, and the cars were honking and swerving to avoid me.

When Xavier finally found me I had run almost to Doheny, a distance, I'm now told, of about five miles from Jacklin's mansion. He leaped out of the limo and grabbed me around the waist, dragging me kicking and screaming into the waiting car. I thrashed wildly in his captive embrace, and I was later mortified to learn that I accidentally broke one of his teeth with my flailing elbow.

"Now calm down, Christina," he said in an even

tone but through clenched teeth as he held me in a grip that was surprisingly strong. "Just calm down. Jesus, if I had known you were going to react this way I would never have done it. Please, Christina, come to your senses, will you?"

I finally stopped thrashing and fell limp in his grip, my heart pounding and my chest heaving with exertion. He put his arm around me, and my head fell against his shoulder like a rag doll's. I broke down entirely, and for the second time in two days I found myself weeping and bawling like some cuckolded schoolgirl, wailing out my heartbreak in the comforting shelter of Xavier's arms.

I heard him order the driver to move on, and when we hit the bright lights of the Strip I was grateful to have the tinted glass to keep out the inquiring stares of the tourists in front of the Roxy. By the time we reached Schwab's, I had calmed down considerably and was finally able to ask the question that had been ringing in my brain since the moment I had seen Paul's face on the screen.

"Xavier," I said, my voice breaking as I spoke, "what happened?"

"I don't know much more than you do," he said in a low, soothing tone. "I found out entirely by accident. I ran into his agent, who's a friend of mine, and we just got to talking. When she told me, I called the studio immediately and they told me Reese had a print of the film. So I asked him to set up a screening for you. Believe me, I had no idea it would do this to you. You must really love this boy, bozo though he appears to be."

"Paul has an agent?" I asked. I could hardly believe it. He had always avoided agents like the plague, complaining that they were parasites and bloodsuckers who had no inkling whatsoever of what it meant to be an artist. He absolutely refused to put his career in one of their hands, even though he knew that without one he would probably remain an unknown outsider.

"Katy Gleason," Xavier said. "The hottest talent pusher in town." He gave me an even look. "What Reese said was no joke, lover. Your boy is going to be an enormous star. They've already paid him more for this picture than any newcomer has ever gotten, and they gave him top billing over Cindy and Gloria, who are no small potatoes. The studio is hyping him like they haven't hyped anyone since Brooke Shields. He's going to be enormous, Christina. More than you ever imagined."

Although it was very difficult for me to make sense of all this—my high-minded, classical Paul, selling out to the *movies*, peddling his flesh in the meat market like all the other ambitious pretty boys—I had to admit that explained a number of the mysteries that had been troubling me so. His long absences, for example, must have coincided with the shooting of the film, with story conferences, publicity engagements, principal photography and the hundred other steps that go into the making of a movie. And his tight-lipped depression; it must have been caused by shame, shame that he had sold out his ideals in the crassest way possible, shame over his inability to admit to me that he had forsaken his own art—and possibly his soul as well—for the questionable glory of temporary stardom. It also, of course, explained the nature—if not the source—of his mysterious contract.

It was something of a relief to have all that explained, but it didn't make me feel any better. For one thing, it neither brought Paul back nor gave me much of an opening to try to get him back—if, in fact, that was what I wanted. And I still hadn't the faintest clue as to the most important question of all: *Why?* Why had he done it? Why after all those years of proud struggling, after all the discipline and the mind-breaking labor of perfecting his mime routines, did he suddenly give it all up to go in a direction that he seemed never even to have considered before? Why had he sacrificed everything he knew and loved—me included—for probably nothing more than a little fame?

Xavier, of course, had none of these answers, and I didn't want to involve him any more than he already was in an affair that was so obviously distasteful to him. It was enough that he cared about me sufficiently to want to inform me despite the fact that he thought Paul useless and decidedly beneath me.

I asked him to drive me home and he did so, dispatching me at my door with a kind embrace. I spent an hour or so at home on the telephone, trying every place I thought Paul might be staying, but I turned up nothing but complete blanks. No one had seen him, no one had heard from him. It was as if he had already gone into hiding in anticipation of his impending stardom. Finally I gave up—for that evening, at least—and fell into an exhausted sleep on the couch without even bothering to remove my "blackest" dress.

The next morning I called Katy Gleason. Apparently she knew me by reputation (or perhaps knew of me through Paul), for she took the call immediately.

"I want to talk to you about Paul," I said. I was in no mood for niceties.

"Not on the phone," Katy said. Her voice was rich, and had an honest quality to it that encouraged me. "Come to my office in two hours."

"I'm coming right now," I said, and hung up the phone without giving her a chance to protest.

Within half an hour I was walking through the door of Katy's office, which was in the prestigious Artists and Writers Building in the heart of Beverly Hills. The outer office was sumptuous in an understated way, a muted sort of high-tech decor that looked as if it had been lifted whole from the pages of the *Architectural Digest*. When I told the receptionist who I was, she announced me immediately and I was told with no further ado that I could go right in.

Katy's inner office was a glass-and-metal wonderland, positively agleam with those shiny alloys that are so admired by American industry. It had a hard-edged look to it that put me off a bit, but my critique of her taste in interior design was forgotten the second I laid eyes on Katy herself.

I am used to the company of beautiful women. My mother spent half her life turning down the photographers and agents who were constantly begging her to enter this beauty contest or pose for that magazine. Beauty, in fact, is taken almost entirely for granted among my friends and acquaintances—it's one of the first prerequisites for permanent membership (as opposed to the temporary variety, which can be obtained with mere wit, brains, or achievement) in what the world's journalists are so fond of calling the haut monde.

But I had never seen a beauty like this Katy Gleason. She had one of those triangular, Siamese cat faces, with the hollowed cheeks and oversized eyes that make one think immediately of a high-fashion model. But where a model's beauty often has a porcelain, hands-off quality to it (one imagines her splitting up the middle if asked to spread her legs too far), Katy's was substantial and firm without being overly athletic. Her hair was deep black and her eyes brilliant green, and when she stood up I saw that she had the kind of body that makes men moan in the dark—full, yet somehow lithe at the same time, and positively rippling with sexual energy.

I could not help but wonder if the explanation for Paul's mysterious behavior lay right here in this office. Certainly she looked to be woman enough to turn any man's head, and I could rather easily imagine her seducing Paul right out of his art and right into the movies. But there was something about her that made me think this unlikely, and it wasn't long before I discovered that my hunch was right.

"Hello," she said in that melodious voice. "Paul certainly wasn't exaggerating when he told me how beautiful you are."

"You have me at a distinct disadvantage," I said. "You see, Paul never told me about you at all."

"I know that," Katy said. "And he swore to me that he never would."

"I'm not surprised."

There was a brief, awkward silence which under the circumstances made me extremely uncomfortable. So I simply blurted out, "I want to know who's responsible for what happened to Paul."

"You don't waste time, do you?" Katy said.

"Not when something's as important to me as this is."

She nodded. "I understand." There was another long pause, at the end of which she looked me squarely in the eyes, holding mine with hers in a steady gaze that very quickly turned into a sort of caress. "I don't know very much," she said, "and before I tell you what I do know, I'd like to get to know *you* a little better."

Now I understood at least this much: Paul had definitely not left me for Katy. She was unmistakably on the gay side of the sexual fence, and now she was unmistakably trying to seduce me. I didn't mind. I go to bed with whom I please in this world, and if a lovely woman happens to catch my fancy I have no qualms whatsoever about indulging a sexual appetite that is decidedly bipartisan. In fact, some of the lushest of my erotic adventures have been with women—I am reminded immediately of the island of Antigua, of the wonderful month I spent holed up there in the Admiral's Inn (where Lord Nelson once trysted with Lady Hamilton) with the sculptor Eloise Bryant; and of an absolutely sensational night with a lady politician (who shall remain forever nameless) after a party for the president at Sardi's.

Who but a woman, after all, is better equipped to bring pleasure to another woman?

I answered her by turning the corners of my mouth into a barely perceptible smile. When she beamed broadly in return, I knew that I was not doing this solely as a way to buy information about Paul, but also because I already liked this woman very much and would probably have been trying to seduce her if she hadn't seduced me first.

Now she got up and walked deliberately over to a small built-in refrigerator tucked in a corner underneath a surprisingly ample bar. She pulled out a bottle of wine and showed it to me, saying, "Château Montelena, their 1973 Chardonnay. The little David from the Alexander Valley that slew all the French Goliaths at that famous blindfold test in Paris. Could I ask you to take your clothes off?''

I stood up without hesitation and began to remove my jeans and blouse, while Katy buzzed the receptionist and instructed her to hold all calls. By the time she hung up I had stripped naked, and she turned from the phone to favor me with another of her dazzling smiles.

"Beautiful," she said. "Glorious. Here, have a glass of wine while I join you."

She poured me a glass of the golden Chardonnay, and I sipped it lightly, moistening my lips with the velvet fruitiness of it and looking fixedly over the rim of the glass as Katy began to strip. She was dressed simply but tastefully (how rare to see someone in Hollywood who really knew how to dress!) in a tailored blouse and medium-length print skirt, and now, as she removed each piece with slow, sure, tantalizing hands, I could see that the clothes were showcasing a body that was a paragon of sexy perfection. As each new garment came off to reveal first her creamy, rounded breasts, then her flat and languorous belly, and finally the lovely little triangular thatch above her vagina, I took another sip of the wine, letting its admirable smoothness hone and polish my insides while the sight of Katy's magnificent equipment had my pussy already turning warm and eager.

"Lovely," I said as she pulled her panties down over her slender, tapered legs. "Lovely wine, lovely lady."

Once again she smiled that enchanting smile. "I'm a bit of a wine fancier," she said. "It's almost a fetish with me, if you know what I mean."

I didn't know, but I was beginning to understand. She pulled an attractive-looking bunch of grapes out of the refrigerator, then pulled one of the plump little balls from its stem and began to circle it slowly, delectably with the tip of her tongue. The sight of that caress and the promise it contained ignited me instantly, and it seemed as if I could already feel the velvet fire of her tongue as it sought and found the lush groove of my tingling pussy-lips.

Then she abruptly swallowed the grape, and the effect was of a hypnotist snapping his fingers to bring me out of a deep trance. I must have looked a little startled, for Katy laughed—again that golden, musical laugh— and said, "These are the grapes that make the wine . . ."

". . . that makes the client's girlfriend," I finished the sentence for her, and then found myself laughing just as pleasantly as she was.

"Please," she said. "Please don't think I planned this. Not before you walked in the door, at any rate."

"Shh," I said, walking over to her and putting a finger to her lips. "I know."

She kissed my finger lightly, then quickly ran her tongue along the underside of it as I gasped with the renewed promise of that delicate gesture. Again it was as if I could feel her tongue teasing my hot little clitty, as if somehow the nerves from finger to vagina had been connected directly, and stimulating the one brought the same heavenly delight to the other.

"Mmm," I heard myself murmuring as a little electric thrill coursed through my already heaving belly. It was all I could do to keep myself from grabbing her by the hair and stuffing her face into the slick and creamy confines of my pussy. Remember that I had had virtually no sex for a long time, and that I am not a woman who takes any joy whatsoever in abstinence. Katy's loving ministrations were turning me weak with desire, and it was only with the greatest difficulty that I kept myself at least somewhat under control, knowing that the longer I held out the greater would be the eventual release.

Now she took my finger, the same one she had been tantalizing with her wonderful tongue, and plunged it directly into the hot tunnel of her mouth, closing her soft lips around it and letting it rest lightly on the surface of her tongue. I moaned again as she began to move back and forth on it—the illusion that I had suddenly been endowed with a penis acted as a further prod to my already stirring insides, and I twirled the finger in the soft warmth of her mouth just as so many pulsing cocks had twirled in mine.

She made a small "o" of her lips and drew them along the full length of my penetrating finger, finally allowing it to slide entirely out of her mouth. She smiled at me. "You've done this before," she said.

I nodded, and was instantly transported back to Antigua, to the raw and sultry heat of the Caribbean and the cooling shade of the room I had shared with Eloise. I remembered it all in the sharpest detail: the caressing sound of the water as it lapped around the poles under the pier, the way one gleaming white sail bisected the view from our window, the musical cries of the fishermen as they joked and argued in their marvelous and mysterious *papiamiento*.

But mostly I remembered Eloise, the way the sun lay like a golden blanket along the soft contours of her body, the sweet smile that creased her face when she closed her eyes to rest after her orgasms, and the spicy, pungent taste of the love-juices that flowed so copiously from her delectable little pussy. Eloise had not been my first woman either, but she was the first with whom I had taken an active role, with whom I had been more than just a consenting adult.

God, what a week we had! The air of romance about the Admiral's Inn acted as a sort of aphrodisiac, and we spent hours every day rolling like a pair of frisky colts in the suite where Nelson himself had rolled with Lady Hamilton. We touched and licked and moaned and fingered, luxuriating in one another's bodies, delighting in the sensation of nipple meeting nipple, of breast flattening against breast, of hair entertwining and silken bellies rubbing up against each other. They were sweet and significant lessons that Eloise taught me, a sort of private seminar in the secrets of the body, secrets which when unraveled led to the most delectable and lush of sexual pleasures.

She taught me, for example, that there were unexpected places in my body that once touched could be counted on to provide the most delicious of surprises. She instructed me in the easy sensitivity of the rib channels, the heavenly stimuli of the belly button, and in the magnificent pleasure available to an anus made receptive by lubrication. She showed me how a woman could be driven half mad with longing with a certain kind of kiss, and how the soft sucking of a clitoris could bring on the most thundering of orgasms. She even astonished me by bringing me to a shattering climax without touching anything but the bottoms of my feet.

More than anything else she taught me how to make my body *available*, how to relax completely and open myself to the sensual feast that was the reward of the truly vulnerable. Since that time I have been a true libertine, without reservations, without taboos, free of the poisonous timidity that keeps so many women from the enjoyment that their own bodies can provide. Because of Eloise I am totally without sexual fears and sexual pretensions, totally myself, totally eager, and totally erotic. With Eloise I found myself as honestly, as truly, and as completely as I ever have with any man.

And now I was opening myself up to another woman again. I snapped out of my reverie and opened my eyes, just in time to see the gloriously naked Katy pop one of the Chardonnay grapes into her mouth and chew it with a slow, sucking certainty that was like a clarion call to my aroused body. With the grape still in her mouth she grabbed my finger and inserted it once again, rolling it through the crushed grape pulp, kissing it, withdrawing it, and licking it with that curiously exciting tongue stroke of hers. I could feel my pussy churning out the oils of my arousal, could feel my thighs growing damp with the flow as my other hand came alive to run lightly along the contours of her luxurious body, tracking lightly down her rib cage, then gloriously *in* at the waist, then flaring out over her urn of hips and back along the perfect hills of her smooth buttocks.

"That's it, darling," she whispered, nodding her head and closing her eyes as I continued to roam along the highways of her body. "Feel me. Touch me. Love me."

Her words pierced me like hot spears, going directly to the secret wells of my womanhood and inspiring a series of little flutterings in my belly that were the first harbingers of the storm to come.

"Touch me, Christina," she moaned, and the words ran up the length of my spine, sending messages of furious desire to my fevered brain.

"Feel me, Christina," she breathed, and the words were like strings on my fingers, making them dance over the silky surfaces of her skin.

She closed her mouth once more over one of my fingers and drew her lips along it until it withdrew. This time she did not let it go, but rather guided it down, enticingly down toward the throbbing triangle of her mound of Venus, past the protective mountains of her outer labia and into the wellsprings of the lush valley beneath. We gasped in unison as my moistened finger made contact with the hardening ridge of her clitty, plowing through her own warm cream to rub lightly along the full length of her love-cord.

She threw her head back and let out a long, low

moan, evidently beside herself with delight at my delicate caresses. Her growing passion was feeding mine, and I moaned in response, dipping my finger once more into the soft meat of her vagina and thrilling with shared delight as I watched her writhe with pleasure.

Suddenly she literally *slid* away from my finger, reaching behind her to pluck a handful of the golden Chardonnay grapes. She held them up in front of me, and it was almost as if I could see the brilliant sun of the Alexander Valley, the voluptuous rolling hills and the lush vines laid out along the Silverado Trail—nature and man locked in the oldest embrace of all. She smiled as I stared at the ripe little globes, a slight dew of perspiration forming on her upper lip, her nipples spiked and distended and her body fairly glistening with the light of yearning.

Then she slowly, deliberately crushed the grapes in her hand, the movement suggesting a sexual power that had only been hinted at up to now. I stared in fascination as she moved toward me, a step at a time, our eyes locking in an understanding that would only be increased by consummation. She stopped just in front of me, and it was as if our naked bodies were the termini to a pounding force that reverberated back and forth between us. I don't think I have ever experienced anything quite like the surging intensity of that contact-without-contact; she might just as well have been massaging me with a thousand hands.

"Stand still," she whispered, and she held up her open hand to show me the crushed grape pulp in her palm. Then she methodically began to smear the golden juices over my body, which recoiled at first from the cool wetness but then relaxed as the soothing moisture began to penetrate my open pores.

She rubbed the pulp along my shoulders, then in a

long, silken stroke down to my breasts, her dampened palms cupping underneath them and pushing them magnificently *up*. My already stiffened nipples now hardened still further as they felt her cool touch, which was softened deliciously by the residue of Chardonnay pulp in her hands.

"My God!" I gasped. "I've never felt anything like that! Never!"

She smiled again and continued her wonderful ministrations, smearing the pungent liquid over the heaving contours of my belly and abdomen, then continuing down to outline the "v" of my pussy and to coat the insides of my thighs, which were now trembling with anticipation and tingling with the mixture of the crushed grapes as they mingled with my own flowing stream of juices.

Then she moved closer, until her nipples touched mine and sent a thrilling spark of real contact shooting through my overheated body. She moved from side to side so that the nipples brushed against one another, and I nearly fainted from the force of the desire that welled up in me, threatening to drop me to my knees in front of her.

"Please," I begged. "Don't tease me like this. Oh God, I want you so much!"

"My beautiful darling," she purred. She stepped even closer and put her arms around me, pulling her to me in a steamy and passionate embrace. I groaned aloud and flattened myself against her, crushing my breasts to hers, feeling her sweat now mix with the exquisite wetness of the spicy grape juice.

Then it was Katy herself sinking to her knees in front of me, letting out a loud sigh as she trailed her tongue down the valley between my pounding breasts, down

over the satin skin of my torso and belly, down . . .
down . . . down . . .

"Oh!" I cried out as her tongue suddenly lashed like
a snake at my tingling pussy, sliding between the shel-
tering hood of the lips and stroking quickly—just the tip
of it—along the length of my erect clitoris. It was like a
flash of lightning along the sensitive little node, teasing
it, arousing it, sending a thrilling jolt of sensation through
my loins—and then it was gone!

"Again!" I moaned. *"Do it again, Katy! You're
driving me crazy!"*

Again her tongue flashed out. Again it parted my
outer pussy-lips, and again it slithered down to bury
itself in my little valley, to stroke and tease maddeningly at my throbbing clitty.

"More!" I barked, and then groaned out my desire
as she licked me once again.

By now I was quite beside myself with passion. I put
my hands in Katy's hair and wrung them desperately,
tangling my fingers in her silky curls, twisting and
pulling as I ground my aching pussy into her face. I had
to have more and more of that divine stroking! I had to
feel her smooth tongue running along the channel of my
clitoris, massaging it, prodding it, setting it afire! I
looked down at her, and the sight of her head against
my abdomen, the tip of her nose touching the twining
curls of my pubic hair, her tongue lashing in and out as
it stroked my pussy up the ladder toward climax, was
like an amplifier, doubling and then tripling the strength
of the sensations that were running wild through my
body!

Then she looked up at me, and ran the tip of her
glistening tongue along her lips. Her eyes were fairly
gleaming with her lust.

"Lie down, darling," she said.

In an instant I was on my back on the lush carpet, my hands going automatically to my own breasts, pressing them together and massaging them as I watched Katy go back to her desk and pluck another bunch of grapes. She crushed them in her hands as she had the first batch, then knelt next to me and once again rubbed the velvety juices all over me. Still kneeling above me, she brought her head down and began to lick the pulpy juice off me, lapping like a hungry kitten at my moistened skin, stopping occasionally to plant a sucking kiss on my hungry belly.

Soon she was inching her way down to my vagina, burrowing into it and rubbing her lips up and down the length of my distended little clitty. I could barely stand it—the pulsing, maddening pressure of her mouth on me, the hot force that slammed through my body with each stroke, the mound of sensation growing at my loins that now threatened to overcome me—it was as if I were being stripped of the very glue that held my body together, as if soon I would simply come apart, melt into a mass of undifferentiated cells, a victim of my own desire.

"*Katy!*" I screamed out. "*I want you too! Come to me, Katy! Please, darling, come to me!*"

She needed no further urging. Immediately she was up on her knees and turning her perfect buttocks to face me. I slid my feet under her slightly spread legs and grabbed her hips in a strong grip, pulling her back toward me until my mouth was in contact with the hot, oily lips of her lovely pussy. It was like plunging into the soft and meaty depths of some exotic fruit, and smearing one's lips with that pungent nectar that was to me a form of ambrosia. At precisely the same moment I felt her bury her mouth into the crevice between my tingling cunt-lips, and at precisely the same moment we both closed our mouths around the throbbing little cords of our love-mounds.

God, but it was delicious! We sucked and rubbed at each other, mirroring one another's movements almost exactly, our faces buried in the secret caves of our mutual passion, our tongues stroking, our lips massaging, our teeth taking maddening little scrapes along the raw flesh of our grinding pussies. With each sucking motion of her mouth, I felt the powerful sensation of my impending orgasm building inside me, growing stronger and stronger, and I could tell by the way that her pussy was beginning to oscillate that Katy was nearing her climax, too.

On and on we went, our mouths and vaginas fused in a passion so elegant, so magnificently fertile, that I wished it could go on forever. The strong-sweet odor of her creamy lubricants, the soft, lush feel of her satiny pussy-lips, the delightful sensation as my lips closed on the delicate little node of her clitoris, and the echoing motion of her mouth on mine as we pumped and drove at each other was like a concerto of desire being played by an orchestra whose pitch and tune were absolutely perfect.

"Yes, darling, yes!" I heard Katy gasp. *"Oh God, I love your sweet mouth! Do it to me, darling! Don't ever stop!"*

Her urging drove me on to even greater efforts, which were immediately echoed by her own. We were breathing in unison, cooing and sighing in counterpoint as we sucked one another with greater and greater frenzy, pushing one another closer, ever closer, to a mutual and simultaneous climax that we both knew would be extraordinary.

"Come with me, Katy!" I managed to blurt out

between mouth strokes. *"I'm almost there! Come with me now!"*

"Yes, darling!" she cried. "I'm coming too!"

With that my orgasm hit me, driving through my body with all the heady power of a runaway bulldozer. I could feel my legs stiffen and my back arch with the strength of it, and it was all I could do to keep my mouth riveted to Katy's throbbing pussy as she too screamed out her climax.

It seemed to last for hours, this roiling, churning dual orgasm, and when it finally faded—in both of us at the same time, I might add—Katy collapsed on top of me and then rolled off my sweat-streaked body to lie next to me on the plush carpet. We lay like that for some time, the silence broken only by the sound of our panting, which gradually quieted until our breasts stopped heaving and we were breathing normally again.

"Sensational," Katy whispered finally, turning to look at me and favoring me with that look of understanding and communion that comes only after sex. "Just sensational." Her wild green eyes had softened considerably in the aftermath of her climax, and her face shone with a sort of devotion that was all the more powerful for being purely temporary.

"Agreed," I responded. "It almost made me forget why I really came here in the first place."

"Me too," Katy said. She picked her languid body up off the carpet now and walked slowly back to her desk. The sight of her wonderful buttocks jiggling so enticingly as she walked almost made me want to go after her again, but I knew we would have other opportunities, and now the urgency of my mission in regard to Paul was beginning to return.

"Back to business," Katy said, sitting up on the top of her desk and popping another grape into her mouth.

"Back to business."

She gave me a look that was distinctly sad. "Remember," she said, "I told you I didn't know much."

"I remember," I replied. "Please, I'm not expecting anything of you. Just tell me what you do know."

Our eyes met as she gave me a level, even stare. "Paul's been bought," she said.

"I know that . . ." I began.

"Wait a minute," she said, holding up her hand to stop me. "I don't think you quite understand what I mean."

"Please, Katy," I came back. "Spare me the mysteries. Just tell me what's going on."

"When I say 'bought,' I don't mean just paid for his work in one picture."

"A multipicture contract?" I said, scarcely believing it. Multipicture contracts, I knew, had gone the way of Irving Thalberg and Cecil B. De Mille. No one offered multipicture contracts these days, and no one would take them even if they were offered.

"No," Katy said. "Something even more outlandish."

"What could be more outlandish than a multipicture contract?"

"I'm not sure," she said.

"Will you stop talking riddles?" I cried out, suddenly exasperated. "You're his agent, aren't you? You conduct his business, don't you?"

"Not this time, I didn't," she said. "This was something Paul did entirely on his own. I wasn't even consulted."

"But *what is it?*" I was nearly screaming.

"Look, darling, I'm trying to help you. I'm telling you everything I know. Paul's been bought, and he's been bought body and soul. It's not just his acting that's been bought, it's *him*. It's Paul himself."

"What is this?" I said. "Some sort of medieval fantasy? People don't just sell themselves!"

"Paul did."

I started to protest, but I couldn't find the words. The whole thing was beginning to get a nasty, almost monstrous sound to it, and Katy's answers were doing nothing but raising new questions. I struggled for a moment with a mounting panic, a feeling that somehow Paul was lost to me forever, that I might not ever see him again except on a movie screen. But I controlled myself and managed to order my thoughts sufficiently to ask the next question:

"Who bought him?"

"I don't know," Katy said, shrugging her shoulders. "It's all very obscure."

"So it seems."

The thought crossed my mind that Katy might be lying to me, that she might know more than she was telling, or even that she might have a hand in what was being done to Paul. But when I looked at her and saw the genuine concern in her eyes, saw the way her shoulders were slumping in defeat, I knew that she was telling me as much of the truth as she knew. I got up and began to put on my clothes, keeping my back to her so that she would not see how distraught I really was. Then I felt the softness of her hand on my shoulder, and when I turned around to face her I could see tears beginning to well up in her eyes.

"Look," she said. "That really is all I know. But you're a very fine lady, and I want to help you if I can. Why don't you go home and let me see what I can find out?"

I looked at her for a moment, then nodded silently. I had my own resources, of course, and I would certainly use them. But I had to admit that Katy was at this point much closer to Paul than I was, and probably had more direct access to knowledge about his mysterious sellout. I had the feeling that I had found in her not only a marvelous and creative sex partner, but an ally I could trust.

I reached over to her desk, plucked one of the golden Chardonnay grapes from the bunch, and held it up in front of her.

"Here," I said. "I think you're going to need some more strength."

I gently inserted the grape in her mouth. I nodded as she smiled at me in understanding, then gave her a brief, chaste kiss, turned, and walked out the door.

CHAPTER FIVE

The next morning I called in my hairdresser, my manicurist, and my masseur and had them all apply their considerable skills (I got them, after all, as a birthday present from the Queen of Goa, a good friend) to prepare me for what lay ahead. I was going back to work, in a sense, and I wanted to be at my best in all possible respects, especially the physical. I do not deceive myself—I know that my appearance has gotten me into doors that would have been fortified to the nth degree against anyone less fortunately endowed, and besides, I know how important it is to go into a new story feeling absolutely at the top of my game.

From the outset, that was my attitude: that the unraveling of the mystery of Paul's—what should I call it? sellout or disappearance or change of life?—would be treated simply as another story; fascinating, no doubt, and challenging, but no more so than, say, the capture of those oil tanker pirates in the Seychelles or the behind-the-scenes machinations in the toppling of the government in Paraguay, both of which I had taken part in. To maintain that attitude, I had to quash my feelings and muster up all the objectivity I could, because I knew that my love for Paul could do nothing but cloud my vision and retard whatever progress I might be able to make toward the solution of this bloody mystery.

Once I had been primped, rubbed, and clipped to near perfection by my adorable caretakers, I went right to work, starting, as usual, with my favorite tool in these preliminary rounds, the telephone. First I called Reese Jacklin, who—amazingly enough—could tell me nothing more than the name of *Quicklime*'s producer, one Tony Jacobs. Jacobs was a nodding acquaintance of mine from some embassy party or other, and when I called he remembered me immediately. But he knew nothing, or so he claimed. He said he had simply been ordered by the president of Constellation Films to use Paul as the lead in the picture, and ordered in terms that brooked no argument whatsoever.

"What could I do?" he said, and I could almost see him shrugging as he shifted his cigar from one side of his mouth to the other. "My hands were tied."

I thanked him and immediately called Constellation, tapping my fingers on the phone table and fuming silently as I ran the telephone maze of secretaries, receptionists, and palace guards who kept the executives from talking to anyone but their mistresses. I finally got through to Desmond Starkey, Constellation's president by reminding his personal secretary that I was part of a group that had bankrolled the first seven pictures the studio had ever made.

It was hardly worth my time. Starkey had much the same story as Jacobs, that he was simply acting under orders.

"We're not independent anymore, you know," he said. "We're just a division of Amalgamated Industries. They tell us what to do."

"Even down to the lead actor in a tacky little racing film?" I said. "I find that hard to believe."

"Believe what you want, Christina," Starkey said. "It happens to be the truth. I get a phone call one day from the home office, they say 'use Paul Bayard in *Quicklime*.' So I use him. I make it a point not to argue with the home office."

"All right, Desmond," I said. "Thanks for nothing."

"Anytime, sweetheart," he said cheerfully. "And don't be a stranger."

We hung up. Just as I was about to dial the home office of Amalgamated Industries (located, appropriately enough, in Cleveland) the phone rang. It was Katy.

"My God," she said, "I've been trying to get you all morning. The line's been busy."

"So have I," I said. "Hacking myself a pathway through the corporate jungle."

"Amalgamated?"

"I was just about to call them."

"Don't bother. You won't get anywhere."

"How do you know?"

"Because," she said, "I've already talked to the fellow who keeps their wheels greased out here. He guarantees me that no one in Cleveland really knows what's going on."

"Not even the chairman of the board?"

"No one."

"Hmm," I said brilliantly. "Who is this wheel-greaser of yours?"

"His name is Leonard Snider. He's a lawyer, and he has some sort of connection with both Amalgamated and Constellation, although I've never been able to get him to tell me precisely what that connection is. Some sort of liaison man, I imagine."

"Sounds positively opaque," I said. "What's his phone number?"

"You don't have to call him," Katy said. "I've already made you an appointment."

"Fantastic!" I said. "You know, if you didn't make so much money as it is, I'd hire you."

"Don't make me offers until you hear about the *kind* of appointment it is," she said ominously.

"Uh-oh."

"Exactly. What it boils down to is that I got you an invitation to one of his parties. They're quite notorious."

"Doesn't sound so bad," I said. "Especially after some of the parties I've been to." I immediately recalled the Pirates of the Caribbean party that Xavier had thrown once, in which each of the guests ended up coupling dog style with someone and "walking the plank" into a swimming pool full of Dom Perignon. Or the Olympics Benefit sponsored by an aging athlete who had once won three gold medals, and which featured a decathlon unlike anything ever seen outside the pages of the Kama Sutra.

"I'm sure I'll be able to manage it," I told Katy.

"I'm sure you will, darling," she said. "But I'm going to come with you, just to be on the safe side."

"Wonderful!" I said, truly meaning it. We made the arrangements and chatted for a moment about trivialities before hanging up. Once the phone was back on the hook, I sat back in my chair and relaxed inside for the first time in days. I have an instinct for the right track—an instinct which is indispensable to the work I do—and now I felt as if things were finally going somewhere. This Leonard Snider sounded very promising indeed, and I silently thanked Katy for the referral, knowing she had saved me much work and frustration in dealing with the corporate melange. And I knew too that Snider was just a man, and no matter how loyal and tight-lipped he might prove to be, I had yet to meet the man who would not talk to me . . . sooner or later, if you know what I mean.

The party was due to begin late Saturday afternoon, so Katy picked me up at noon in her Corniche, putting the top down for the two-hour drive to Santa Barbara, where Snider lived. Santa Barbara is one of those towns about which people are always saying that it has the highest per capita income in the country, which instantly incites arguments with aficionados of Shaker Heights, Great Neck, and Tiburon, and which is due primarily to the fact that a great many successful movie people live there in blissful semiretirement.

But to my surprise, Katy did not turn off the highway at the Montecito exit, which leads to the heart of the Santa Barbara movie colony. Instead she drove on through town and out the narrow road toward the San Marcos pass. We went up the coast range, up past Camino del Cielo with its magnificent view of the ocean, past the sprawling ranch which Jane Fonda and Tom Hayden keep as a weekend retreat, and down into the oak-studded greenery of the Santa Ynez Valley.

Just before we reached Lake Cachuma and the little town of Paradise, Katy turned off onto an unmarked but well-graded dirt road which was set off by a double stand of eucalyptus trees on either side. Black Angus cattle grazed peacefully in the tall yellow grass, lifting their heads to bellow at us as we roared by. Finally we came to a circular driveway, and parked in front of the immense one-story ranch house on the other side.

Snider himself greeted us at the door; he was a tall, rangy man who reminded me a bit of an old-fashioned secretary of state. He smiled at me pleasantly when

Katy introduced us, looking much more like rural gentry than the sexual madman Katy had described.

"Come on in," he said in a relaxed baritone. "Party's just getting started."

I have heard those words at least ten thousand times in my life, and they almost always conjure up the same scene: people standing around in little groups of threes and fours, nibbling exotic little tidbits and smoothly swooping drinks off passing cocktail trays as they engage in a low-key contest to see who can be the more quietly impressive. "Sedate" is the word I want, with just a slight buzzing undertone of repressed sexuality and eager anticipation.

Consequently I was not in the least prepared for the sight that hit me when I walked in the door. There were some fifteen to twenty couples in Snider's hockey rink of a living room, and another ten or so outside, gathered around and in a swimming pool that looked to be only slightly smaller than Red Square in Moscow. And nowhere did I see a shred of clothing, nowhere did I hear a sound that was even vaguely conversational. What I did see was a writhing, almost undifferentiated mass of naked human bodies, pushing, pumping, slithering and sliding along the freshly waxed floor like some kind of ballet gone madly horizontal; what I did hear was an odd mixture of passionate whispers, groans, and delirious screams.

In one corner of the room a man with the body of a weight lifter was standing erect, inserting his monumental cock into a woman who was at least six inches taller than he while at the same time he lifted two other women entirely off the floor by their crotches, one in each hand. In another corner the blackest woman I have ever seen—so black as to be almost purple—was straddling the body of a gorgeous American Indian in full war paint, while simultaneously reaching her head back to lap at the pussy of a woman who must have been the world's most magnificently preserved senior citizen. In the middle of the floor a group of eight people had formed what looked like a human train while the poor woman who was unfortunate enough to play the caboose wailed for someone to come couple her. Outside I could see two men standing on the diving board, fencing exuberantly with their monstrous cocks while the sexiest water polo game I have ever laid eyes on went on inside the pool itself.

I have to admit it: I gaped. I have been to enough orgies to know what the word "orgy" generally means in reality—two or more couples screwing simultaneously in two or more different rooms. I have been to private clubs in London, Hong Kong, and Lagos that make Plato's Retreat look like a baby-sitting cooperative. I have been to the weddings of porno kings and Super Bowl victory celebrations. But I have never seen anything like the passion play that was going on in that house, have never experienced a sexual circus that was so absolutely without inhibition.

All in all, it looked like something Hieronymus Bosch might have drawn on commission for *Playboy* magazine.

As I continued to try to adjust my unbelieving brain to receive and process the messages my eyes were sending it, I found that my body was responding unbidden. Unmistakable and undeniable little flutterings were beginning to bounce about in my belly, and I felt a twitching between my legs as my pussy began to dilate of its own accord. Instinctively my one hand began to climb up my rib cage, up and up until it rested enticingly on the hill of my breast, while my other hand went under my skirt and up my leg toward my already pulsating vagina.

At the same time I felt a hand on my ass, gently rubbing and kneading the creamy flesh of my buttocks. Under other circumstances I would have responded immediately—one way or the other—but in this setting it seemed so entirely natural and even innocent that I didn't even turn around to see who it was. Besides, I was too busy staring at the mass of humanity in front of me, sorting out sexual details as my brain began to distinguish one incredible coupling from another.

I was particularly intrigued by a tiny, perfectly proportioned and well-muscled little man who I later discovered to be one of the country's most successful jockeys, a two-time winner of the Kentucky Derby. He had two women lying face down on top of one another, and he was screwing them alternately in perfect rhythm, withdrawing from one and then plunging his surprisingly hearty cock into the other—in, out, in, out, up and down and back and forth while both of them squealed their delight. I was tempted to tear off my clothes and add myself to this pile, but I thought first it would be a good idea to find out what had happened to Katy.

I needn't have worried. With one quick scan of the room I found her, already gloriously naked and on her knees, that luscious tongue of hers snaking into the creamy pussy of a woman with a diamond in her nose and a pair of lacy little tattoos around her nipples. The woman's face was vaguely familiar to me, and when she closed her eyes and threw her head back in delight at Katy's ministrations, I realized I had seen her in just that position, but with a sequined jump suit on and a microphone in front of her. It was Belinda Jay, a jazz singer whose exquisite talent had made her a star in Europe while she remained virtually unknown in this country.

I was glad to see Katy well occupied, but at the same

time I was curious as to what our host might be doing. I looked around until I saw Snider standing near a grand piano with all his clothes still on, sucking contentedly at a pipe. I wondered for a moment if he ever actively participated in these sexual whirlwinds of his, or if he was simply the ultimate voyeur, getting his pleasure vicariously from the pleasure of others. Nor was my question answered when a slender, beautiful redhead came up to him, unzipped his pants and unceremoniously drew out his still-limp pecker and stuffed it whole into her mouth. Amazingly, Snider hardly moved a muscle, continuing to observe the goings-on with that detached air of his, hardly taking notice as the redhead gulped and fondled him with her lush lips.

But I had no further time to indulge my curiosity vis-à-vis our host. Once again I felt that hand—or perhaps a new one—begin to massage the already trembling orbs of my buttocks. By this time I was well on the road to full arousal, my breasts heaving and my breath coming in ragged little gasps, and I could no longer ignore the insistent message of this anonymous touch on my eager behind. I turned around to find myself staring into the deep brown eyes of one of the most gorgeous men I have ever seen—a male model, probably, or perhaps a professional womanizer. His body was like a statue, a paragon of rippling perfection, and the smile on his face had the serenity of an angel's combined with the tantalizing sexual mischief of a servant of Beelzebub.

"Hello," I said, my breath nearly catching in my throat. "And who might this be touching me?"

"Aw, shit," said the gorgeous piece of manhood. He turned on his heel and walked away.

I had inadvertently discovered one of the rules of Snider's little soirees. One was perfectly free to indulge oneself in whatever sexual activity that struck one's fancy; there was absolutely nothing verboten in the way of pleasure and satisfaction. But the one inviolable law if one was to indulge was never, never to ask anyone else's name. This form of discretion was actually quite sensible, as Snider's parties tended to attract the crème de la crème of the world's glamour elite, and of course each guest had a vested interest in his own anonymity. I only wished I had been told that rule explicitly. It would have both spared me considerable embarrassment and perhaps gained me the attentions of that lovely man.

The loss of my Adonis only served to arouse me that much further. Luckily, there were a number of people who were not about to let me wander about unattended. A friendly looking woman came up and smilingly (but silently) helped me unbutton my blouse (oh, the glorious freedom as my breasts were exposed to the warm air!), and someone else slipped my skirt and panties off from behind.

Thus liberated, I went off in search of a partner or two. I didn't have to look for long. Before I had gone three steps I felt a collection of hands reach up and grab me by the calves and ankles, and within a few seconds I had been pulled down onto the floor and into a marvelously seething pile of warm humanity.

I got into the spirit of things instantly, twisting and writhing in that wonderful mountain of flesh, my hands reaching out to grope and finger and explore as other hands rubbed and prodded me everywhere at once. I felt breasts press against my tummy, muscular thighs rub up and down the sides of my rib cage, hardened cocks poke at the little doorway to my anus. For once in my life I could have tolerated what has always seemed to me the cruelest handicap: blindness. For in this sensual feast, this chorale of pure sensation, the one thing I could have done without for a few moments were my eyes.

I continued to swim happily about in this ocean of flesh, my aching pussy growing more and more demanding as the juices of my excitement continued to flow. To understand how thoroughly I was aroused, imagine your favorite lover, your most skilled paramour not only multiplied by ten, but a hermaphrodite as well, with the sexual equipment of both genders caressing your entire body, lodging in all the secret places of your desire at one and the same time. Imagine having one hand on a perfect, lush breast, another pumping up and down a hardened shaft of male love-flesh, while your lips alternately caress a warm, creamy pussy, and the sensitive skin of a pebbled scrotum. Imagine the mingled fluids, the sweat and the juice and the drops of semen smeared all about your body so that you slide over the moving flesh like a seal on a wet rock. Imagine all that, and you'll begin to understand why this marvelous party of Snider's had me fairly dizzy with delight.

Finally my urgency overcame me. My vagina was dilated to the utmost, and my belly was heaving and throbbing with the strength of my desire. I had two orgasms in quick succession before I could reach out, grab hold of the nearest and hardest cock, and plunge it to the hilt into my over-wrought pussy. I had another orgasm as the unknown cock entered me, and still another as I felt someone's groin make contact with the pulsating knob of my clitoris.

Soon I cried out in disappointment as I felt that wonderful prick withdraw from me, leaving me empty and still moaning out my need into the sunlit room. But I was not left long in that condition, as someone rolled me over and I felt another, even plumper cock penetrate me from behind, reaming out the softened walls of my vagina as it plunged in and out. In a moment I was up on my hands and knees, bucking back and forth on that wonderful rod while someone else knelt down in front of me and offered me his sleek prick, which I gathered hungrily into the warm cavern of my mouth.

By now I was quite beside myself. I wanted every hole plugged, every cavity filled. I wanted to feel warm flesh all over me, feel myself being flooded, inundated, feel myself being rocked and plundered and buffeted until I dissolved in a stream of fiery orgasms. My pussy was firing now like a machine gun, little bulletlike climaxes that grew stronger and stronger until they melded into one gigantic, cosmic orgasm that left me drained, limp, and satisfied—a grinning, mindless heap on Snider's oaken floor.

I don't know if I fainted or merely fell asleep, because the next thing I remember was hearing Snider's cheerful baritone saying, "All right, everybody—game time."

I had no idea what he meant, of course, but given the uproarious time everyone had had up till then, I could only suppose that this "game time" was some sort of traditional grand finale to the party. We all picked ourselves off the floor, a forest of glistening naked bodies, and stood there grinning at each other like children at a birthday party while Snider rounded up those guests who were still outside. I happened to catch a glimpse of Katy, who was holding hands with Belinda Jay while the singer idly massaged the agent's breast. We winked at one another, then turned our attention back to Snider, who had just returned to the room.

"Good," he said, smiling contentedly at the crowd around him. It was becoming more and more evident that Snider was simply an organizer, a ringmaster, a man who took his pleasure from programing rather than from participating. Well, I thought, to each his own. I only knew that I would never be able to simply stand and watch as he had apparently done all afternoon. I never have been able to bear the sidelines when there was a chance to get in the game.

"All right," he said, "what'll it be this time?"

"How about 'Explorers and Amazons'? said the weightlifter, who was still fingering away at one of his lovely dumbbells.

"We did that last time," Snider said. "A little originality, if you please."

"What about 'Star Travel'?" offered the gorgeous young man who I had almost enjoyed earlier on.

"Or 'Ballet,' " said the jockey.

"Or 'Romans and Visigoths'?" suggested Belinda.

By now it was obvious to me that Snider's games were forms of sexual fantasy, to be indulged in en masse. It sounded like a marvelous idea as far as I was concerned, but I wondered how everyone was to come to agreement as to the fantasy itself, especially when it seemed that everyone in the room had his or her own pet theme.

Snider solved the problem simply by taking the decision out of his guests' hands. "Actually," he said, "I think I've got a better idea. Let's do 'The Court of Marie Antoinette.' "

"Without costumes?" complained the beautiful older woman. "How?"

"*With* costumes," said Snider. "It's a little surprise I've been saving for you."

He clapped his hands and two servants appeared, rolling out a metal rack lined with elaborate eighteenth-century costumes, which looked astoundingly authentic even bunched up as they were on the rack. While everyone oohed and ahed and said "marvelous," Snider moved in to preside over the distribution, handing courtier's garb and powdered wigs to the men (except for the jockey, who got the most outlandishly colorful jester's suit I had ever seen), and lovely, frilly hoop skirts with enticing decolletage to the women. Everyone had a wonderful time helping everyone else on with their beautiful costumes, but there were three of us—Belinda, Katy, and myself—who had apparently been left out.

Not for long, though. When everyone else was dressed, when they had finished strutting like peacocks and complimenting one another on how marvelous they looked, Snider clapped his hands for attention.

"All right," he said when everyone else had quieted down. "Now we come to the leading players in our little drama. First, the eminently wicked Madame de Pompadour." He took one of the three remaining dresses, a magnificent thing of pink velvet with blood-red roses brocaded on the bodice, and presented it to Belinda, who put it on amidst enthusiastic cheers.

"Next," said Snider, "the reigning duchess of love, the elegant Marie du Barry." A second dress, a symphony of powder-blue satin and white lace, went to Katy, who filled it out so elaborately as to impress even this jaded crowd.

"And now," Snider went on, "the star of the show, the paragon of amour, lover of kings and destroyer of empires, the Queen of France—Marie Antoinette!"

He took my hand and led me over to the rack, to the one remaining dress, which he took down and held out for my approval. And I must admit, the dress was a thing of breathtaking beauty: a cascade of silk in royal purple, embroidered with fleurs-de-lis and accented with a sash of dashing pink. I started to take it from Snider, but he stepped away from me.

"No, my queen," he said softly. "You must not soil your hands with this worthless garment."

"Then bring me my ladies!" I said imperiously. I was catching onto the rules of this game and beginning to enjoy it immensely. The smile on Snider's face as he bowed low told me that I had indeed caught the spirit of the thing, and when he clapped his hands two of the women stepped forward to help me on with the dress. I could not help but notice that it had Velcro fasteners along each side, presumably for quick and easy removal.

Once the dress was in place the crowd murmured its appreciation. And with all due modesty, I must say that I looked positively stunning—my hair up off my neck, the beautiful dress showing off my color most admirably, my breasts revealed by the low decolletage right to the very points of my nipples. For a moment I almost wished I had been born two hundred years earlier, so that I could have dressed like that every day of my life.

"Now," said Snider, bringing me back to reality, "we begin. Today Queen Marie and her trusted friends"—with a sweeping wave he indicated Belinda and Katy—"are holding auditions for new lovers. Anyone of aristocratic blood is welcome to try out, but be fore-warned: A horrible punishment waits for those who fail."

He looked around the room, a glint in his eye that I found rather disturbing. I even wondered briefly if he would bring a little touch of sadism to this play of his. But the smiles and tittering of the guests relieved my fears on that score.

"First," he said, "the court entertainers will prepare the ladies for the audition."

Immediately the jockey, the weight lifter, and the

Indian stepped out of the crowd and walked toward us. I saw the weight lifter begin to nuzzle at Belinda's neck, while the Indian boldly put both his hands inside the bodice of Katy's dress, drew out her lush breasts—the crowd gasped as they popped into view—and began to tweak and fondle the nipples into an excited hardness.

As I watched this stimulating sight with growing interest, that wonderful little jockey dipped his head under my dress and started to lap at my oh-so-willing pussy with a tongue that was apparently as well-trained as the horses he rode. I responded almost immediately, moaning my approval as I watched the further advances of the weight lifter and the Indian, each of whom had now hiked the dresses of their respective ladies up above their waists, revealing pussies that were already growing wet with lubrication.

As was mine. The educated tongue of that sweet jockey was traversing the entire length of my crotch, burying itself up in the crevice between my buttocks, then trailing down over my dilating pussy hole to stroke tenderly along the hardening button of my clitoris. It wasn't long before he had me so marvelously excited that I was pulling my own breasts out of the bodice of that elegant dress, and massaging the aching globes until the nipples stood straight out at attention.

"The Queen is ready!" Snider barked. "First suitor, to the front!"

My friend the jockey withdrew—somewhat reluctantly, I noticed—and a strapping fellow in a powdered wig stepped up, his torso still covered with a formal waistcoat, but with his pantaloons removed and his aristocratic cock jutting up proudly from his loins. I was already so creamy inside that no further lubrication was needed, and so eager to have my hungry vagina filled with that magnificent instrument that I fairly thrust

myself at him, spreading my legs wide across the make-
shift throne on which I was sitting and feeling him slide
into me with one smooth, powerful stroke.

At the same time I could see the two men who had
been cock-fencing on the diving board rip the dresses
off Belinda and Katy, turn them around on their hands
and knees, and begin to plunder them from behind. It
was as if I could feel what was happening to them as
well as my own sensations, could feel the entrance of
all three cocks and the buffeting of all three powerful
loins. I closed my eyes and met each thrust of my
aristocratic lover with an answering thrust of my own,
goaded to even greater exertion by the chants and the
cheers of the crowd.

"*Oui*," I sighed, suddenly feeling thoroughly French
and thoroughly the queen. "*Oui, mon amour! Comme
ça!*"

In what seemed like a matter of seconds, I felt my
suitor stiffen and heard him grunt out his climax as his
cock jerked and throbbed inside me. I bucked up and
down madly to wring out the last juices of his orgasm,
and found that I could not stop even when he finally
withdrew. I myself was nowhere near my orgasm, and
now my little pussy was empty, leaving nothing but an
aching void.

But my host would not allow me to remain that way
for long. "Next!" he yelled. "Can't you see the Queen
is waiting?"

At once another eager suitor stepped up. I yanked at
the Velcro fasteners and tore my dress off, then turned
around, grabbed the arms of my "throne," and bent
over so that my torso was at a 90-degree angle to my
waist, thus giving this new aspirant the greatest possible
access to my throbbing vagina. He didn't hesitate. He
stepped immediately into the breech, skewering me

with the full length of his wonderful rod, and beginning immediately to fuck into me with long, powerful strokes.

But this candidate didn't last much longer than the first, yelling out his orgasm after only a few strokes while I fumed in impatient frustration. When he was finished and had withdrawn abjectly, I stood up, turned to the crowd and said:

"Is there no man here strong enough to satisfy his lonely queen?"

A silence fell over the crowd. I noticed that Katy and Belinda had evidently been more fortunate than I, and that they now lay on the floor, spent and only half-conscious, their naked bodies intertwined with those of their victorious suitors. In other parts of the room those who could no longer stand to watch and wait were indulging themselves in every imaginable manner of copulation, but even this stopped as my urgent plea rang through the room.

Finally a man stepped forward, the gorgeous thing who I had put off earlier with my inopportune request for his name. He was smiling softly, and as he advanced toward me his hand was going up and down in strong, regular rhythm on his hardened cock. Finally he reached me and bowed so low that the point of his delectable prick was almost jabbing him in the chest.

"At your service, my queen," he said.

I needed to hear no more. I took him by the hand and led him to a spot in the middle of the room and lay down on the floor as the crowd formed a circle around us. In a flash he was poised over me, and I drew my knees back until they were just under my chin so that he could penetrate me to the fullest. Just the sight of him had pushed me several steps nearer orgasm, and now, as he entered me, I felt the unmistakable surge of my impending climax beginning to build in the pressure cooker of my loins.

When I opened my eyes I saw that the crowd had already melted away; so inspired were they by the sight of my magnificent suitor beginning to saw in and out of me that they returned anew to their own randy activities. I closed my eyes again and concentrated with all my might on the feeling of his glorious cock heaving and throbbing within me, contracting the muscles of my loving cunt around it, feeling the walls pulse maddeningly in time with its insistent beat.

"*Oh!*" I cried out as the sensations welled up inside my like lava in a seething volcano. "*Oh! . . . Oh! . . . Yes, my love! . . . Just . . . like . . . that!*"

I threw my legs around him, clenching my thighs in a vise grip on his sides and clamping my ankles together so that he was locked inescapably inside me. I heaved and thrust against him, beating my heels on his back and clutching at the powerful muscles of his arms as inch by inexorable inch my orgasm rose inside me. This was the one I had been building toward all day, the one I had unconsciously been saving for him and him alone, and now it hit me, the force of it driving my pumping hips mad with fury, sending me shimmying up and down the full length of his pole in a mindless, senseless adagio that threatened to drown me in the sweet fluid ocean of pure sensation, pure feeling.

"*Oh God!*" I screamed out into the room as my back arched up off the floor and my body went stiff from the power of this incredible climax. I knew my lover was coming, too, and this served only to multiply the strident power of what I was feeling. I soared on the energy of that orgasm, feeling myself leave my body and drift out into a cottony, star-studded carpet, shoot-

ing through time and space like a soul released from
earthly torment, alone and unchained.

"By the way," I heard him whisper as my body
collapsed on the floor underneath us, "since you were
wondering earlier: my name is Leonard Snider."

"Why didn't you tell me?" I said as we drifted side
by side in the pool on a pair of air mattresses, sipping
Polish vodka and grapefruit juice—a great après-sex
pick-me-up, by the way—contained in exquisite glasses
of Swedish leaded crystal.

"First things first," he said. "In my life, partying
always comes before business."

"But who was that fellow who was organizing everything?" I asked, genuinely curious.

"A neighbor of mine," Leonard said casually. "His
great-great-grandfather had the original land grant for
this entire valley. His wife doesn't mind him coming to
the parties, but she absolutely forbids him to fuck anybody but her. So he doesn't fuck anybody at all."

"Imagine that," I said, then lapsed into a meditative
silence, which my adorable host soon broke.

"Katy told me you wanted my help with something,"
he said. "Some kind of trouble."

In my work I have developed a policy of being as
forthright as possible unless there is some good reason
to be otherwise. I looked closely now at Snider, at the
young Adonis who had satisfied me so utterly only an
hour before, and wondered if I should try to beguile
him. My instincts told me that he could be a treacher-
ous and formidable opponent if his own interests were
at stake, but that under these circumstances he would
not feel himself challenged and would thus respond best
to a direct approach.

"I do need help," I said. "I want to know what
happened to Paul Bayard."

He gave me a startled look.

"You want to know what *happened* to Bayard?" he said. "Well, nothing's *happened* to him except that he's about to become the biggest international star since Eastwood."

"Exactly my point," I said. "International stardom is not Paul's style."

"What makes you so sure?" he said.

"I know him quite well," I said. "We were once lovers."

"Did you ever stop to think that you may not have known him as well as you thought?" Snider inquired, attempting to take the offensive again.

"No," I said, and I meant it.

"Well, think about it a bit," he shot back. "I've yet to meet an entertainer who wouldn't kill for the chance to be where Bayard is right now."

"Let me put it another way," I said. "What would happen if Paul suddenly decided not to be an international star?"

Again that careless shrug. "He has no choice," Snider said. "He's under contract."

"To whom?" I said immediately. We were finally getting to the heart of the matter.

He gave out a weary sigh, as if being pestered by the insistent questioning of an intelligent but naïve child. "To Constellation Films," he said.

"You mean to Amalgamated."

"Yes, to Amalgamated. They're one and the same thing, as I'm sure you know."

"Then why is it that no one at Amalgamated seems to know anything about it?" I said sharply. I had him in a corner now, and I had no intention of letting him escape.

He shifted uncomfortably on his air mattress and took

a long sip of his vodka. "I couldn't tell you," he said finally, doing his best to hide his obvious discomfort.

"Mr. Snider," I said, narrowing in. "I came here because a very close mutual friend of ours told me you could help. Now, you've certainly gotten what you wanted out of this little arrangement . . ."

"Are you telling me you didn't enjoy the party?" he said. "If so, then you're a better actor than your boyfriend."

"I'm not saying that," I said. "I did enjoy it, and very much. I'm only saying that now I need to have what I want."

Snider rolled over on his side and gave me another long look, but this time there was genuine fear in his eyes. I could see that my questioning had definitely hit an exposed nerve.

"All right," he said finally. "I'm going to tell you everything I can, but only on two conditions."

"Yes?"

"First, you must never tell anyone where you got the information."

"That goes without saying," I said. This was something I had learned from my work as a journalist: Never ever compromise the source of your information—not if you intend to use him again, at any rate. "What's the second condition?"

"That you do absolutely nothing to follow up," he said. "The entire thing stops here, with your curiosity satisfied and . . ." He stopped in midsentence.

"And?" I said.

"Your life intact." He said it casually, but it was followed by a meaningful glance. "Understood?"

"Understood."

"All right," he said, seemingly relieved. "I'll tell you what I know, which is not everything by any stretch of the imagination. If I knew any more, I probably wouldn't be talking to you at all.''

"Please," I said. "No more preambles. Just the information." Despite myself, I was beginning to grow impatient with this verbal ballet.

"Paul Bayard *is* under contract," he said. "But it's a private contract, to a private individual.''

"What are you talking about?" I said. I had never heard of such a thing.

"Just what I said. And, by the way, you'd probably get more accomplished, and faster, if you'd listen more and interrupt less.''

"Go on," I said, properly chastened.

"Actually, there's not much more to it. Bayard's 'talents,' if you'll pardon the expression, were bought on a private basis by someone very powerful who also happened to be very impressed. That's all I know.''

"Who?" I said.

"I told you, that's all I know.''

Suddenly Snider rolled over, dropped off the raft into the pool, and began to swim toward the other end with a smooth, powerful underwater breast stroke. I followed after him, bent on outlasting him with the help of lungs conditioned by years of scuba in the waters off Grenada. When he finally came up for air, I was right next to him.

"I don't believe you," I said.

"Look," he said, "you don't want to get mixed up in this. It involves things that are way too big for you.''

"Like what?" I said.

"I've told you what I know," he said. "Isn't that enough?''

"No," I said, "It's not enough.''

"So you're not going to abide by the agreement?''

"The first part, yes. But not the second.''

"You have no idea how much you're going to regret that decision," he said.

"Be that as it may," I said. "I want to know everything."

"Not from me," he said.

"Who, then?" By now I was practically pleading. "Just give me a next step."

He gave me that look of assessment again, undoubtedly trying to weigh my trustworthiness against the value of his own anonymity. "No names," he said eventually. "I'll give you a place. From there it's up to you."

"Now we're getting somewhere," I said. "Where do I have to go?"

"San Cristóbal de las Casas," he said.

"Where on earth is that?" I said.

"In Mexico. The state of Chiapas, near the border with Guatemala."

"Mexico?" I said in surprise. "Chiapas? Isn't that place known for its drug trade?"

"You ask too many questions," he said, and dove underwater again.

I followed again, thinking furiously as my body took over what for me is the automatic function of swimming. I was confused, certainly, and for the life of me could not understand what possible connection Paul could have with drugs in an out-of-the-way place like San Cristóbal. It could very well be a subterfuge, I realized, an attempt on Snider's part to mislead and ultimately frustrate me out of my objective. But I thought not. There must be a reason why Snider was vague.

When he came up for air—again, long before I felt the need myself—I grabbed him by the hair and planted a fervent kiss on his lips. I could feel his lovely cock begin to swell in his bathing suit as I crushed him to me.

"Just one more question," I said when we broke the kiss. "Then we'll play some more." I reached down between his legs and ran my hand meaningfully across the underside of his balls. "How long is the term of Paul's contract?"

He looked at me with what I can only call genuine delight as he reached around behind me to unclasp the top part of my bathing suit, leaving my breasts to float buoyantly on top of the water.

"It's for life," he said, an unreadable glint in his eyes. "They don't make them any longer than that."

CHAPTER SIX

There were no commercial flights to San Cristóbal. Xavier offered to fly me down in his Lear, but when I checked on it I was told that the runways there were too short even for executive-sized jets. So I took a Mexicana flight to Tuxtla Gutiérrez—a horrible industrial town in the middle of a raspy desert—and from there hired a local pilot to fly me up to San Cristóbal in his prewar Cessna.

The flight itself turned out to be just as beautiful as Tuxtla was ugly. It took us sailing up the side of the magnificent range of mountains that starts there in Southern Mexico and runs all the way down to Panama. From out altitude, which seemed to be no more than treetop level plus a hundred feet or so, I could see long, elegant ribbons of waterfalls winding through mountain forests, and a thin mist that laced its way through the trees so that the whole scene was somehow reminiscent of a Japanese paradise. Occasionally my eyes were tantalized by marvelous little foot trails that ran mysteriously off into the woods, and once or twice I thought I saw Indians trotting along the trails, carrying loads of firewood at least as big as they were, using nothing more than a strap attached to their foreheads.

By the time the pilot landed in a little Alpine meadow at the top of the mountain, I was enthralled. Everything around me was brilliant green and dotted with yellow flowers, and a creek ran peacefully through the little meadow that had been dignified with the name of an airport. By the side of the creek a gaggle of Indian women dressed entirely in white laughed and talked as they washed clothes and beat them dry on the blue rocks that also served as their chairs. It was the sort of wonderfully primitive place that under less pressured circumstances I might have chosen for a private retreat, or a romantic holiday with a special lover.

But I had business. The pilot very graciously drove me from the airport into town, a magnificent old colonial *pueblo* with a weather-beaten seventeenth-century cathedral facing the village square. I took a hotel on the other side of the plaza, a charming old place with fresh flowers in the courtyard fountain and wildly colored tropical birds cawing madly from their wrought-iron cages.

I drank a *manzañita* in the courtyard, and for the first time began to wonder what I was actually going to do now that I was there. I hadn't the faintest idea who to talk to—even Xavier's almost universal network of contacts did not reach into this remote little spot—and very little notion of where to start. Now I found myself regretting that years ago I had turned my schoolgirl nose up at Spanish and concentrated on learning French.

Luckily, the hotel manager spoke English and was able to find me an interpreter, a winsome young mestizo boy with the improbable name of Tolerante Dos Rios. A part Quiché Indian, Tolerante was sixteen and had one of those angelic Mexican faces with the Walter Keane eyes. I immediately took him to my room so as to avoid being overheard, but when I boldly told him

that I wanted to meet whoever
local drug traffic, and would pa
he was so startled that he forgot h

"*Quieres conocer al Cubano?*"

I didn't need Spanish to understan
and now I was just as surprised as h
there's a Cuban in charge of the trade he

"*Sí, señorita*," he said. "Back in the
where they grow the *mota* and the *opio*, the Cu an runs
everything."

"I want to meet him," I said.

"This is not easy," he replied.

"I didn't expect it to be easy. If you can arrange a
meeting, I can fix it so you'll never have to work
again."

He gave me a wary look—I suppose he was entirely
unused to having women speak to him that way. But
when I opened my wallet and gave him a hundred-
dollar bill—"for your trouble," I said—he brightened
immediately.

"I come for you tonight," he said. "I take you to the
Cuban."

"Perfect," I said. "And thank you, darling." I leaned
over and planted a motherly kiss on his forehead, where-
upon his face lit up in a tremendous blush and he
literally sprinted from the room.

I spent the rest of the day seeing the sights: strolling
through the Indian market, picking among the baskets
of green chilis, mangoes, and the bright red pepper
called *aji*, buying several pairs of the crude, massive
golden earrings that the women haul down from the
secret mountains in cardboard boxes; then a short trip
outside town to a series of caverns that were even more
spectacular (although somewhat smaller) than the famous ones at Carlsbad, New Mexico. By the time I

was after dark, and I found myself running my rented car to the hotel in fear that I had missed Tolerante.

But he was there, dressed in white peasant pants and white serape, his hair combed and slicked back, his face shining clean. He looked so adorably innocent that I had the urge to take him in my arms and cuddle him half to death, but I remembered his reaction when I kissed him that afternoon and managed to stifle myself.

"We must hurry, *señorita*," he said when he saw me. "The fight is already started."

"What fight?" I said. He had mentioned nothing of this in the afternoon.

"*Los gatos del monte,*" he said. "You'll see. But please, we must hurry. *Apúrese, señorita.*"

"Wait a minute," I said when we were outside. "What does this fight, whatever it is, have to do with the Cuban?"

"His cat is fighting tonight," he said. "He will be there, I know."

Without another word of explanation he started off across the square, and there was nothing I could do but shrug and follow him as best I could. He led me past the church, then through a maze of impossibly narrow streets and even narrower alleyways, finally stopping in front of a silent, darkened tire shop to wait for me to catch up. When I reached him, Tolerante drummed his fingers on the corrugated metal door, and within a few seconds I heard a muffled voice say something in Spanish. Tolerante answered, then took my hand and led me around to the back of the shop.

There a door creaked open and Tolerante ushered me into a large, brightly lit room that must have served as the shop's garage during the daytime. Once my eyes adjusted to the sudden glare, I could see that the room was ringed with people, an amazingly mixed crowd that included Mexicans in fancy-dress *guayaberas*, solemn Indians in their white cotton clothing, a few Caribbean-looking blacks, and one woman who I could have sworn was German, although she was dressed in the bright wools of the Indians of Guatemala. The room was surprisingly quiet, as people talked in matter-of-fact tones, and only an occasional laugh rose above the conversational hum.

Then I noticed a stack of cages standing apart in one corner of the garage. Inside the cages were various felines, but in versions I had never seen before, not even in the pages of *National Geographic*. The animals had long, low bodies reminiscent of weasels, with triangular heads, sharp, pointed noses, and faces that reminded me of raccoon, but without the mask. Some walked restlessly around their cages while others appeared to be almost somnambulant, but they all exuded a mysterious sort of tension, like athletes before an event or, perhaps more aptly, like coiled snakes.

"Los gatos del monte," Tolerante said when he saw me staring at them. "Soon they will fight."

"What about the Cuban?" I said.

"I don't see him now. But he will come, I am sure."

Before I could open my mouth to ask another question, a hush fell over the room as two Indians walked across to the cages, opened them, and dragged out two of the mountain cats by the scruffs of their necks. The cats remained quiescent in the restraining grasps of their masters, who now walked over to the center of the room and stood on opposite sides of a large wooden box with side rails just high enough to keep the cats in while still low enough to allow the audience a good view.

The tone of conversation in the room rose perceptibly now, an anxious, excited buzz that foretold of the violence to come. I saw bottles being raised to lips and money passing from hand to hand as bets were placed. The air was growing thick with the sweet smell of fresh marijuana. Tolerante passed me a cigar-sized joint and a mason jar filled with an ominous-looking clear liquid of some sort. I took a hit on the joint, feeling the fragrant, skunky *mota* go instantly to the back of my brain, which immediately lit up in grateful response. I then took a healthy gulp of the stuff in the mason jar, which had the furious punch of airplane fuel mixed with an aftereffect that whispered of the secrets of the Mayans.

The scene was beginning to have a decidedly sexual effect on me. The tension and suppressed violence of the exotic mountain cats, the tableau of the excited crowd and the two solemn Indians presenting their animals, and stimulation of the weed and the liquor (which I knew to be the notorious *mezcal*), were combining in me to send erotic little messages beaming through my body and out to the surfaces of my breasts and inner thighs, which themselves acted as antennae, picking up the unmistakably sexual overtones being emitted by the crowd. Even before the action started I could feel myself start to groan inside, could feel the excited little tremors running through my belly, and I wondered how I would get through the evening without a man to pour myself over. I found myself now hoping fervently that the Cuban would show up, for more reasons than one.

Suddenly the room erupted in an explosion of noise. The two Indians simultaneously flung their cats into the box in front of them, and in a flash the vicious little animals were at each other, rolling and spitting, howling and clutching as they went for each other's throats. At the same time, all the stored tension and excited anticipation of the crowd was released, and in the din that followed it was hard to distinguish one animal's cry from another's.

As for me, the sight of those two slinky animals tearing at each other acted like an electric prod to my already overcharged insides. The part of me that managed to remain detached wondered at this sudden eroticism in the face of violence, for I have never been the type to derive any sort of pleasure at all from the pain of animals, although there are many in my circle of acquaintances who do. But the *mezcal* and the sweet weed were evidently tapping something inside me that had remained hidden up till then, something primitive and bestial, an ancient sexuality that was tied to life and death in a way we moderns can scarcely understand.

But this is intellectualism. The plain fact of the matter is this: I was incredibly excited by the fight between the two mountain cats, excited in a way that was all the stronger for being entirely new to me. As the animals continued to have at each other, launching themselves full force at one another's faces, parrying for balance, looking for that mortal opening at the soft underside of the throat, I found my breasts tingling and heaving, my heart pounding, and my tongue unconsciously flicking over the surface of my own lips.

"How long does this go on?" I said to Tolerante.

"*Hasta la muerte,*" he replied. "To the death."

"And where is the Cuban?"

"I do not know, *señorita.*"

He must have noticed the heaviness of my breathing, the glazed look in my eye, the faint line of perspiration that had begun to form on my upper lip. I may even have taken the initiative myself—I no longer remember. What I do remember is the sensation that charged through me as I felt his delicate, slender fingers at the back of my neck, massaging the muscles gently, with an astonishingly knowing touch. Under other circumstances I undoubtedly would have reacted, would have removed his hand with a gentle smile, perhaps, or even have scolded him. But no such thought crossed my mind at that moment. The delightful, insistent massage was exactly what I needed, and almost immediately I found myself backing up so that the rounded crests of my buttocks brushed lightly against his groin.

"*Sí, señorita*," he murmured, and I could feel his breath on my neck. He was timing the pulses of his massage so that they coincided with what was happening in the box—each time one of the elegant little cats lunged at one another, Tolerante's marvelous fingers closed on my tender neck muscles. Each time one of the cats let out a mighty yowl, he would press his groin that much more tightly against my trembling buttocks. Each time one of the cats made a desperate plunge for the other's throat, he would flex his long, slender pole against me, laying it against the crevice of my ass-cheeks and penetrating that vulnerable spot ever so slightly.

As I tore my eyes from the cats and looked about the room, I could see signs that many of the spectators were being affected the same way I was. There was a group of obviously wealthy Mexicans who had probably come from the capital just for this spectacle, and I saw now that a number of men had hiked their ladies' skirts above their waists and were running their hands along the insides of their cinnamon-colored thighs as the women writhed and wriggled in transported ecstasy. In another corner a group of Europeans—the men dressed rather comically in safari suits, the women resplendent in silk evening gowns—were nuzzling passionately at one another, and here and there I saw the flash of a bared breast, the glimmer of an exposed thigh. The German woman, who was evidently some kind of veteran of these shindigs, was rubbing her breast with one hand and massaging her pussy with the other, while a gorgeous and regal Latino sank to his knees in front of her and began to clutch wildly at her churning hips. Of all the people in the room, only the Indians remained unmoved, their taciturn eyes still glued on the struggling cats.

In the meantime, Tolerante was gluing himself to me. His hand was rubbing even more insistently at my neck, and I could feel his chest against my shoulder blades, his thighs against the backs of my own, and most of all his marvelous little prick rubbing up and down along the crack in my ass-cheeks. I pressed back against him with greater and greater fervor, my buttocks beginning a slow, grinding rotation as I groaned aloud at the delightful contact.

"Mmm," I purred as I ground into him. "You feel marvelous, darling."

"*Señorita*," he sighed, and despite my yearning I was touched by the sweetness of it. "You are so beautiful. I want you so much."

I closed my eyes and leaned back against him even harder, feeling his rigid cock throb as it tried to bury itself in my buttocks. With my eyes closed the hissing and growling of the animals mingled with the screams and sighs of the overwrought crowd to become an erotic symphony in my brain, a symphony that even now was beginning to rise to an inevitable crescendo. When I opened them again I saw that the audience had now reached more advanced stages of erotic involvement, saw, in fact, that what few inhibitions remained were being shed one by one.

The party of Mexicans had lost all pretense of continued interest in the cats (who, by the way, had reached some sort of impasse in their struggle and acted much like exhausted boxers who spend the late rounds of a fight simply clenching and clinging to one another). One of the women was on her knees, lapping gently at the underside of her lover's cock with long, smooth strokes of her velvety tongue while another woman who was stripped to the waist and whose breasts were jiggling enticingly was just beginning to prod at the same man's asshole with a slender finger. Staccato "ai"'s and whispery *"mi amor"*'s emanated from the group, sounding for all the world like the movements of small animals in a fern-choked jungle.

The Europeans were now prancing about in various stages of undress, and it seemed that in their group no genital was left exposed without some hand to cover it, or some mouth to engulf it in its warm, moist tunnel. I particularly remember the sight of one reed-thin Frenchwoman, standing alone a bit apart from the group, her dress torn to tatters by her own fierce clutching, swaying to some invisible wind as she clawed at her pussy with her whole hand.

The German woman now seemed to be bent on outdoing everybody. Her dress was hiked up almost to her neck, and she was being held in a horizontal position by two reluctant-looking Indians who must have been her servants, while her elegant lover buried himself between her legs, sucking madly at her vagina as she threw her knees over his shoulders and began to kick him wildly in the back.

"Ja!" she screamed as she kicked him, her voice cutting like a knife thorugh the general commotion. *"Ja! Ja! Ja!"*

By now even the stoic, silent Indians were beginning

to shift their interest from the animals in the center of the room to the wild goings-on along the peripheries. Two of them were casting hungry glances at the solitary Frenchwoman, and over near the cat cages I saw one elderly man unveil an astonishingly virile cock and start to stroke the hardened rod in easy, measured rhythm, his eyes glued on the Mexican woman with the bared breasts. He must have been sending her some kind of urgently sexual telepathic message, because just as she grew bored with playing with her companion's ample butt, her eyes locked with those of the old man across the room. Without hesitation she strode over to where he still stood stroking his proud cock, and with an ecstatic groan she knelt in front of him and buried his dark pole in the warm valley between her heaving breasts, which she then pressed tightly together to form a sheath around the Indian's cock.

"My God!" I moaned as my senses registered the sights and sounds of the sensual banquet taking place all around me. I pressed back still harder against my wonderful little lover's loins, panting out my desperation as my buttocks rotated wildly in a frenzy that was rapidly growing out of control. I had to have satisfaction! The massive orgy going on in that room was stripping me of my sense of judgment, was turning me wild with desire! I had to feel this man-child's luscious cock inside me, pushing at the resisting walls of my tight cunt! I had to have him, and to hell with the consequences!

"*Tolerante!*" I gasped. "*Please! Touch me! Touch me all over! Touch my breasts, my ass! Make love to me!*"

"*Sí, señorita,*" he said in a husky whisper. "*Así, mi amor! Asi!*"

As he spoke I felt one of his hands snake around my

waist and drift up my chest to gently cup the underside of one breast in his palm. At the same time the hand that had been rubbing my neck so dreamily now sought out my other breast, so that soon both hands were clasped over my heaving mounds, the fingers alive on me, pressing the cloth of my dress against my nipples until the little berries stood out proud and firm against the restraining garment.

"Yes," I sighed. *"Yes, my little lover! Touch me like that! Oh yes, you feel so good!"*

He went on massaging my firm breasts, brushing and pressing at the nipples through my dress until I could stand the heavenly teasing no longer. I took both his hands in mine and literally stuffed them into the bodice of my dress, the touch of his fingertips on my bare skin igniting me still further. In another moment he drew both my breasts up and out of the restraining garment, exposing them to the exciting stimulus of the pleasantly cool night air and at the same time providing unimpeded access for his amazingly practiced fingers, which now tweaked and rolled and pressed at my nipples with an urgency that was making me positively weak with desire.

"That's it," I moaned in passion, wriggling my buttocks in tight little circles against the hardness of his prick. How I wanted that cock inside me! How I wanted to open my legs to admit him, swallow him, wring the pungent juices from that lovely penis of his! I knew in that moment that I had passed the point of no return, that if it was fated to be I would gladly make love to him then and there, with the growls of the cats and the squeals of the ladies ringing in my ears! The feel of his fingers on my sensitive nipples, the wonderful surge of his cock as it parted the cleavage between my pumping buttocks, the delightful sensation of his hot breath along

my shoulders and neck . . . I was absolutely alive with passion, and my moistened quim was begging for satisfaction, for the release I knew this lovely little Mexican boy could provide me!

"Señorita," I heard him whisper, and his voice was like a hot poker penetrating my brain, "I want you! I want to make love to you, señorita! You are so beautiful . . . so beautiful! I must have you!"

I moaned again and closed my hands over his, pressing them that much more firmly against my pounding breasts. He squeezed them tightly now, kneading and rubbing them, pressing the hard little buttons of my nipples so that jolts of sensation coursed along every nerve, every fiber of my aching body. I threw my head back so that it rested on his shoulder, and instantly his mouth was on my neck, his lips alive with desire, warm and tantalizing, singeing the sensitive skin of my neck as they played deliriously along the surface.

At that moment I opened my eyes and saw that the sensual fiesta in the audience had progressed still further. The bare-breasted Mexican woman had brought the Indian man to orgasm simply by rubbing his cock between her breasts, and she was now smearing the semen all over her belly as she licked the residue from the delicate little slit at the tip of his cock. The Indian's eyes were gleaming with lust, with the pride of a sexual conquest the likes of which had not been seen since Malinche seduced the great Cortez, and he glowered over her now with all the virile power of a triumphant chieftain.

The German woman was still being slavered at by her gorgeous lover, who was buried between her legs while her thighs clamped mightily around his ears. Apparently unable to take a passive role any longer, the two Indian servants who were holding her had stripped off her serape and her cotton blouse, and were now sucking greedily at her monumental tits. Her eyes were glazed and her head was lolling back and forth with the strength of her uncontrolled passion, and her hips were bucking wildly up and down, pressing her yearning cunt against the face of the man who was eating her so divinely.

By now the Europeans were entirely naked, and they had formed one of the most creative daisy chains I have ever seen, with the solitary Frenchwoman at the head of it, cupping one lustful Indian's balls in her hand while the other plundered her from behind. The others were strung out behind her in an astonishing array of sexual attitudes, each one connected to the other by one or more genitals as shouts of "*alors!*" and "*comme ça!*" issued loudly from the group.

The Mexicans seemed to have outraced everyone, for in their gallery lay a pile of exhausted, half-dressed bodies, legs draped over panting chests and weary heads lying across the soft bellies of satisfied women. One of the satiated men—a comical little character who looked amazingly like Cantinflas—now raised his head and blew a kiss to the Frenchwoman, then sank down again in a blissful torpor without bothering to see if his salute had been acknowledged.

Seemingly forgotten in all this sexual carnage were the two cats in their arena in the center of the room. But they did not remain forgotten for long. Suddenly one of them began to recover his energy, and with a mighty yowl he lunged at the other, teeth bared and a look of crazed aggression in his eyes.

All attention now turned to the center of the room, responding as one to the crazed urgency of that sound.

As its last echo died in the room the German woman screamed out her orgasm, and it was nearly impossible to distinguish one sound from the other. The Mexican woman tried to turn her face toward the arena, but her Indian grabbed her head and thrust his cock back into her mouth, his hips now pumping the hardened instrument into her with brutal fury. But all the other Europeans stopped their writhing and squirming to watch the suddenly revitalized fighting in the center of the room.

As for me, the sound of that mountain cat's howl penetrated me with the same smashing impact as if it had been a rigid cock. I shivered, my eyes glued on the two animals as the aggressor backed off again and stiffened in readiness for what I knew would be the death lunge. At the same moment, Tolerante reached down, lifted my dress above my waist, and pulled down my panties in one swift motion. Instinctively I spread my legs and bent over double, exposing my trembling cunny to him as I continued to watch the deadly tableau in the arena, hypnotized and fascinated by the impending kill.

Then came one of those time-frozen moments: the stronger of the two cats immobile but poised, savoring the certainty of his victory while cruelly prolonging the fatal act itself . . . the vanquished preparing himself for the end, but still refusing to turn belly-up in submission to his would-be killer . . . Tolerante waiting behind me, his prick unsheathed and ready for the inevitable penetration . . . my vagina twitching and throbbing as it waited the agonizing few seconds for the welcome invasion of my lover's cock . . . And then . . .

In a flash the scene came alive. The winning mountain cat leapt at his exhausted victim, bowling him off his feet and instantly sinking his piranha's teeth into the soft and unprotected throat. In the same instant Tolerante pressed forward, plunging his slender cock past my swollen pussy-lips, parting the inner labia with a sure thrust and burying the hardened rod to the hilt in the warm cream of my vagina as I moaned out my approval.

But in that same moment, as the cat dug his teeth into his victim's throat and began to twist about in preparation for the kill, as Tolerante began to move slowly inside me, I suddenly came awake. It was as if I had been in a deep trance, mesmerized by the horror and violence and gritty sensuality of the scene I had been witnessing, trapped immobile in the dance of contrasts, the ballet of life and death. Now, though, I truly realized what was happening. I could no more go through with this brutal consummation than I could kill that pretty little mountain cat with my own hands.

I moved forward suddenly so that Tolerante's cock slid out of my lubricated pussy. I straightened up quickly and turned to face him, almost laughing at the surprise and hurt registered on his face. I took his hand in both of mine and said urgently:

"Not here, lover. Not like this."

Before he could answer I reached down and stuffed his cock back into his pants. Then I took his hand and literally dragged him out of the room, keeping my eyes averted from the arena and trying not to hear the horrible cries of the dying cat. No one noticed us leaving, so raptly were they watching the death scene being played out in front of them, and when we finally reached the street I took a deep breath and thanked God that I had snapped out of my trance before fully implicating myself in this minor tragedy.

This is not to say that I had lost all desire. In fact, the reverse was true, for my overwrought body was still feeling all the pounding sensation that the events of the last half hour had inspired in me. Now that we were outside and alone, my desire welled up in me with even greater strength than before, especially now that I had been entered so lovingly and then been forced to cause his untimely withdrawal.

"Quick!" I said to my astonished young lover. *"Back to the hotel! I must have you! Now, do you understand? Now!"*

Before he could reply I grabbed his arm and started to sprint down the street, practically dragging him along with me as I ran. Inside, my body was screaming: *Now . . . oh, God, I've got to have him now . . . I've got to feel him inside me . . . I'm burning . . . oh God, get me to that room!"*

It seemed as if it took hours for us to reach the hotel, but in reality it must have been no more than a few minutes, because by the time we ran up the stairs to my room and locked the door behind us the flame in my body was burning as high as ever. Vivid images from the cat fight streamed through my brain—the two stalking animals and their murderous eyes, the outrageous German woman and the white heat of her desire, the lovely old Indian and his unmerciful cock as it plunged in and out of the willing mouth of that bare-chested Mexican woman, the French with their exuberant daisy chain and the played-out Mexicans—all these combined in me to make my nerves come alive, make my whole body throb in a dance of primitive passion.

I quickly stripped the wide-eyed Tolerante—poor boy, he still must be wondering what to make of me—of his shirt and pants, trailing wet, urgent kisses down the length of his body as I removed his clothes. I took his hand and led him to my bed, flinging him down on his back so that his still-hard cock stood up like a flagpole. Without further ado I stripped off my panties, lifted my dress, and plunged myself down on him, groaning with sweet agony as I felt his cock slide up into my dilated pussy.

"*Oh yes!*" I cried. "*Oh, God, yes! That's what I want! Fill me, darling! Fuck me! Let me feel you inside me!*"

I put my hands on the bed beside him to support my weight as I raised my hips high in the air, so that just the very tip of his delightful cock remained embedded in me. Then I lowered myself down on him in a long, silken stroke, going as slowly as I could, savoring each glorious second, each glorious new inch of pure pleasure! When I felt my ass-cheeks contact his groin and the sensitive skin of my pussy-lips touch the hard muscles of my abdomen, I ground myself down on him, feeling the lips of my vagina part to allow that heavenly contact between his muscular belly and the tingling cord of my excited clitoris.

I stopped for a moment, letting him savor the sensation of being buried completely inside me, and then I began to move slowly back and forth, reveling in the sweet friction of his skin on my clitty. Then, before I brought myself too dangerously close to orgasm, I lifted up again, poised still in the air for a long moment, and then lowered myself back down onto him, crashing into his loins with a hearty plunge that had both of us gasping with delight.

"*That's it, my little lover . . .*" I said in a husky voice. "*Just like that! Oh, Tolerante, you feel so marvelous! I want you to stay inside me like this! Never leave, do you hear? Oh yes, my love!*"

Soon the words merged together to become nothing

more than a passionate babble, to which Tolerante responded with little urgings of his own in Spanish. I continued to maintain the same delicious cycle of stroking: hips high in the air, then smoothly down until he was once again buried to the hilt in my hungry pussy, then a back-and-forth motion along the hardened muscles of his groin. Now he was responding, too, bucking up to meet me as I lowered myself down onto him, then twisting the muscles of his stomach and abdomen so that they formed a little peak, along which my aroused clitty slid as if had been grafted there.

"Mmm . . ." I whispered. "Yes, my little love . . . how did you learn to do that? . . . that's just delightful . . . oh, yes!"

"Ai, mi amor . . . mi linda amor . . ." he groaned as he continued to buck up against me, his thrustings growing ever stronger and more urgent. My pussy had closed around his cock like a velvet vise, holding it in a firm grip, caressing it, making it swell with passion as it continued to saw up into me. I felt his hands creep up the outsides of my thighs to rest on my churning hips, pulling them up and down with even greater fury as he rose to meet me, and now the rustlings deep in my belly were growing stronger, collecting and building to the crescendo that foretold of my coming orgasm.

Now his hands left my hips, rode up my sides and landed squarely on my breasts, his fingers immediately forming little "o's" around the nipples and his thumbs pushing them delightfully in. I felt the alarm ring through my body, and I began to shudder and tremble in anticipation of the climax that was moving closer with each second, with each renewed thrust of his supple young body. I knew now that I would be able to hold out no longer, that any second I would pour my hot juices out over his straining muscles.

"Ah! . . . Yes! . . . Yes! . . . Oh . . . my . . . God! . . ." I spit out through clenched teeth as the orgasm hit me, coursing through my trembling body with all the power of a tidal wave. At precisely the same moment I felt my sweet young lover stiffen, felt him arch his back in one final thrust, felt his delightful cock swell and throb as he pumped his semen into me like a fire hose gone berserk.

Then all was quiet. I gently pulled myself off him and lay down at his side, nuzzling up against the smooth skin of his neck as I stretched my satiated body out in the double bed. I could feel his panting breath along the side of my face, could feel his divine young muscles relaxing in the aftermath of his climax. Outside I could hear crickets calling, and the cooing of the birds in their cages—a lovely, peaceful counterpoint to the impassioned wildness of the evening. By the time I leaned over to kiss him, to thank him for that delightful fuck, he was already sound asleep, his breathing coming in regular little whistles that reminded me of the wind rustling through the misty forests of Chiapas.

Later that night I awoke to feel the insistent hardness of Tolerante's cock as it came alive along the skin of my thighs. In a dreamy half-sleep I rolled over to accept him, keeping my eyes closed and murmuring incomprehensibly as he made love to me with a gentle, rolling motion that made me feel like an island shore being caressed by a warm and placid sea. Within a very few seconds I had come to orgasm, a long and lovely climax that had me soaring like some enchanted bird through the awakening sky.

We made love all that night, exploring one another's bodies with all the tremulous excitement of new lovers. By the time we finally fell into an exhausted sleep, Tolerante had grown up in my arms, had become, in effect, a mature and understanding man, worthy of the best a woman like me had to offer, and wise in the ways of love.

CHAPTER SEVEN

By the time the morning sunlight hit the top of the cathedral, my mind had returned to business. Somehow that long, dreamy night with Tolerante had made me more determined than ever to find out what had happened to drive Paul into that mysterious and seemingly hopeless captivity, to turn that powerful love of ours so suddenly and irredeemably cold.

"Tolerante," I said as we sipped coffee and munched on fresh *bolillos* in the courtyard, "take me to see El Cubano."

He shook his head immediately. "No, *señorita*," he said. "This I cannot do, not even for you."

"And why not?"

"Because, *señorita,* one does not seek out El Cubano. If he wants you, he comes to you."

"How unsatisfying," I said. I reached into my purse, took out another hundred-dollar bill, and stuffed it in his shirt pocket. Then I leaned across the table and gave him a long, passionate kiss, sliding my tongue between his teeth and rolling it enticingly around the moist cavern of his mouth. He remained stiff for a moment, then began to respond, sucking at my tongue like a hungry kitten at his mother's tit.

"All right, *señorita*," he sighed as I finally broke the kiss. "I will take you. But I cannot guarantee that we will find him. Even if we do, I don't think he'll talk to you."

"I'll take the chance," I said.

"I don't think you understand, *señorita*. It could be very dangerous for you to go into the mountains."

"I'll take the chance," I repeated.

He gave me a long look, then seeing that I was absolutely resolute, he sighed and nodded. "All right," he said in a resigned tone. "*Vamos*."

We got into my rented car—one of those horribly noisy German jeeps that everyone finds so cute these days—drove through town, and headed south on the highway toward the Guatemalan border. After a half hour's drive along the excellent Pan American Highway, Tolerante suddenly directed me to stop at an unmarked spot by the side of the road. There was a small foot trail that led off into the forest—for the life of me I still cannot figure out how he could tell one of these tiny footpaths from another—and without a word Tolerante started off down it, leaving me no choice but to follow in silence.

We walked for what seemed like hours through the still forests, seeing no signs of life whatsoever. Thankfully I had worn a pair of baggy jeans and an army shirt, for everywhere it seemed that thorns and brambles reached out to grab at me. Finally, when the noonday sun had burned the mist off the clinging trees, the trail began to broaden and I thought I heard voices in the distance.

In another few minutes we emerged into a large clearing, where a dozen or so stone huts with thatched roofs were pouring smoke through the unadorned holes that served as chimneys. Immediately a tiny Indian woman appeared at the door of one of the huts, then walked quickly toward us. Tolerante met her halfway, and the two talked urgently in a language the words of which thundered with antiquity, while I stood off to the side trying to hide my nervousness.

Finally I saw Tolerante nod solemnly, and then he turned and walked back to me.

"*Está bien,*" he said. "The old woman will take you to see El Cubano."

"And you?"

"I go back to San Cristóbal."

I frowned at this news, for a moment not knowing whether I should feel relieved that I was finally going to see the Cuban or apprehensive about being abandoned here by Tolerante. But I could see that I had absolutely no choice in the matter.

"All right," I said. "I'll see you at the hotel."

"*Sí, señorita,*" he mumbled, giving me a look of such intolerable sadness that my heart nearly broke. I reached to touch his cheek, but before I would he spun on his heel and walked off down the forest trail. Within moments the trees had swallowed him.

It was the last time I ever laid eyes on that marvelous boy, who had touched me so deeply in such a short time.

Now the tiny Indian woman—she could not have been more than four feet tall—motioned that I should follow her. We crossed the village, the woman beating off the wretched, furiously barking dogs as we passed, and soon plunged back into the forest, following a trail that, unbelievably, was even narrower than the comparative superhighway on which we had come. The old woman immediately broke into a surprisingly rapid trot, so that I had some difficulty just keeping her in sight, let alone keeping up with her.

After an hour or so of this, we suddenly broke out of the woods into another clearing. In this one there were no houses, only a blackened, ash-strewn field which had once obviously borne some sort of crop. The woman stopped at the edge of the clearing and let out a howl so astoundingly similar to the ones I had heard last night from the *gatos del monte* that an inadvertent sexual thrill passed through me.

In a moment the call was answered, and soon a couple stepped out of the woods on the other side of the clearing. Their appearance was so strikingly different from anything I had seen since coming to Mexico that I almost gasped in surprise: The man was at least six and a half feet tall and black as a panther, while the woman, who resembled him somewhat, was a statuesque Negro-Latin mix with a round face, startling eyes, and skin the color of milk chocolate.

They walked quickly across the clearing toward me as the old Indian faded away into the woods. They were holding hands, and their quiet confidence with one another led me to assume that they were lovers, or perhaps husband and wife. Finally they reached me and I looked from one to the other, barely able to hide my admiration for these two nearly perfect physical specimens.

So this is El Cubano, I thought. *Maybe I'm finally going to get some answers.*

"Miss van Bell," the gorgeous giant said in flawless English, with just a hint of a Cambridge accent. "We've been expecting you."

"You have?" I said. "How? Why?"

He ignored my questions completely. "I am Nacimiento Santos," he said, "and this is my wife, Julia. Please come with us."

Without allowing me a word he took his wife's hand and led me up a small hill on the other side of the clearing. When we reached the top he pointed down the hill to a large field in a bowl at the bottom. Even from that distance I could see that I was looking at what amounted to a marijuana plantation, the plants—all of them from ten to fifteen feet tall—waving in a gentle breeze, foot-long flowers crowning the tips and reaching for the benevolent sun.

"Very impressive," I said, and I meant it.

"It's actually quite sad," he said. "Come with me and I'll explain."

They led me down the hill to a tiny shack at the edge of the marijuana field. From there I could see a corps of Indians tending the plants, some trimming and picking yellow leaves from the bottom stalks, others carrying bucketfuls of water with that now-familiar forehead strap. Evidently what the Cuban had here amounted to an industrial installation—lack of machinery notwithstanding—and I found myself wondering how much he paid his peons for their obviously considerable labor.

We stood outside the shack, watching silently as the workers went about their business. Finally the Cuban spoke:

"This is our last field," he said, and I could hear the sadness through his steely voice. "I came here ten years ago from Cuba, with orders from Fidel to organize these Indians, to make them see how the *puercos* in Mexico City were conspiring to keep them poor and miserable. And I did a good job. I cut their corn production in half and applied that labor to planting *mota,* which we then traded for guns and money. We had a real revolution going. We were *winning.* The army didn't dare follow us here, where the forest is one of our most powerful weapons, and we controlled everything outside San Cristóbal. We even elected one of our people Governor of Chiapas. Oh yes, we were strong.'' His eyes shone as he remembered his triumph.

"What happened?" I said.

"The DEA." He spat out the words as if they were some kind of deadly poison.

"Are you talking about paraquat?" I asked, remembering the hubbub that the spraying of Mexican marijuana had caused. "You mean they killed all the plants?"

"Pah!" he said bitterly. "They never touched a plant. But they killed the trade as effectively as if they had really sprayed the entire country."

"You mean it was a hoax?"

"The hoax of the century. You see how this field is protected? You feel how the winds blow everything up the hill, how no plane could possibly fly lower than the field to seed the wind with that poison of theirs? All our fields were that way. We were never touched by paraquat. The only thing that killed us was the scare."

Now I understood. I myself had never smoked much Mexican marijuana, as I preferred the fragrant Thai and the potent Afghan sinsemilla grown on the Kona Coast. But I had heard the talk. I had heard the news of lung damage, of paraquat testing and chromosome breakage and what-have-you. I had not paid it much attention at the time, but now that it was laid out in front of me I could understand that no American potsmoker would have bought Mexican marijuana during those days of fear. I could see how clever, how diabolical the government had been in playing on the paranoia of the health food generation, knowing the yogurt-eaters would never touch anything that had been tainted with chemicals, even if the tainting were nothing more than sheer invention, sheer propaganda.

We sat in silence for a moment, looking down at the

field that represented the last gasp of hope for Santos' personal revolution—or so I thought at the moment. As we sat I occasionally glanced over at him, seeing the almost holy determination in his eyes shine through the unutterable weariness. I saw now that Julia was looking at him in the same way, and abruptly I suspected that this lovely young woman, a teenager probably, had known no other existence than this for over half her life. Nacimiento Santos had become her entire world—her hero, her raison d'être, her friend, her lover, and this last thought stirred in me a pang of the one emotion that I hardly ever feel: jealousy.

Then another thought occurred to me. "*Señor* Santos," I said, "you said awhile ago that you'd been expecting me. And yet you let me find you without your knowing why I came. Why? If I were you, I would let no one find me."

"A dangerous policy, I agree," he said in that curious accent. "And you're right, I don't know why you came. But I do know that anything important enough to bring you to me must be important enough to deal for."

"You're offering me a deal? But what could I possibly do for you?"

"I know you well enough to know that you have influence."

"I know many influential people," I said. "That doesn't mean I have influence."

"No?" he said, turning to look at me with a cool, challenging stare.

"It depends on what you want me to do with these influential people."

"Just tell them what I have told you. Tell them what your government has done to a country of poor, ignorant Indians who will starve if they have nothing to live on but corn. The *mota* is the only chance they have to improve their lives."

"You want me to tell my friends to support a Communist revolution?"

"Communism has nothing to do with it. I stopped being a Communist six months after I got here. 'Isms' mean nothing to these people. They need food, and they need self-reliance. And what they need, I need."

He was looking directly into my eyes, and the dedication, the sincerity in his expression was undeniable. It was evident that he had somehow been absorbed by these secretive and implacable Indians, and that in that process he had given up his political orientation to become something of a missionary.

"All right," I said after a long moment. "I'll do what I can."

For the first time I saw him smile, a flashing, blazing smile that lit up his face like a black diamond. He reached over to touch my hand, and it was as if he had put his strong fingers directly on the entrance to my vagina, so strong was the sexual thrill that coursed through me.

"Thank you," he said softly, still smiling that magnificent smile. "And, now, what can I do for you?"

"Among other things," I said coyly, throwing him a teasing glance, "you can tell me who your buyers are. Or were."

"Why would you want to know that?" he said, frowning slightly.

I told him about Paul, about the mysterious contract, and obliquely about the lead that had brought me to Chiapas in the first place. He listened intently, and when I was through he sighed deeply.

"I'm afraid," he said, "that you've got the wrong

drug. The man you're looking for, the man who apparently 'owns' this lover of yours, does not deal in *mota*."

"But you know who he is?" I asked hopefully.

"No. I just know his reputation. And I'm not trying to frighten you, but I think you would be much better off if you simply found a new lover."

He turned again to look at me, and I caught his eyes and held them. I am quite good at reading truth or fiction in people's eyes, and if Santos was lying, then he was far and away the best liar I had ever met. Realizing that, I was struck with a feeling of hopelessness and utter disappointment—it seemed now as if Paul were farther away from me than ever, as if I would never solve this wretched mystery, and as if the entire incident was lodging in my brain like a fishbone in the throat.

My thoughts must have registered on my face, for in a moment I felt Santos' hand in mine again. I looked up at him to see his face softly lit by a gentle, compassionate smile.

"Come," he said softly. He helped me up, then released my hand and started walking down the hill, indicating with a gesture that Julia and I should follow. When we reached the edge of the marijuana field, he stood up on tiptoe, grabbed one of the fifteen-foot plants by its neck, then pulled the foot-long flower down toward him. A look of calm and peaceful ecstasy passed over his face as he closed his eyes and rubbed the fragrant blossom all over himself, smearing his face with the heavy golden pollen and sticky resin.

When he was finished he offered the flower to me, and I followed suit, immersing my face in it, inhaling its delightful perfume, feeling the pollen cling to my lips and eyelashes. When I finally turned the flower over to Julia—who immediately began to repeat the ritual in which Santos and I had just indulged—Santos bent over and kissed me lightly on the eyelids, the tip of my nose, and finally my lips, licking the resins from them, then feeding them back to me with his tongue as it entered my mouth.

What a wonderful sensation! It was as if my head were immersed in a fragrant cloud of perfumy marijuana, my eyebrows and lashes dusted with the sweet pollen, my taste buds inundated with the thick flavor that was being planted in my mouth by his gentle tongue. I sucked now on that warm flesh, feeling my head grow light as the insistent weed penetrated my brain, my body, my pores, down to the very cells themselves, the center of life. At the same time the tip of his tongue was rubbing gently at the back of my throat, thrilling me with little sparks of desire that were growing more urgent by the moment.

I knew that I would have to have this marvelous black man, and soon!

In a moment I felt him gently withdraw his tongue from my mouth, and I opened my eyes to see what he would do next. My question was answered when he dipped his face in the rich flower again, then walked over to his wife, who turned her ecstatic face up to his. In a moment they were kissing passionately, a kiss that spoke of an intimacy so powerful, so total, that I was almost ashamed to watch; and I even wondered momentarily if I should somehow make a graceful exit and try to find my way back to San Cristóbal.

But I needn't have wondered. Santos soon broke the kiss with Julia—I noticed that he had stayed with her no longer than with me—took her hand, and led her over to where I was standing.

"Now," he said in that soft, strong voice, "my two ladies. If you please."

I looked at Julia, carefully examining her face for any sign of jealousy, or of mindless submission to her husband. I saw neither. What I did see was a bright, eager, innocent face, a face that radiated beauty and devotion to this man, whom she obviously loved with all her heart. I was touched deeply by that face, that smile, and I soon found when she licked the pollen from her lips, parting them just slightly to allow the very tip of her tongue to pass over them, that I wanted her every bit as much as I wanted him.

"Come to me, Julia," I whispered.

She obeyed instantly, stepping over to me and opening her arms wide to accept my embrace. As her body melted into mine, I could feel the pliant softness of her breasts as they met my own; and as we kissed, our tongues mingling in delightful play that was laced with the heady flavor of the marijuana, I found my hand beginning to rove of its own volition over the smooth roundness of her buttocks. This touch she answered by beginning a slow undulation of her hips, so that I could feel the shy softness of her mound of Venus as it made contact with my own love-flesh.

By this time the beast was stirring within me, and it was all I could do to keep from taking over the program, as it were, and attacking the two of them simultaneously. But I realized that I was on someone else's ground, that Santos was to be the conductor here, and that I would probably enjoy myself all the more if I simply surrendered to him, accepted his pleasure as my own, and availed myself of the lush fruits that were being offered to me in the form of their two glistening bodies.

I stepped away from Julia and waited for Santos to introduce the next movement in this sexual concerto of his. While Julia and I watched raptly, he took a dried corn leaf and rolled the most enormous joint I have ever seen from the blossom he had picked. He lit it and inhaled deeply, closing his eyes and grinning that marvelous grin of his, then passed the joint to Julia, who took a hearty toke.

Then it was my turn. I inhaled the grass and instantly felt it fill my veins with its secret joy. I felt as if the weed were making love to me itself, massaging me just underneath my skin with a thousand subtle fingers, a thousand tongues.

"Excellent!" I murmured, closing my eyes to savor the juice of it. "My compliments."

"Open your eyes," Santos urged.

I did as he asked, seeing that in the meantime Julia had stripped herself and was standing naked, like some magnificent bronze statue in the afternoon sun. She stood there with her arms outstretched and her legs spread wide while I gaped unashamedly, almost sobbing in my desire for her lush body.

"Santos . . ." I groaned. *"My God, she's so beautiful . . . I want her so . . ."*

"Patience, my darlin' " he said, and for the first time I could hear the rolling accent of the Caribbean in his voice. "Everything will happen, darlin'. Just be patient."

I moaned to myself and unconsciously cupped a hand under one of my breasts, beginning to massage it idly as I kept my eyes glued on the rich chocolate brown of Julia's body. As I watched, Santos picked another blossom and walked slowly over to her, as she spread her gleaming legs that much farther at his approach. When he reached her he put his hand down so that the blossom he was holding came to rest squarely between her legs, and Julia immediately began to ride back and forth on it with a slow, tantalizing motion, her pussy-lips just grazing the soft, furry flower, her eyes closing and a lazy, seductive grin beginning to spread across her face.

"*Sí,*" I heard her whisper as she rocked gracefully back and forth. "*Sí, déme la flor . . . la linda flor . . .*"

I was hypnotized by the lushness of this sexual scene being played out in front of me, fascinated and stimulated almost beyond control by the lovely Julia as she swayed so elegantly over the golden bloom. Only half conscious of what I was doing, I raised my other hand to my breast and now began to poke and tease at both nipples through the material of my fatigue shirt. Santos glanced over at me and smiled approvingly as he continued to hold the flower for Julia, whose lips were beginning to pull back to bare her teeth in a lusty grimace.

"Take off your clothes," Santos said. "She's nearly ready for you. Aren't you, love?"

"*Sí,*" she murmured. "*Traígamela.*"

Within ten seconds I had stripped off my clothes, and I smiled as the warm mountain sun caressed my skin on the outside while the *mota* continued to work on me from within. Santos beamed his approval, then beckoned me to come closer to the writhing Julia. By the time I reached her, her head was thrown back in ecstasy and her body was beginning to tremble as the flower continued to tickle at her aroused clitoris. Her nipples were standing straight out from the ends of her regal breasts, hardened and spiking at the balmy air like a pair of antennae.

I didn't need to be told what to do at this point. With a sob of triumph I sank to my knees in front of her, just as Santos removed the flower from between her throbbing legs. I groaned aloud as I swiped the tip of my tongue along her tender labia, tasting the heady mixture of the viscous marijuana resin and her own pungent juices.

"*Mmm* . . ." I murmured, nearly beside myself with the glorious sensation of that fragrant flavor on my tongue. "*. . . so delicious . . . so sweet . . . I've never tasted anything like this . . . marvelous . . .*"

I could no longer control myself. My own pussy was pouring out lubricants like a gushing fountain, and I could feel the lush juices inundating my thighs as I knelt before the sighing Julia. Abandoning all restraint, I buried my tongue in between her labia, feeling the marijuana pollen tickle my lips as I sought and found her erect clitoris. Even there, even in that secret cavern the marijuana had penetrated, and the fragrance of the mixed odors was enough to nearly make me faint with desire. I could feel Julia respond to my penetration, writhing and thrusting at my mouth, groaning out her pleasure, her pussy beginning to oscillate in tiny circles against my lips as I sucked at her tender clitoris like a madwoman.

At the same time I felt something hard and warm against my cheek. Without loosening my mouth-grip on Julia's moistened vagina, I opened my eyes and looked off to one side. Sure enough, Santos had stripped himself naked and was now laying his magnificent black cock against the side of my face, so that it shone there in the sun like a scepter of some Nubian prince. Underneath it he was holding still another marijuana blossom, which he was rubbing against his cock so that I could see the shiny crystals of THC adhere to his ebony skin.

Immediately I reached out for that lovely cock, circling my fingers around the underside of it and beginning to pump it with long, even strokes. My mouth was still buried in Julia's vagina, my tongue sweeping furiously along her hardened clitoris as her body trembled and quivered about me. By now the heady *mota* was suffused throughout my body, and in my fever I had the startling illusion that I could feel what I was doing to Julia as if she herself were actually doing it to me. My own clitty came alive with this fantasy stimulation, hardening and beginning to throb just slightly in rhythm with that of the Cuban girl.

"*Ai . . . ai . . . ai . . .*" she chanted like a metronome gone mad as she rocked her vagina back and forth against my face. I reached my free hand around her and began to prod gently at the crevice between her perfect buttocks, which made her respond with a lengthening stroke and a quickening tempo. I could feel that she was nearing her orgasm, so I rose up to meet her, pushing my mouth against her pussy with greater and greater pressure, hearing her moan with delight.

At the same time my hand was pumping up and down even more furiously on Santos' rock-hard cock. "*Yes, my little darling . . .*" he breathed as I settled into a steady rhythm, timing my strokes to coincide with my licking at Julia's clitty and my exploratory little nudgings at her anus. "*That's right, darling . . . fuck me . . . with your hand . . . like that . . . oh, yes . . . just . . . like . . . that!*"

By now the flavor of the marijuana was beginning to fade as it was drowned out by the flood of juices from Julia's ripe pussy. I wanted more of that divine flavor, and more! Remembering that Santos had rubbed his cock with one of the *mota* blossoms, I now withdrew my mouth from Julia's vagina and quickly closed it around the end of Santos' magnificent instrument, at the same time inserting a moistened finger between Julia's labia so that she would feel no loss. And, indeed, she acted as if there had been no change whatsoever, continuing her bucking and writhing and even quickening the pace as my finger made contact with her rigid little clitty.

The taste of Santos' cock in my mouth was simply heavenly. As I rolled my tongue around the fleshy head of it my saliva was inundated once again with the marvelous pungence of the marijuana resins, and once again my body responded as if to the call of trumpets. I moved my mouth back and forth along that lovely organ, squealing with delight as I felt the head of it scrape the back of my throat. My finger was still imbedded in Julia's pussy, the tip of it now beginning to circle around the opening of her vagina while the rest of it lodged firmly against her moving clitoris. She was shaking wildly now, her entire body trembling out of control, whispering and groaning out a mad area of desire.

Now I pulled my mouth from Santos' cock and sunk it once more into Julia's wonderfully moistened little pussy. At the same time my hand reached out to fold itself once more around Santos' hardened penis, stroking up and down it in an accelerated tempo that soon had him groaning aloud. His cries mixed with Julia's, spraying out into the clear mountain air like so many swallows, echoing down the hillside until it seemed that the mountains themselves had joined our lustful game.

I went on that way for some time, my mouth and hand alternating between Julia's writhing pussy and the wonderful tumescence of Santos' cock. My own body was alive with stimulation, infused with the powerful *mota* so that it felt as if the three of us were wired together in a shared circuit, sensations passing back and forth among us so that my dizzied brain still had trouble distinguishing who was actually doing what to whom. Back and forth my mouth flew, sucking first at the thrilling hardness of Santos' strident prick, then at the throbbing warmth of Julia's pussy, back and forth, back and forth in rhythm, until . . .

Suddenly Santos withdrew from me, leaving my mouth empty as my finger continued to work at Julia's vagina. I opened my eyes and looked about me in confusion.

"Santos . . ." I groaned out, "what are you doing? Don't leave me now, darling . . . please!"

"No, mi amor," I heard his rich voice say. "I won't leave you. Don't worry."

I looked down and saw him sitting on the leaf-strewn ground beneath me, his marvelous pole standing proudly up from his groin like a mahogany bowsprit. Without further hesitation and with a passionate moan I sank down onto it, feeling the proud flesh sear into my willing pussy, splitting the walls apart and sending a shock of delight thundering through my body. At the same time I grabbed Julia's hips and pulled her along with me, so that my mouth was still glued to her streaming vagina as she thrust herself against my face with even greater fury than before.

Santos supported his weight with his hands behind him on the ground as I began to rise and fall on him, shimmying up and down the full length of his gorgeous cock, imbedding the wonderful pole in me and feeling the maddening friction along my pussy walls as it withdrew once more. This up-and-down motion nearly undid poor Julia, who ground her pussy against me with the strength of a wildcat, her belly throbbing and rolling as if with some internal earthquake, her hands twisting in my hair, her teeth clenched, her face soaked with perspiration as she finally screamed out her orgasm.

Santos continued to buck up and down, meeting my every thrust with a powerful parry of his own, splitting my aching vagina as I went on riding him, groaning with ecstasy at every penetration and sighing deeply with every withdrawal. My own climax was approaching fast, and now I could feel Santos begin to stiffen in anticipation.

Finally it hit us, our twin orgasms slamming into us at one and the same moment. I rammed myself down onto him, grinding my buttocks against his groin, wringing every last drop of semen from his twitching cock as I prolonged my own shattering orgasm in the process. When it was all over I lay back against him, feeling his cock begin to grow soft inside me while Julia lay down along my belly, the three of us happy, panting, and exhausted on the marijuana-strewn soil.

I stayed a week in the mountains with Santos and Julia; and it is now a time that is lost in a haze of marijuana, slow days, and torpid sex with the two Cubans. I must admit that I became entirely absorbed in Santos and his milieu, so much so that during one of our languid ménages à trois, as Julia lay under me, sucking and nuzzling at my breasts while Santos entered me from behind, I found myself crying out in Spanish. This, of course, left them both grinning from ear to ear, and left me determined to teach them a few poignant words in French, which I did.

While all this was going on I did my best to get some information from Santos, repeatedly trying to establish some connection between him and Paul's mysterious "owner." But as often as I asked him, he denied any knowledge beyond what he had already told me: that if this major dealer was involved in drug traffic, it was in some drug other than marijuana; for he, Santos, knew and dealt with everyone at the top rung of that particular ladder, and would certainly have known about anything as extravagantly unusual as Paul and his contract.

"It must be opium," he would say. "If I were you, I'd go to Thailand."

With this clue planted in my mind, I soon grew itchy to continue my search. He dispatched Julia to guide me out of the mountains and back to San Cristóbal, but when we reached the highway she refused to go another step. We bid each other a fond goodbye, and then she faded back into the forests which had become her only home.

CHAPTER EIGHT

I flew back to Los Angeles and caught a flight to Thailand without so much as changing clothes. At this point, Thailand was the only lead I had.

I skipped Bangkok entirely (except for the mandatory two-hour layover at the airport) and flew directly to Chiang Mai. Bangkok was old news to me, and I didn't think I could bear another trip to the Floating Market or another meal at the Rang Toa. Besides, the opium trade originates in the mountains north of Chiang Mai, and I felt I had a better chance of making a meaningful contact if I went right to the source.

Thankfully, Chiang Mai is considerably cooler and more tolerable than Bangkok. I checked into the Chiang Hotel, determined to stay only as long as it took me to arrange a trip up into the mountains. Since I knew that nothing in Thailand moves at Occidental speed, I calculated that I would have several days to a week there. In the meantime, I would relax and play the tourist.

After a brief rest, I asked directions to the Varorot Market, the principal outlet for goods and crafts from the hill tribes. With any luck, I would be able to find someone to guide me to the Meo people. The desk clerk gave me directions with the same patience and graciousness that one gets from any Thai who does not live in Bangkok, and I quickly caught a Vespa-powered *samlor* to take me there.

Knowing that nothing was going to happen as fast as I wanted it to, I resolved to put my mind into the Oriental time frame and enjoy each moment as much as I could. And the streets of Chiang Mai proved to be truly enjoyable. Flowers were everywhere, brightening the shop windows and street corners, perfect complements to the easy smiles and radiant mountain complexions of the people themselves. Chiang Mai is considered the northern capital of Thailand, so it was a natural congregation spot for all the hill tribes, who now filled the streets in what amounted to a perpetual parade, the dazzling colors of their clothing suggesting springtime in an Alpine meadow.

The *samlor*—which is really just a jitney that has succumbed to the twentieth century—took me past the Poo-Ping Rajinives Palace and the Wat Phra Singh, a fourteenth-century monastery that is the oldest Buddhist temple in northern Thailand. Finally, after nearly running over what must have been half the population of some obscure mountain tribe, the driver deposited me at the Varorot Market, taking my fare and disappearing immediately into the forest of humanity in the street.

I walked through the market at an easy pace for a while, stopping here and there to bargain for the delicate wood carvings and bright cotton fabrics that were the staple crafts of the area. Finally, in a dim booth far off the mainstream of the market traffic, I found what I was looking for: a beautiful ivory carving with a hand-painted scene that must have come from some Thai erotic folk tale. In it a Thai woman, her perfect moon of a face alight with ecstasy, was lying on her back, her

knees raised almost to her chin and her legs spread wide
to allow the entry of her lover, whose virile cock jutted
out smartly from his silk robes. There was a tender
eroticism about the painting that struck me suddenly
with pangs of longing for Paul, for the feeling it com-
municated was almost exactly like that Paul and I had
generated during the first weeks of our affair. I bought
the carving without even bothering to bargain (which
disappointed the woman in the booth more than if I had
actually cheated her), resolving to give it to Paul once I
had eliminated whatever—or whoever—it was that was
standing between us.

I paid the woman and turned to go, then turned back
to her on a sudden impulse. I speak only a few words of
basic Thai, and of course she spoke no English, but by
pointing and gesturing I was able to make her understand what I wanted: a trip to the mountains, to the land
of the Meo. When I mentioned that name her face lit up
in a broad smile, and she pointed at her own chest,
telling me that she was in fact a Meo herself.

"I don't believe it!" I exclaimed, then hurried to
assure her with grunts and sign language that I was
happy, not angry; for the Thais do not often raise their
voices unless they are being profoundly emotional. With
a few more gestures and handclaspings, we established
that a relative of hers, perhaps a husband or a brother
(she indicated gender by pointing to the man's cock in
the picture on the carving I had just bought), would
guide me to the Meo's principal village as soon as he
was ready to leave Chiang Mai. All I had to do was
check with her at the same time every day from now
until then, and be ready to leave at a moment's notice.

In fact, it took over a week for her brother (husband?) to get himself ready for the journey. I spent that
time reading everything I could find about the Meo,

then buying the brightest colored clothing I could find, for the books told me that the hill people considered most Westerners hopelessly drab.

Finally, after a week or so of faithfully checking every day, the woman at the market indicated that her brother (or whoever he was) would be ready to leave that afternoon. I was to meet him in front of the market with whatever gear I would be carrying.

I took a samlor back to the hotel, then dressed in the brightest of the muslins I had bought in the shops. I checked out of the hotel and went back to the market, expecting to find my guide waiting in front with a herd of mules and a tribe of cousins. But no such sight awaited me when I got there, so I killed time browsing around the stalls that lined the street.

Some three hours later a Toyota Landcruiser pulled up to the curb in front of me, and a grinning Thai said, "Miss van Bell?" in perfect English. To hear my name spoken in English, in that place, and by that mouth, gave me quite a start, and all I could do was peer in the window.

"Are you . . ." I managed to stammer.

"Touby Lyfoung," he said, still grinning as if in triumph, although over what I hadn't the faintest idea. "You're going with me."

"Yes, I guess I am," I said. And that was all there was to it. I threw my bag onto the overhead rack and climbed in. I turned to him and opened my mouth to speak, but he anticipated my question.

"Born in Anaheim," he said, grinning what turned out to be a perpetual grin. "Right next to Disneyland."

We went north by jeep to Chiangrai, a small city in the mountains. From there we would go by mule caravan to Mae Salong, a village near the Burmese border where Touby lived and where the biggest opium processing center in the area was located. As we drove along, Touby filled me in on the history of the opium trade in the area: how the growing of the poppy had been the spine of Meo existence since time immemorial; how first the French, then the Nationalist Chinese, then the Americans had tried unsuccessfully to eliminate the trade and then had inexorably, each in turn, become enmeshed in it; how bitter experiences with these capitalist powers had turned the majority of the Meo toward Communism and armed rebellion. It was a complicated story, full of the intrigues of the CIA and the Chinese generals, and by the time he finished it we had already arrived in Chiangrai.

It seemed that once Touby was in motion there was no slowing him down—within two hours of our arrival in Chiangrai our caravan was outfitted and we were ready for the trail. The trip—through some of the most outlandishly gorgeous mountains I have ever seen—took two rather severe and tiring days, but Touby was very solicitous, and with the exception of a bit of distant rifle fire things went smoothly enough.

Touby had been such a perfect gentleman, in fact, that when we finally reached the crest of the trail and looked down into the little valley where Mae Salong lay, I was surprised to suddenly have him look me up and down with an expression that is as international as it is transparent. When he lifted me off the mule, his hand slid down over the firm flesh of my ass and lingered there just slightly. I chose to ignore it for the moment, and stood patiently while he continued to survey my personal geography.

Soon he took a step back and looked me up and down, his grin growing even wider, if that was possible. "You look just right," he said, and there was a mysterious tone of satisfaction in his voice.

"Just right for what, if I may ask?"

But Touby didn't answer. He simply turned and began leading the mules down the trail toward the village, leaving me to go beside them on foot. As we descended we passed through fields of tall and brilliant poppies, where Meo women in formal-looking black robes were splitting the pods and drawing off the gooey resin that was the world's first painkiller. When they saw us the women came running from the fields, fawning over Touby as if we were some sort of royalty and paying charming attention to me as well—touching my clothes, my hair, my hands, twittering and grinning gaily in obvious approval.

"They like you," Touby said. "Very important."

"I know," I said. "Thank them for me and tell them I'm very honored."

Touby's broadening grin told me I had said exactly the right thing, and when he translated what I had said into Meo, the women were beside themselves with delight. In other circumstances I might even have been a bit suspicious, for it seemed to me that they were overreacting to my presence, but I attributed it to a natural effusiveness on their part and let it pass.

Now Touby led me into the village, which was little more than a series of thatched huts arranged in a semi-circle around a one-story masonry building. As we walked, the women came from everywhere to surround us, welcoming us in the same way as had the women in the fields. Later I found out the reason for their reverence for Touby—his father had been a revolutionary leader, the last of the great Meo *kaitongs*, or little kings, and Touby, after being born in exile in the

United States, had returned to take up the reins when his father was killed by the Chinese.

Later still, of course, I would find out the reason for their immediate and elaborate acceptance of me.

But for now the thing that struck me most was the absence of men in the village.

"Are you the only man here?" I asked Touby.

"The rest are fighting," he said. "They come only at night."

I wanted to ask him more, but he took over the role of questioner, leading me into one of the darkened huts and sitting me down on a gorgeous hand-woven rug.

"Now," he said. "Why have you come?"

It was a direct question, and I knew he would want a direct answer. I poured out my story, explaining that I had come to seek a contact with the agent of Paul's "owner," whoever that might be. When I finished I studied his face. It was passive, expressionless.

Finally, after what seemed an eternal silence, he said, "There's an American who comes every year to transport the crop. His name is Gerald Laslow."

My heart skipped a beat. This surely must be the man! "When does he come?" I asked breathlessly.

"He will be here in three days," Touby said.

"Fantastic," I said, sure that I had finally picked up the trail.

For Touby's part, my business seemed entirely unimportant. He got up and walked out with a wave of the hand and a brief "Stay here for now. I'll see you tonight."

As soon as he was gone, the hut filled up with women. They sat in a ring around me, talking and laughing in their wonderfully musical voices, occasionally reaching out a hand to touch my clothes or stroke my hair. Two more women stationed themselves at the door to the hut, as if to guard me.

Despite the kindness and charm of the attention I had received so far, I was beginning to get a bit nervous. There was something possessive, almost proprietary about Touby's attitude, and now, with this retinue of giggling Meo women surrounding me, I felt almost like a prisoner. The fact that Touby seemed entirely indifferent to my own purpose in being there only made me that much more uneasy, as if he had his own use for me, some plan that involved me without necessarily needing my permission.

At the same time, Touby was the only ally I had in this territory and the only real chance I stood of hooking up with Gerald Laslow. When the time came for the Meo leader to reveal his true intentions, I knew I would have to at least appear to be cooperative, no matter what scheme he had in mind.

I found out soon enough. I was kept inside the hut for the rest of the afternoon, fed a delicious but indescribable meal, then preened and combed and fussed over by the ladies who had been left to attend me. Then, as if by prearranged command, they disappeared, filing out the door one by one, leaving nothing behind but a trail of giggles. I was left entirely alone.

"What the hell is going on here?" I said aloud to myself. I was actually getting a bit frightened.

"Nothing to it," I heard a man's voice answer, and then Touby stepped into the hut, resplendent in a formal silk robe of brilliant yellow with a bright red undergarment that looked something like a tunic. "Are you ready?"

"Ready for what?" I said.

Now it was his turn to look genuinely puzzled. "For the kidnapping," he said.

"I beg your pardon?"

"The moon has risen, hasn't it?" he said. He stepped back and took a look outside. "Sure it has. Let's go."

"Touby, what are you talking about? Go where?"

He gave me a long look, as if trying to figure out if I was really as dumb as I sounded. Then, apparently satisfied that I was, he said, "You really don't understand, do you?"

"No," I said. "I really don't."

"Then why did you wear a wedding gown for this trip?"

I looked down at my clothes, which I had selected simply for their brightness. Suddenly the whole thing became clear to me. The shopkeeper in Chiang Mai had sold me a Meo wedding gown, undoubtedly thinking that I was going to marry someone from the tribe. And Touby's sister must have misunderstood, must have told him that I was looking for a Meo to marry. That explained his indifference when I told him I was looking for Laslow—he probably assumed that I was just being coy, that I wanted him to make the first move.

I burst out laughing. "Oh, Touby," I said. "This is an awful mistake." I explained to him my theory of what had happened.

"Makes sense," he said. "Too bad."

"Why too bad?"

"Because now you've got to go through with it. You've got to let me kidnap you. That's how we get married around here."

"Touby," I said, "I have no intention of becoming either your victim or your wife."

"You have to," he said.

"Why? Why do I have to?"

"Because if you don't, they'll kill you."

"Who'll kill me?"

"The women. That's what they do to someone who jilts her betrothed."

I had no further time to digest this, because Touby quickly walked over to me, applied some martial arts trick to my neck that effectively paralyzed me for a moment, then tied my hands behind my back with a silk cord. I tried to kick him, but he simply dodged me, picked me up, and carried me out of the hut. Outside a mule was waiting for us, his saddle and bridle bedecked with flowers and studded with silver. Obviously, this was to be a very formal kidnapping.

I kicked and screamed bloody murder, but soon realized that the Meo would think that all part of the ceremony. There was really very little I could do. So I kept quiet, allowed Touby to place me on the mules, and did some furious thinking as Touby climbed on behind me and kicked the mule into action.

Within a few seconds I had calculated that I was in no real danger so long as I simply went along with this charade. On the other hand, real rebellion at this point could easily get me killed. And what harm would it do if I "married" Touby? No civilized court would recognize such a marriage, so my leaving Meo country would be tantamount to an annulment. And leave Meo country I most certainly would do, just as soon as I made my contact with Laslow.

Besides, Touby's hands had now snaked around my waist and were resting peacefully just below my breasts. I had not made love—not voluntarily, at any rate—since I had left Chiapas. And the moon was full, the night warm and flower scented, and Touby both an interesting and a charming paramour. What did I have to lose?

I thought. And the answer came immediately: absolutely nothing.

So I relaxed and leaned back against my host/captor/ fiancé, basking in the strength of his wiry arms. He embraced me tightly, and I could feel his sweet cock begin to balloon under his robes and poke tentatively at the crack in my buttocks. The slow swaying motion of the mule caused the smooth leather saddle to rub enticingly at my pussy-lips, which were already beginning to dew up in excitement. Night birds sang sweetly as we rode out of the village and up a narrow mountain trail, so that the whole experience was rapidly turning into an erotic serenade.

"Touby," I said dreamily as I moved his hands up under my trembling breasts, "is this really the way the Meo go about getting married?"

"It used to be," he said, his hands gently massaging my welcoming tits. "It's the old, old way. But it's not done much anymore these days."

"Then why are you doing it?"

"I'm in the line of the *kaitongs*," he said. "It's expected of me."

"I see," I said, then lapsed into silence, content to merely feel Touby's hands playing over the firmness of my breasts and to feel the delightful stimulation of the saddle on my eager little clitty. I was completely relaxed now, and even looking forward to the idea of having this, my first and perhaps only marriage, be to a Meo Chieftain, a man who I might never see again in my life. At heart, I suppose I am still a romantic; and it was hard to imagine anything more wildly sentimental than being kidnapped and wed by an Asian prince.

Besides, I found myself looking forward immensely to the consummation.

We continued to ride up the winding trail, Touby's

hands playing a concerto on my breasts as we jiggled along. The steady motion of the saddle against my aroused little pussy was driving me half-crazy, the insistent stimulation seeming to tease and whisper of the greater stimulation still to come. I could feel Touby's soft, sweet breath against the back of my neck, and occasionally he leaned forward to take maddening little nibbles at my ear lobes, as I groaned my approval out into the perfumed air.

"Oh, Touby," I breathed. "I think I'm beginning to like this."

"Just wait," he said. "Just wait."

A few minutes later we reached what seemed to be the crest of the trail. Touby turned the mule around and we sat dead still for a moment, looking out across a range of beautiful peaks and valleys that, in the hazy moonlight, gleamed like something from a Japanese painting. Now sure of my cooperation, Touby untied my hands and lifted me off the mule, taking me by the hand and leading me down a narrow footpath toward a clump of trees.

Inside the little stand of trees, almost entirely hidden by the spreading branches, was a tiny cottage—a shrine, actually—the outsides of which were intricately carved in a Meo erotic motif. I stopped to examine the carving, which was so lifelike that my heart began to pound in my chest at the sensual orgy depicted there. Everywhere there were Meo ladies, some elaborately robed and others charmingly naked, and they formed an intricate chain with the fiercely garbed warriors who were fucking them in nearly every orifice. Here a gorgeous princess, her eyes shining with mysterious ecstasy, bent double over a young poppy plant while a perfectly formed young captain approached her from behind, his cock advancing in front of him like a conqueror's sword.

There a lovely couple stood naked in a silver river, the woman's legs locked around the man's back and her arms around his neck as she plunged down on his hearty prick. In another area a woman lay spread-eagled and delirious with excitement as an enormous tiger with an amazingly gentle expression lapped tenderly at the flanges of her pussy, while in the dead center of the mural an outrageous god had each of his seven cocks buried in one of seven queens. The whole thing was done in gold, silver, and gemstones, and had been carved with such elaborate care and great skill that I knew this place must have been an ageless and sacred shrine.

"My God!" I gasped, scarcely able to resist the urge to plunge my own fingers into my dampened pussy. "This is incredible!"

"Let's go in," Touby said, taking my hand and guiding me up the steps.

The shrine was designed so as to be partially open to the night sky and to the long view of the surrounding mountains. So in a sense, as a Meo princess I would have stars for a bridal veil and the whole world as my domain. A sentimental notion, I realize, but I challenge any woman in the same situation to feel anything but syrupy. For me, I was absolutely enraptured by this marvelous fantasy.

The floor of the darkened shrine was covered inches deep in fresh poppy petals, which made a soft, rustling sound as we sat down. Touby lit a candle, which cast its glow over the brilliant carpet of flowers beneath us, a gentle, rolling sea of color and silken texture that fairly invited one to sink into its luxuriant depths. I could feel the smooth, caressing touch of the petals against the exposed skin of my legs, and I idly trailed my hand through them, delighted at the sensation.

Now Touby set the candle on a small table in the center of the floor. On the table I could see a small silver bowl, a flat instrument something like a file, but made of polished hardwood, and a long ivory tube, delicately carved and inlaid with gold filigree. Touby beckoned me to come near and pointed at the bowl, which was full of a black, resinous goo that I recognized immediately.

"Opium," I said. "Of course."

Before I had time to think about it further, Touby impaled some of the black mass on the wooden needle, then heated it briefly with the candle. When smoke began to rise from the opium he quickly bent over it with the ivory tube, inhaling it all in one long drag. Then, still holding his breath, he moved over to my side and covered my lips in a deep, passionate kiss, exhaling the marvelously fragrant smoke so that it traveled deep into my lungs.

"Mm," I sighed as the rosy smoke penetrated me. "How lovely."

"Again," he said.

Once more he went through the timeless procedure, but this time, as he favored me with his opium-laced kiss, he moved his hand up under my breast at the same moment. The effect was wonderful, as if I were being massaged externally and internally at the same time. Already my blood was turning warm from the powerful opium, and Touby's gentle touch on my heaving breast only raised my temperature that much further. I rubbed my thighs together to accentuate that marvelous sensation of suffusing warmth.

I don't know how many times Touby went back to the little silver bowl, or how many opium kisses he favored me with. I only know that I was soon floating in a semiprivate paradise, aware of nothing but the dreamy glow of the opium and the gentle ministrations of Touby's hands. In that state, I felt my desire bloom in me like some slow-to-open night flower, but it was a desire that was clear and patient, without any of the usual sense of urgency. I knew that Touby and I would soon have one another, and I felt as if we would be able to fuck for weeks—gladly, calmly, in a measured cadence that would guarantee us a height of ecstasy that few people ever reach.

"Touby," I said after a time. "Undress me, Touby."

Without saying a word, he reached for me and stood me on my feet, standing before me and smiling a smile that was very different from his typical everyday grin. With one smooth movement he pulled my dress over my head, then quickly removed the cotton tunic underneath. The surprisingly warm air caressed my naked skin, wafting over it in exactly the same way that the opium was wafting through my veins—in fact, in that state I had the impression that I could actually *see* the air currents conforming to the shape of my body.

"Beautiful," Touby whispered. "I never thought you would be this beautiful."

"I'm beautiful inside, too," I said. "Come over here and find out."

I stretched out my arms to him, and he locked me in a warm embrace, pressing my body against his and kissing me softly. I began to move against him, rotating my hips in small, lazy circles, feeling his burgeoning cock rub against me through his robes. Then he stepped away from me and quickly stripped, gazing at me all the while with that beatific smile of his.

And what a glorious body! In clothes he looked small and slight, the heavy veins that ran up his arms the only clue to his considerable strength. But now, seeing him naked in the moonlight and ankle-deep in poppy petals,

I realized how perfectly proportioned he really was, how smoothly down into the groin area where his cock stood proudly at attention, then down into legs that had been sculpted by half a lifetime of walking these mountain trails. His skin glowed a golden color in the soft candlelight, and when he stood stock still, as he was at this moment, it was easy to imagine him the model for a statue of the young Buddha.

"Now," I said, and I'm sure my eyes must have been shining with the desire that the sight of him aroused in me, "come here."

He walked slowly over to me, stopping when he was just within reach. His cock pointed at my trembling belly like a spear at a target. Suddenly I could no longer stand even this small separation, and I was overcome by an urge to meld myself to him, to sink into his gorgeous body like a diving osprey into a warm ocean, to bathe myself in the golden glory of his skin, his touch.

"Oh, Touby," I groaned. *"Come to me, darling . . . don't leave me alone here . . . come to me . . . take me . . . make love to me . . ."*

Without waiting for a response, I took a step toward him and put my hands on his shoulders. I was beside myself with desire, with an aching need for him, and even though I knew that I should probably let him orchestrate our lovemaking, I simply could not help myself. Propping myself on his shoulders, I rose up on my tiptoes and poised myself so that his cock lay along the outside of my vagina, not yet penetrating it, but parting the lips of my pussy and wedging itself against the erect little node of my clitoris.

"Mmm, yes, darling," I sighed as I felt the marvelous friction. *"That's it . . . let me feel you . . . let me feel that wonderful cock of yours . . ."*

I began to move my hips slowly back and forth, feeling the delightful sensation of his rigid cock rubbing gently at my tingling clitty. By adjusting my weight on the balls of my feet, I could increase or diminish the amount of pressure on my love-cord, and this was the only thing that kept me from coming immediately. My pussy was yearning for his entry, pouring out a stream of creamy lubrication as if in invitation, but I was determined to hold off, to prolong this magnificent sensation as long as possible. In this sense the opium came to my aid, numbing my aroused nerve endings just enough to keep me from having a shattering orgasm right then and there, but at the same time giving a richer, more solid quality to the stimulation itself.

For his part, Touby seemed to be holding up rather well. He was moving back and forth just slightly, enough to maintain the heavenly pressure against my clitty, but not so much as to bring me to premature climax. His rhythm was steady and solid—no missed beats, no tremors, nothing to indicate that he himself was nearing orgasm—and he cooed the most amazing sounds (Meo, of course) into my ears as he rocked back and forth with me.

"Yes, darling . . ." I moaned in return. *"Oh, you feel so good against me . . . I love it, darling . . . don't stop . . . don't ever stop . . ."*

In another few moments I lost all control. I began swaying powerfully against him, sinking my full weight down on his cock as I slid along the length of it, grinding my steaming pussy against his groin, then sliding out again to feel the bulbous head bury itself between my cunt-lips. My legs began to grow weak as a series of ecstatic sensations threatened to overcome me, and soon I found myself shaking and trembling with the sheer power of it.

"Oh! . . . Touby! . . . Oh! . . . Oh! . . . My . . . God . . ." I groaned through clenched teeth. I wrapped my arms tightly around his back and pressed myself against him with all my strength as a series of machine-gun orgasms swept through me, each one a spark that threatened to ignite a magnificent internal explosion. I sank my teeth into his neck and felt the warm taste of a drop of blood on my tongue, and this, in my opium-induced haze, only served to incite me all the more. I bucked and moaned and threw myself against him like a crazed mare in heat, bathing myself in this heavenly chain of orgasms.

But even when the last of them died down and I had to prop myself against Touby to keep myself from collapsing, even then I knew we were just beginning. Touby had not yet come, for one thing, and I knew that I had reserves of sexual strength that had not yet been tapped.

Touby must have sensed that, because after only the briefest of pauses, he picked me up, carried me across the room, and lay me down on a poppy-strewn bed. Then he bent over me—smiling, as always—and began to scoop more petals off the floor, sprinkling them slowly, daintily, one at a time over my sweat-streaked body. I began to come alive again as the soft little petals fell to caress my breasts, my nipples, my tingling belly, and I looked down, entranced, to see them fall and lodge themselves in the wiry curls of my pubic hair.

"Touby," I laughed. "What in heaven's name are you doing to me?"

"Old custom," he said. "Groom covers bride with poppies, bride shuts up and enjoys."

"Really?" I said. "Well, what happens if bride decides to do *this*?" In one swift motion I rose up, grabbed his wrists, and pulled him down on top of me. In another moment we were rolling merrily through the poppy petals, spraying them this way and that, thoroughly enmeshed in a kaleidoscope of pure sensation—skin against skin, the silken petals clinging to our bodies, our hair, our eyelids, and all the time laughing and wrestling like a pair of puppies at play.

Finally we rolled back onto the bed. I lay on my back and Touby knelt above me, his eyes aglow with rekindled desire. As I lay panting beneath him, he picked up a single poppy petal and began to brush it back and forth against my nipples, which were already so erect that I thought they could hardly stand this extra stimulation. While he continued to tease the hardened little cherries of my nipples, he picked up another petal and ran it lightly along my outer labia, which immediately began to flower open with the delicate friction.

In another few moments of this I was fully dilated, fully open to him, and he probed gently with his finger to ascertain my readiness. When my aroused pussy seemed to gobble his exploring finger of its own accord, he withdrew with a smile, then spread my legs as wide as they would go and entered me with a smooth, even thrust of his hardened cock.

"That's it . . ." I cried. *"Come inside me, darling . . . come inside me . . . yes . . . yes . . . I love to feel you like that . . . fuck me, darling . . . fuck me . . ."*

And fuck me he did! Responding to my fevered urgings, he began to saw in and out of my welcoming pussy with long and measured strokes. It seemed to me that I could feel him plunge into me all the way up to my belly, my ribs, filling my aching cunt with the hard flesh of his cock, stirring me with it until I began to boil inside with the pure hard fury of it. In my opium dream I had the feeling that I was an empty balloon, an airless bag, and that his magnificent prick was inflating me, pumping me full of oxygen, giving me life.

Much more of this, I thought to myself dreamily, and I'll probably burst.

I closed my eyes tight and drew my knees up under my chin, exposing the entire plane of my eager pussy to him. He responded by burying himself in me as deeply as he could, his groin pulling up against my tingling cunt-lips and massaging them maddeningly as he plunged in and out with greater and greater fury. My teeth were clenched and my head was thrashing from side to side, my hair brushing against his face like a thousand tiny whips, and I was babbling incoherently, grunting and mewling out my ecstasy in a language that is as universal as it is incomprehensible.

"Jesus Christ!" I heard him gasp in decidedly un-Meo-like tones. "Where were you when I was in the States?"

"Nowhere near Disneyland, I can tell you that," I managed to answer.

Somehow this sounded so comical coming from a Meo chieftain in a mountaintop fuck-shrine that I almost burst out laughing. But I was a bit too far gone for comedy.

"Touby," I said. "I love you dearly, but please stop making jokes and just fuck me!"

"At your service," he said.

Now he plunged into me with renewed vigor, his groin still fused with my throbbing clitty, his cock ripping through me like a fast boat on a surging ocean. I responded in kind, throwing my legs around his back and locking my ankles tightly together, my cunt now closing around his wonderful prick like a velvet trap. Now we were truly locked together, our bodies joined as if they had been welded, a single machine lubricated by sweat and by the juices of sex, a growling, churning engine, piston and cylinder, trying to tear itself apart, driving itself to its own destruction.

"*God . . . Touby . . . yes . . . yes . . .*" I chanted, hardly knowing what I was saying in my sexual frenzy. "*Fuck me . . . fuck me, Touby . . . like that . . . yes . . . oh, yes . . .*"

A few seconds later I felt that familiar itch begin to rise in my belly, and I could tell from the greater strength of his exertions that Touby was nearing orgasm as well. We continued to thrust at each other, stoking the fires of climax that were roaring up in each of us, driving one another ever nearer to our mutual release. Soon it was on me, a long, steady massive climax that was almost exactly opposite the short, staccato bursts I had experienced earlier. It hammered in me like the throbbing of a bass drum, slamming outward, then seeming to turn to vapor and escape through every pore of my sweat-soaked body.

At the same time I felt Touby stiffen, felt his gorgeous cock begin to throb and spew its oily load into me. The timing was absolutely perfect! We screamed in unison into the warm night air, and for a moment I had the feeling that our shouts were being answered approvingly by the spirits of every couple who had come to consecrate this peculiar but marvelous little shrine. I had the feeling that a thousand years of lovers were watching us, and that someday, if I ever came back to this place, I would find Touby and myself etched into the mural on the wall outside, enshrined there forever.

"*Oh, Touby . . .*" I sighed when our orgasms finally faded. "*That was marvelous . . . just marvelous . . .*"

"You weren't so bad yourself," he said. "For a white girl."

I laughed easily, feeling thoroughly relaxed, thoroughly at home with this man who I realized was now my husband—in Meo country, at any rate. But the laugh did not stop when I did! In fact, it seemed to grow and multiply until it sounded like many voices laughing, as if the carved figures had come alive and were sharing our mirth. For a few seconds I put it off as some new opium fantasy, but when the laughter grew in volume, refusing to die away, I finally opened my eyes and sat up.

There, in front of my eyes, filling the hut with their presence and their laughter, were at least a dozen Meo tribesmen, all dressed in their traditional splendor!

I quickly moved to Touby's side, casting my eye about for my clothes, for something to cover myself with. Finally I crouched behind him, letting his body shield me from their eyes.

"Touby," I whispered in his ear, "who *are* they?"

"My three brothers," he said, "my two uncles, and my seven cousins."

"Well, tell them I'm charmed to meet them, and I'll see them all at the reception."

Touby said something in Meo, and the men once again broke into uproarious laughter.

"Touby," I said dangerously, "why are they laughing?"

"They think you made a joke," he said.

"Well, tell them!" I barked. "Tell them it is most definitely *not* a joke!"

"They wouldn't understand," Touby said. "This is a very important part of the ceremony. And I had to go through hell just to get it diluted this much. They only agreed because you're a foreigner."

"Touby," I said, "I think you'd better tell me what you're talking about."

"Didn't you read it in your books?" he said. "The part about Meo weddings?"

"I never got that far," I said.

"No wonder. Well, at a Meo wedding—right after the kidnapping, that is—all the adult males in the groom's family come to, um, sample the bride. It's an old, old—"

"No," I said. "I don't care how old it is, I am not about to fuck your entire tribe."

"I know that," Touby said. "Just calm down. I told you I got the thing diluted."

"Oh, good," I said. "Does that mean I only have to fuck the uncles?"

"You don't have to fuck anybody," he said. "Nobody but me, that is."

"And what do we do with this family reunion of yours?"

"They watch," he said. "That was the best deal I could make for you. They watch."

"And if I don't feel like putting on a show?"

"They kill you."

"I see," I said. "Amazingly efficient system of justice you people have." I gave him a long, cold stare, then turned my gaze to each of the relatives in turn. Finally I let out a long sigh.

"This is going to be one hell of a honeymoon," I said.

Actually, it turned out to be nowhere near as bad as I had expected. Once my arguments died down and it became obvious that things were going to proceed as negotiated, Touby's uncles et al sat down in a circle and settled into an attitude of polite and quiet watchfulness. In fact, they even managed to impart an air of solemnity to the whole thing, which I thought would have been impossible, but which they managed to pull off quite well.

As for me, I have never been one to shy away from an audience.

So within a few minutes Touby and I were locked together again, his cock pumping in and out of the creamy depths of my pussy. I decided to put on a good show for the uncles, so I threw myself into this Oriental fuck-fest with renewed energy and spirit, literally shimmying up the length of Touby's marvelous pole, then sliding slowly, languorously back down again. A few minutes of this and I was off to the races for the third time that night.

We went at each other like that all night long, rolling and heaving through the poppy petals, changing positions and orifices as the mood struck us. We abandoned ourselves completely to the rite of consummation, forgetting even the presence of Touby's relatives as we explored and plumbed one another's bodies until every last drop of sexual juice had been wrung out of us.

When it was all over, when we simply could not move our bodies any more, we fell asleep, joining the uncles, brothers, and cousins who long before us had grown weary of the vigil.

CHAPTER NINE

I bided my time for the next few days, turning in an Academy Award–winning performance as Touby's wife and even learning a few words of Meo. Knowing that I would be leaving as soon as I made my contact with Laslow, it was quite easy for me to play the role, and I think I won over the Meo women fairly handily. After the honeymoon night in the shrine, the men were no problem whatsoever, and I could tell that a few of them were getting ready to make me offers of their own, if I should ever tire of Touby.

Actually, I rarely saw the men. The neighboring Yao tribesmen had recently decided to align themselves with the capitalist forces who were attempting to wrest control of the opium traffic from the Communist Meo. The Yao had allied themselves with elements of the Taiwanese army who had been run out of Mae Salong by the Meo and who had now established an encampment just across the Burmese border. This new Yao-Taiwanese offensive meant new fighting for the Meo, and the air was constantly being rent by the sound of mortar fire. The men, Touby included, were out on what amounted to a perpetual bivouac.

175

In the midst of all this, the opium harvest went on at its timeless, unhurried pace. The women spent all day in the fields, coming back to the village after dark with canvas sacks full of the resinous poppy juice. After a day or two of being left alone in the village, I begged relief from the boredom and asked to be taken to the fields when the women went out. After a brief discussion they consented, and the next morning I was handed a sack and a small curved knife and told to go with them.

I spent the better part of that day in the poppy fields, winding my way through the well-kept rows of head-high flowers, slitting open the polyps underneath and squeezing out the black gold inside. It was fascinating work (for a few hours, at least), and it was easy to understand how the opium poppy had become the sine qua non of Meo life, the center of its religion, the mainstay of its economy, and, of course, the motive power of its recreation.

Just when I was beginning to grow bored with the monotonous repetition of the harvest labor (I have never been known for my patience with manual tasks), I heard loud cries from the other end of the field. When I looked up, I saw that the women at that side had stopped their work and were congregating, looking down the hillside and pointing excitedly at something I could not see from where I was stationed. I dropped my sack, went over to that side of the field, and looked down. On the trail far below I could see the tiny figures of a train of mules, with a man walking alongside the lead animal. Even at that distance I could tell that the man was not a Meo.

Laslow! I thought, my heart suddenly beginning to beat faster. At last I was to meet the man who could hopefully lead me to Paul's "owner."

It took him another hour to reach the village, during which time the women returned to their work, seeming to double their speed. When he finally reached the crest of the hill and came abreast of the field, the women stopped again and fell into an excited single file behind the mule train, chattering gaily as they followed him into the village. I had not yet had a good look at him, or any chance to present myself.

When we reached the village, Laslow tethered his mules and disappeared immediately into one of the huts with the headwoman. The rest of us took up a position outside the hut, waiting for Laslow to emerge. When he did, I caught his eye at once.

He was a tall man, well-built and powerful looking, with a weathered face. He exuded the wild, sad feeling of a man who had seen too much, who knew humanity in all its baseness and depravity as well as in all its glory. There was also a dark, brooding sexuality about him that attracted me immediately.

He broke loose from the headwoman and walked over to me, his forehead wrinkled in a deep frown. "Who the hell are you?" he demanded.

"Christina van Bell," I replied. "I've been waiting for you."

One eyebrow shot up immediately. "Oh?" he said. "And who would you be working for?"

"That's just what I wanted to ask you," I said.

"Young lady," he said, "Miss Whoever-you-are, I hope you know that you're playing a very dangerous game." His tone was calm, but there was a threatening undercurrent to it.

But I was not about to back down. "So are you," I said.

He stared at me for a long moment, trying, I suppose, to figure me out. I stood my ground, staring back at him coolly. He broke first.

"All right," he said. "Let's talk."

He led me into the headwoman's hut, giving instructions in Meo that we were to be left alone. Once inside, I explained why I had come: my search for the holder of Paul's contract; the inexorable trail that had led me here through Snider, then Santos, then Touby. "I know you work for the man who owns Paul's contract," I said. "I just want to know where I can find him. You won't be implicated in the least."

He sat for a long time in silence, evidently thinking over what I had to say. "All right," he said eventually. "I've got a good setup with the Meo, the first decent setup I've had in my life, and I don't want to see it compromised. But there's nothing I can do for you here. As soon as the harvest is over and I'm all bagged up, you come with me to Penang. Once we get there I can set you up with people who can take you right to the boss."

I was suspicious. "Why can't you just tell me his name and where he lives?" I said.

"Because I don't know either one of those things," he said. "Those answers are in Penang."

I thought it over for a minute, and realized that for the moment I would have to be happy with this rather unsatisfactory compromise. I had no way of knowing whether or not he was telling the truth, but in this situation I had no way of finding out.

"All right," I said. "I'll come with you to Penang. But what do I tell Touby?"

"Are you really married to him?" he said.

"Up here I am."

"Then you can't tell him anything. We'll just have to sneak you out."

"Why can't I just tell him? He's civilized enough."

"He still has to answer to his people. Besides, the Meo have only one form of divorce."

"Death," I said. "I should have known."

"Death," he said, nodding in agreement. "And you certainly should have."

Three days later the harvest was ended. Touby had come back from a series of skirmishes with the Yao to oversee it, and had made me increasingly nervous by gluing himself to my side at all times. Apparently he was taking our marriage more and more seriously, as Laslow seemed to have known he would. I had developed something of an affection for the Meo leader, and I didn't want to hurt him if there was any way it could be avoided. But I could see there would be no way to approach him reasonably, so I held my peace and left my escape up to Laslow.

I knew his mules were loaded with this year's crop of opium resin, so I kept myself as ready as possible, fucking Touby silly at night so that he would sleep deeply, while sleeping with one eye open myself. Nothing happened the first night but on the second, when I was just about to drop off to sleep in spite of myself, I heard a rustling at the door of the hut. Then I saw Laslow's figure silhouetted in the doorway against the moonlight, and I knew that it was time to move. I got up quickly and tiptoed out of the hut, causing not so much as a stir in my Meo husband.

Outside, Laslow had everything waiting. The mules were packed and the front two were decked out in Meo riding gear. We mounted and moved off through the village as I hoped against hope that the mules would not stumble or bray. If so much as one Meo awoke, I knew, I could kiss my life goodbye.

But the escape went off without a hitch, and soon enough we were heading down the trail, putting distance and safety between us and Mae Salong. The night was gloriously moonlit, very similar to that other night— my God, it seemed so long ago!—when I climbed the mountain with Touby and locked my body to his in that beautiful little shrine. Now I could not help but turn and look back, looking wistfully up the mountain, hoping to discern some shape, some familiar landmark that would help me locate that strange and wonderful temple of sex. But the mountains were shrouded in mist, and the shrine seemed hopelessly gone forever.

Yet despite my temporary melancholy, I had the unshakable feeling that I was finally on my way back to Paul.

The next morning we arrived at Chiangrai, where Laslow transferred the raw opium to, of all places, an Air Force helicopter.

"How do you get away with that?" I asked, after the chopper had taken off.

"With what?" he said.

"With using an Air Force helicopter to transport opium."

"You should see the general's new swimming pool," he said.

So that was it, of course. I should have known. Evidently, the military was neck deep in the opium trade, and in that light some of the more absurd aspects of American foreign policy in Southeast Asia suddenly began to make perfect sense. I could not help but wonder how many wars that had been fought in the name of religion, or freedom, or national self-determination had in reality been opium wars, battles to control what is and always has been one of the most lucrative trades on earth.

Realizing that, I also knew that Touby would never again be able to leave his mountains. Somehow, it was not a pleasant thought.

"What happens to the opium now?" I asked Laslow as we walked back to his jeep.

"Bangkok for processing," he said, "then Marseilles for distribution, then on to buyers in Europe and America."

"I thought that route was dead," I said.

"It was," he said, and now I saw him smile for the first time. "I'm reviving it."

There didn't seem to be anything more to say, so I simply climbed in the jeep beside him. A short ride and two plane flights later, we were in Penang, that beautiful Malay island which is known throughout Asia as one of the last bastions of British colonialism.

We took a taxi to the airport terminal in George Town, then a trishaw—the combination of rickshaw and tricycle that is the mainstay of public transportation in Malaysia—to the funicular railroad that takes one to the top of Penang Hill. Penang itself is something of a Southeast Asian melting pot, and the street scenes reflect the mixture of cultures that have come to enjoy the city's tropical beauty and undeniable prosperity. The smell of Penang's streets is almost awesome—frangipani mixes with the Malay *satay* and Indian *biryani,* held together by the heavy tropical air and then stirred to a fragrant stew by offshore breezes. I had been there several times before, and now I was glad to return; doubly glad in that I felt I was drawing nearer and nearer to the end of my search.

Now we rode the funicular up the hill, leaving the heat of Canarnon Street behind as we passed through successive layers of jungle vegetation to the cool and flowery air at the top of the hill. Laslow maintained a suite in the Penang Hill Hotel, and was welcomed warmly by everyone from the porter to the manager. I found this welcome vaguely overexuberant, for up till now Laslow had struck me as one of the most reticent, self-contained people I had ever met, but I realized he had probably bought these people's affection with the proceeds of his opium concerns.

We went immediately to Laslow's suite, which offered a breathtaking view of George Town (whose lights were just now beginning to wink on in the dusk) and the brilliant white sand beaches of the Batu Ferringhi, the "foreigners' mile." I stood watching the peaceful scene for a while, then turned to Laslow, who was sitting on the edge of the bed with his shoes and socks off, rubbing the soles of his feet with a look of exquisite bliss on his face.

"When do I meet your friends?" I said.

He looked at me, startled, as if he had forgotten that I was in the room at all. "Soon enough," he said. "Don't be in too much of a hurry." He continued to rub his feet, the expression on his face growing stranger and stranger. "There's something we have to do first," he added.

Of course there was, I thought to myself. It had seemed all along that he had given in to me too easily, and I should have known that a little sex was going to be required of me somewhere along the way. Well, I had no particular objections—he was, as I said, a darkly attractive type despite his tendencies toward brooding silence.

I smiled at him and started to unbutton my blouse. Immediately a blush rose in his cheeks and he held up his hand to stop me. "Not that!" he barked. Then, a bit more softly, as if he had embarrassed himself, "Not yet, anyway."

"Oh," I said, putting on a bit of a pout as I tried to figure out what his game was. "What do you want me to do then, darling?"

"Come over here," he said.

I walked slowly over to him, exaggerating the movement of my hips as I did.

"Sit down," he said when I was standing above him. "On the floor, please."

I frowned momentarily, then recovered myself and did as he asked. "What now?" I said.

"Rub my feet."

It was all I could do to keep from bursting out laughing. He sounded so pathetic, so strangely deprived when he said it, as if there was no greater hedonism— and at the same time, no greater shame—than having your feet massaged by a willing woman. But I controlled myself, took one of his feet in both hands, and began to rub the soles gently.

"Ah," he said, a rare, slow smile spreading over his face. "That's it. You really know how to do it."

I kept it up, kneading his feet with a steady rhythm, watching in fascination as he closed his eyes and lay back on the bed. In a few more moments I felt the bed begin to move slowly, and when I looked up I saw that his hips were undulating in a slow, almost snakelike motion. His eyes were closed, and beads of perspiration had begun to form on his forehead. Under his pants, I could see that his cock was rising inexorably.

So that's it, I thought. A foot fetishist. Well, I could see nothing wrong with it, so long as it didn't turn into something ugly down the line. I have been known to indulge a few fetishes of my own, so I certainly had no call to feel either superior or particularly alarmed.

"Mm," he groaned, his hips rising and falling a bit faster now. "That's good. Now use your fingernails."

Luckily, my rather long fingernails had managed to escape intact from Meo country. Now I scraped them lightly along the soles of his feet, trailing them along the lines of blue veins. He moaned loudly and began to twist and turn on the bed, his passion growing at approximately the same rate as was the size of his prick.

And I had to admit it: I was beginning to turn on myself. Any sort of genuine sexual stimulation can do it to me, I suppose, and there was no doubting the sincerity of Laslow's desire. From an attitude of amused and somewhat detached skepticism, I was rapidly becoming more and more involved, and now I could feel those familiar butterflies beginning to stir in my own stomach.

"Do you like that?" I purred as I ran my fingernails once again over the soft skin of his soles. "Does that feel good to you?"

"It's great," he panted. "Perfect. Just don't stop. Please don't stop."

The urgency in his voice went straight to my churning pussy, and I could feel the fleshy lips beginning to flower open as I responded to his growing need. His pants were now tenting straight up in the air as his prick grew increasingly rigid, and I began to wonder if he would have an orgasm on the spot.

As if in answer, as if to postpone the inevitable a little while longer, Laslow suddenly sat bolt upright in bed. He quickly slipped his pants off, then his underpants, and I felt my own breathing become more rapid as his enormous cock shot into view. I began to knead and massage his feet once again, leaving my other hand free to climb up his thighs and wrap itself around his rigid pole.

To my surprise, he slapped my hand away. "Not

now!'' he said in a hoarse voice. ''It's too soon!'' He was looking down now at my feet, a glazed and fevered look in his eyes. ''Take your shoes off!'' he ordered.

All right, I thought—turnabout's fair. I started to reach for one of my shoes, to take it off with the same nonchalance with which one normally performs such mundane acts, but again Laslow barked at me.

''Not like that!'' he said. ''Slowly! Do it slowly!''

Now I had to concentrate on making a strip show out of the mere removal of my shoes. And I must say, I did an admirable job, even though I did find it a little difficult to take all this as seriously as Laslow did. First I ran my hand slowly along the outside of one of my shoes, which were the type of glove-leather pumps that leave the top of the foot exposed while hiding the heel, sole, and toes. I suppose, if one were as obsessed with feet as Laslow obviously was, the shoes could have been considered sexy, even peekaboo. At the same time, I moved my foot around and around in what I supposed were enticing little circles.

Apparently I was right. ''That's it,'' Laslow murmured, his eyes growing wider by the minute. ''Just like that. Take it slow. Tease me.''

I continued wiggling and rubbing at my shoe for a few moments, then slowly, with any number of false starts, began to slip it off, starting with the back of it so that my heel was the first thing to come into view.

Again Laslow moaned. ''Beautiful,'' he said. ''Perfect. Now let's see those toes.''

If it had not been for the honest-to-goodness desire in Laslow's voice, I'm sure I would have burst out laughing. But, I reminded myself, this man is very important to me, to my search for Paul, so I'd damned well better take the whole thing seriously. With painstaking slowness I slipped the rest of the shoe off my toes, wiggling them a bit as they popped free.

"Hold it right there," Laslow said breathlessly. "Don't move." He got up suddenly, went to his suitcase, and pulled out a small Polaroid camera. "I want to get a shot of this," he said.

In a flash he was kneeling beside the bed again, the camera poised for a close-up of my foot. All the while Laslow was muttering, "Gorgeous . . . gorgeous . . ." reminding me of a horse breeder looking at a perfect colt. He took several shots in sequence, waiting impatiently for the camera to issue the finished prints, whispering to himself all the while, rearranging my foot in a series of what I can only call poses; all in all he enjoyed himself quite thoroughly.

"Darling," I risked when he seemed to be exceptionally satisfied with a particular shot, "whatever do you do with all these photos?"

He looked at me as if I had asked the most ridiculous question since someone asked Pavarotti if he liked to sing.

"Nothing," he said. "I just like to shoot them. Now shut up and take off your other shoe."

I did as he asked, allowing myself a small sigh as I removed the other pump. Laslow then took several shots of that foot, still muttering and fussing over the light and the angle of placement until he got a shot that satisfied him. Finally he looked up at me with a smile.

"Now come up here on the bed," he said. "Lie down beside me."

I climbed up on the bed and snuggled up next to him, starting at once to nibble at the nape of his neck. Now, I thought, finally we're going to have some legitimate sex here. My own desire was rising rapidly, and I felt in need of a bit of broader attention.

But with the first touch of my lips to his neck, Laslow pushed me away. "Not that way," he said. "Turn around. Head to foot."

Again I did as he asked, but this time I paused briefly to plant a small, rebellious kiss on the head of his cock. I saw him glare at me murderously when I did, but I ignored him and simply continued to turn around. Finally I was stretched out next to him, my face next to his feet.

"Now," he said. "Kiss me."

I began to run my lips along the edge of his foot, taking little nibbles at it and occasionally letting my tongue stick out to trail along it. Suddenly an enormous flash singed my eyes, and I looked up to see the Polaroid which he had left suspended on a tripod. Apparently he had a remote shutter in his hand and was planning to photograph our entire session. Well, I thought, to each his own.

"Don't let it bother you," he said. "Just keep doing what you're doing."

"Certainly, darling," I said. "But I hope you're keeping track of these little favors I'm doing you."

"Don't worry about it," he snapped. "You'll get yours, no problem."

So I returned to the task at hand, planting wet kisses along the top of his foot while at the same time I rubbed and massaged the soles. I heard him begin to groan again at the other end of the bed, so I redoubled my efforts, now wrapping my hands around the arch of his foot and beginning to take the toes into my mouth one at a time.

"Yes!" he cried as I wrapped my mouth around his big toe, running my lips along its soft length and sucking on it gently. "That's it! Oh God, that feels good!"

I continued to suck and lick at his toes, moving from

one to the other, then giving the same treatment to his other foot. By now he was nearly beside himself with the pleasure of it, writhing on the bed with ever-increasing abandon, groaning and whispering passionate little endearments as I went on tonguing him. In the meantime, flashbulbs were going off at about thirty-second intervals, creating a strange slow-motion strobe effect that only exacerbated the general weirdness of the scene. I was beginning to feel as if I had somehow gotten lost on the set of a movie made by some Fellini-esque pornographer, and that any moment a bunch of midgets in drag would burst into the room, strip off their clothes, and jump head-first into a birthday cake.

Then, just when I was beginning to wonder if all this was really worth it, I felt a warm, soft touch on the bottom of my own feet. Laslow had begun to kiss me in return, launching, I suppose, his own version of the old *soixante-neuf*. But the strangest thing about it was my response: I felt immediately as if he were kissing a zone that although previously ignored had all of a sudden become highly erogenous. A tingling sensation started as he kissed me, beginning in the soles of my feet and then radiating up my legs until it homed in on my neglected pussy, stirring my lonely little clitty into renewed life.

He kissed me a few more times, trailing his tongue along the soles of my feet as I responded in kind. Then he stopped for a moment.

"You like that?" he said.

"Darling," I said, a little breathlessly, "I have to admit that I do."

"See?" he said. "And you thought I was crazy."

"Stay crazy, darling," I said. "I love it."

"There's no place on the body as sensitive to stimulation as the feet," he said.

"So I see," I purred. "But darling, let's not have an anatomy lecture just when I'm finally starting to enjoy all this."

He chuckled once, then returned to my feet, which indeed were growing more and more sensitive, more and more open by the moment to this surprisingly sexy foreplay. And I became his shadow, echoing each kiss, each stroke, each nibble with one of my own, feeling the divine little sensations shoot up my legs and spread through my nervous system, igniting my aching body like sparks in dry grass.

Then I felt him inexorably begin to move up, inch by inch, kiss by fevered kiss, over the tops of my feet to my ankles. Again I echoed him, moving my mouth slowly up to the base of his calves, sliding back toward him as I did so. It was obvious what he had in mind here—we were in direct line with one another, passionately kissing our way together, with me moving toward his erect cock and him toward my hungry pussy like trains on a collision course.

"*Mm, yes . . .*" I said as I felt his lips smoothing along my calves, his mouth clinging to me like a suckerfish to the body of a whale. "*Yes, darling . . . come to me . . . my cunt wants you, darling . . . come to me . . . hurry . . . hurry . . . please . . .*"

"It's all right," he said in a suddenly soothing voice. "There's no hurry. We'll get there . . ."

"*Oh, darling . . . you're driving me crazy . . .*" I moaned. "*I can't stand it!*"

It was true. I was growing more and more excited, more and more desperate with each passing second, with each new touch to my trembling calves. My breasts ached as I dragged them along the bed, the combination of the friction and the delightful sensation of Laslow's mouth on my legs making my nipples stand at attention.

At the same time, I was trailing kisses along his legs, brushing through the forest of wiry hairs and taking occasional little nips at the receptive flesh, which somehow still smelled of the mountains, of the harvest of opium.

Closer and closer together we moved, and soon I felt his hand—his hand! It was the first time he had actually touched me!—snake up my legs, grab my panties, and pull them down over my hips. At the same time he pushed my dress up so that both my buttocks and the moistened mouth of my pussy were exposed to him. He grabbed my legs at the knees and pulled them as wide apart as they would go, then went back to kissing his way up my calves, my quaking thighs.

"Yes, darling . . ." I cried. *"Come to me, darling . . . closer . . . closer . . ."*

It was all I could do to keep from jamming back against him with all my strength, grinding my aroused cunny into his waiting mouth. I was absolutely overcome with the white heat of my desire, with the feeling of his hot mouth on my flesh, and I wanted nothing more than to feel his lips make contact with the lips of my hungry pussy, to feel his tongue sear its way into me.

At the same time, I was moving closer and closer to his groin, which was undulating in lazy little circles, pressing the hard flesh of his cock against my belly. I parted his legs at the knees just as he had done to me, and teasingly ran my fingernails along the insides of his thighs, caressing and scraping them, feeling him buck a bit harder against me in response.

"Do you like that, darling?" I cooed. *"Do you like it when I touch you?"*

In answer, he slid his head up suddenly and planted a quick kiss on the flanges of my starving vagina, at the same time inserting his tongue between the yielding labia and running it in one long swipe along my clitoris. Again I had to overcome the urge to simply push back against him as hard as I could, to glue my pussy to the wonderful softness of his lips. But I held myself back, shuddering a bit when he withdrew from me, and groaning as if in protest at my own control.

I also began to flick my fingernails along the base of his balls, teasing the sensitive scrotum and bringing his cock to greater and greater life. I could tell by the increasing force of his writhing that I would not have much longer to wait, so I moved my head back further, drawing closer and closer to the sensitive mass of flesh at his crotch, drawing up my knees so as to provide exactly the right fit.

Slowly, slowly I drew back, moving my mouth along the insides of his thighs, then brushing my lips through the spindly little hairs at the base of his balls. With that first touch of my mouth to the nerve-riddled flesh of his scrotum, he exploded, twisting and turning underneath me, grinding his massive cock up against my neck.

"Christina!" he yelled. "I can't take it any more! Suck me, Christina! Take me in your mouth and suck me!"

"Gladly, darling," I said. "But I want you too, you know . . . I want to feel your mouth on my sweet pussy . . ."

"Yes, yes! . . . anything! Just do it, Christina! Do it!"

But I was not quite ready. I wanted to draw it out a bit, make him wait as he had done to me. So I propped myself up fully on my hands and knees, and began taking long, languid swipes at his balls with the broad surface of my tongue. Over and over I caressed him that way as he cursed and roiled beneath me. Then, finally, when I knew he could take it no more, I nibbled my way up the warm stem of his cock and finally plunged the head of it into my mouth, feeling the hard flesh burrow into me as I heard him groan with satisfaction.

A moment later I felt the splendid touch of his lips again at the entrance to my cunt, felt them nibble and press against my tingling flesh like a snail crawling up a blade of grass. Now I let myself go, wiggling my buttocks in small circles, pushing back against him, harder and harder yet, mashing my eager pussy against the surface of his mouth until I thought I would go berserk with the splendid contact. At the same time I took his lovely cock deeper and deeper into my own mouth, feeling it slide along the softly lubricated flesh and finally lodge itself against the back of my hungry throat.

Now I started to move my head up and down, slowly, rhythmically, pursing my lips around the hardness of his prick, making a soft glove of my mouth and a tight little tunnel of my throat. The top side of his dick lay against my tongue, which caressed it gently as I continued to slide back and forth, reveling in the luscious friction and tasting the first few droplets of precome that issued from the tip of his delightful penis.

As if in answer, Laslow wrapped his lips around the little hill of my love-cord—which was so highly aroused that it was actually palpitating—and began to suck at it gently, sending a powerful surge of sensation coursing through my heaving body. I ground myself against him even more tightly than before, feeling the tip of his nose bury itself in my cunt hole. His hands had moved up around my hips, and they now pushed me back and forth, burying his cock in my mouth on the outstrokes and gluing his lips to my erect little clitty when he pulled me back against him.

In a few moments we had lost ourselves in a symphony of motion, a dance of desire more coordinated than the finest ballet. We were absolutely at one in our movements, a seesaw of pure eroticism, sliding back and forth along the length of one another's bodies, sweating and heaving, bringing each other ever closer to the brink of a thunderous orgasm.

A few minutes later it hit. I could feel his prick stiffen and begin to throb in the soft and yielding confines of my mouth, could taste the load of his thick, white semen as it splashed against the back of my throat. At almost the same instant my own pussy erupted, and a thrilling climax swept over me, amplified ten times by the fact that it was happening at the same time as his. Had I not been so busy swallowing, I'm sure I would have screamed aloud; and even though his mouth was still virtually melded to my electrified little clitty, I could hear muffled yells coming from his end of the bed.

He continued emptying his balls into me for what seemed like hours, and I swallowed furiously—in self-defense, if nothing more. I had placed both my hands firmly under his buttocks, and with the coming of orgasm had inserted one finger into his anus, prodding gently and seeking out his prostate. This seemed to elongate his orgasm tremendously, as I had known it would, and with each gentle poke I felt a new spurt of semen issue from the tip of his cock to slide in an uninterrupted flow down my welcoming throat.

Finally I felt his body go limp beneath me, felt his cock still its motion and then slide gently, reluctantly, out of my mouth. I moved forward a bit so that the contact between my spent clitoris and his mouth would be broken. We lay there in silence for a few minutes, still head to toe, with me on top of him, trying to work up the energy to move further, or to speak.

Eventually I heard him whisper something nearly inaudible in a weak, hoarse voice. I turned my head to look back at him.

"What did you say?" I asked.

He moved until he had eye contact with me, then smiled lazily, the first truly relaxed expression I had ever seen on his face.

"Christina," he said, "you've got the sexiest arches this side of Bangkok."

"Why, thank you, darling," I said, nodding my head in mock courtliness. "I could say the same thing for your marvelous heels."

CHAPTER TEN

Next morning, as we sat on the terrace enjoying the first eggs Florentine and Dom Perignon I had tasted since leaving Marseilles, I began to remember that despite the amusing little soiree the night before, I had come here for a reason. Realizing that, I immediately began to grow impatient.

"When do we meet your friends?" I said. "I'm developing a slight itch."

"We don't meet them," he said. "They meet us. You know the Orient well enough to know that you don't make appointments."

I sighed and took another sip of the champagne, feeling its delightful dryness tickle my palate. "All right," I said, "so it's more of this Far Eastern time-killing. What do we do?"

"There's a festival tonight," he said. "I'm sure Ian and Nicole will show up there. In the meantime, let's take a drive."

So we spent the day touring the countryside in Laslow's Lotus Elan. In the afternoon I took over the wheel, and did a bit of high-speed fooling around on the narrow country roads. Putting that responsive little car through its paces was like a form of therapy, a great release from the accumulated tension of my quest. When we finally turned back toward the city, I felt renewed, revived, ready for anything.

By the time we reached the outskirts of George Town, the sun was setting into the Strait of Malacca and the sky was announcing the day's end with shouts of pink and purple. Then, just as we were entering the city, I saw an extremely curious sight: a Bengali man walking along the road, dressed only in a simple white robe, and with what looked like an enormous knitting needle sticking through the skin of his back! As we passed him, my head pivoted as if my neck were a ball bearing and I gaped at him without shame.

"My God!" I said to Laslow. "Did you see that?"

"Thaipusam," he said.

"I beg your pardon?"

"Thaipusam," he repeated. "It's a Hindu festival that celebrates the birthday of Lord Subramaniam, who was some sort of martyr, I think."

"And that's how they *celebrate*?" I said. "By skewering themselves?"

"Wait until you see it tonight," he said. "It's like a human shishkebab."

"I'm not sure . . ." I began.

"Don't worry about it," he said. "There's no blood. They only do it to show penitence, and they're experts at not hurting themselves."

Apparently the festival was a major one, for as we drove back toward the base of Penang Hill we found all the streets decorated with banners and streamers, all the shops closed, and all the people hurrying purposefully in one direction or another. Tents and wall-less canvas shelters were being set up in vacant lots, and little wooden podiums dotted nearly every street corner. There was an air of anticipation in the street which took hold of us immediately, and we found ourselves hurrying rather more than we might have on a more ordinary day.

We drove back to the hotel, changed quickly, then took the funicular down to the base of the hill. Already the streets were teeming with people, a mix of Hindu celebrants and curious Chinese, Thais, and Malays, as well as a few amazed tourists. The sounds of feverish chanting blended into the incense-thickened air while smoke from thousands of tiny offering pots drifted up in thin clouds to obscure, then reveal, the gaudy decorations draped overhead. We walked along as fast as the milling crowds would allow, our nostrils tantalized by the thousand smells, one of which was the now-familiar sweet-dense odor of opium.

The more we walked, the more frequently I saw people like the man we had seen on the road: Hindu penitents dressed in shining white saris, showing their devotion to the dead hero by means of that delicately brutal self-torture. For without exception, each of them had one or more needles stuck into and protruding from their bodies—some, like the man we had seen on the road, through their backs, some through the skin on their chest or arms, and a surprisingly large number with the needles passed all the way through the flesh of their tongues! The revulsion I had felt at first sight soon gave way to fascination, and to memories of certain incidents in my own life in which I had been shown quite delightfully that pain is often one of the straightest and quickest roads to pleasure.

"You know," I said, "I think I'm beginning to understand this."

"Don't be too sure," he said. "It's just starting."

I was just about to reply when Laslow literally disappeared from my side. It was as if a pair of arms had reached through the crowd and simply plucked him away. When I turned to look for him I saw that that was indeed what had happened, for now he was being embraced by a huge European man who had him in a bear hug and was picking him off the ground, all the time regaling Laslow with a deep, booming laugh.

"Laslow!" he was saying in a rich voice thick with a south-of-the-river London accent. "I'll be damned, I will!"

"Put me down, you idiot!" Laslow was saying, but I could tell that he was having trouble controlling his own laughter. "Can't you see I'm with somebody?" He nodded over in my direction.

"What's the matter, ducks?" the giant said. "You wouldn't be embarrassed now, would you?" He deposited Laslow on the ground. "Let's meet your bird, then," he said.

With Laslow on the ground standing next to him, I could get an idea as to how big the Englishman really was. Laslow himself stood a good six-two, but he looked like an anemic dwarf next to his friend, whose full black beard made him look like a handsome Goliath. For there was not an ounce of fat on this man, only solid, perfectly proportioned muscle and a face that radiated both health and sheer physical power. All in all, I thought, a most awesome sight.

Now Laslow straightened his clothing and the two of them walked over to me. It was only then that I saw that Laslow's friend was accompanied by a stunning woman, a redheaded amazon with a perfect complexion and a body to make men leave home. She must have been at least six feet tall, with breasts in the forty-inch range, and my first reaction to her was one of sheer jealousy.

"Christina van Bell," Laslow said when the threesome reached me, "meet Ian Stenneck."

"My pleasure," I said, disguising my excitement as best I could.

"Could be, love, could be," he said. "We'll just have to see about that, won't we?" He took my hand, holding it with surprising gentleness for such an enormous bear of a man. But he held it just an instant longer than civility required, giving me a transparently flirtatious glance at the same time. Seeing this, his amazon girlfriend stepped quickly up beside him.

"My wife, Nicole," Ian said blandly.

"Your better third?" I said. As Ian and Laslow both chuckled, Nicole threw me a murderous glance, her eyes narrowing like a cat's.

"Just 'better,' " she said in an exaggerated French accent, which was so thick you could have spread it on a croissant.

"All right, lass," Ian said to her. "Save the daggers for later. Now, what are we all up to?"

"As a matter of fact," Laslow said, "I was just about to take Christina to see the dick trick."

"I beg your pardon?" I said.

"The dick trick!" Ian exclaimed, his face lighting up like a kid at Christmas. "Is that bloke still about?"

"As far as I know, he is," Laslow replied.

"Well, let's go!" Ian said.

"Excuse me," I put in, "but would someone mind enlightening me?"

"I would theenk," Nicole said (pronouncing it "sink"), "zat ze lady would already know everything zer is to know about dick tricks."

"Oh no," I responded. "I've never even *been* to France."

"All right, girls, knock it off," Laslow said.

"Exactly," Ian added. "I'm here to enjoy myself, not to listen to a lot of bickering. Now let's go find this bloke. He's really quite daft."

I sheathed my verbal sword—for the moment, at least—and fell into step with Laslow as we moved off down the street. We were on the Pengkalan Weld, which runs along the George Town waterfront, and whenever the crowd cleared we could see what amounted to a parade of sampans on the water, their sails dazzling in the many-colored lights. Fireworks were going off everywhere, splashing their brilliant sparklers against the sky, making the whole thing reminiscent of a scene from the Battle of Fort McHenry. I could almost imagine some Malaysian Francis Scott Key observing the scene, the beginnings of a strident tune now turning in his head.

After a few blocks we ducked back into the Leboh Gareja, then turned again at King Street. This narrow thoroughfare—little better than an alleyway, really—was absolutely choked with humanity, and it took us nearly half an hour to move a single block. But we finally arrived at a corner which Laslow seemed to have had in mind all along.

"There," he said. "There he is. The owner of the world's most incredible cock."

I craned my neck to see through the crowd, twisting this way and that until I finally saw the man Laslow was talking about. He was standing on a hastily constructed platform, and from my vantage point I could see absolutely nothing prepossessing about him. He was a Hindu, small and slight and burnished brown, wearing nothing in the way of clothing but a monk's loincloth. It was next to impossible to tell his age—he could have been an old thirty or a young seventy. The most remarkable thing about him were his wrinkles:

They appeared only around his eyes, and they radiated out, like the rays of some internal sun. At the moment he was standing stock-still with his eyes closed.

"This isn't the trick, I presume," I said.

"Shh," Laslow said. "He's just starting. He's working himself into a trance."

After a few more moments of absolute stillness, the little man opened his eyes. With sure, steady movements he dropped his loincloth . . . to reveal the most awesome cock I have ever seen in my life. It hung down from his groin like an elephant's trunk, at least a foot and a half long and possibly as much as three inches in diameter. I tried to imagine that immense piece of flesh penetrating me, crawling up inside me like a thing alive, but failed utterly. It was simply beyond the powers of my imagination.

My elephant metaphor soon proved to be entirely apt, for the first thing this incredible little man did was to roll this amazing cock up into a coil, much as an elephant does when he lifts a peanut to his mouth. But the Hindu somehow managed to roll his penis into a spiral so tight that it could have been a coiled garden hose, or a sleeping snake. The crowd gasped, of course—what else could it do?

"My God!" I said. "Is this real?"

I heard Ian chuckle behind me. "Just wait, love," he said. "He's only tuning up."

Ian was right. I am still at a loss to explain what the little Hindu did next, even though my eyes were riveted on him and I could see him quite clearly. No matter: The next thing I knew, that enormous cock of his, that bludgeon, had disappeared! Absolutely, entirely, utterly disappeared! He had made a couple of slight, rapid shifts in his stance, but nothing that could have accounted for such a sudden and monumental absence.

Now he stood before us, transformed for all the world into a woman, his dark pubic hair pointing in a familiar "v" to the place where his cock should have been—*had* been, in fact, until just a moment before.

Then, while everyone gaped at him speechlessly, he turned slowly around, showing us first his flanks and then his backside. Still, there was no sign whatsoever of that magical prick of his. After a moment he bent over slightly and began to slowly part the cheeks of his ass, and inch by inch his cock began to peek out at us. He had somehow, in the flash of an eye, managed to bury the thing between his ass-cheeks, hiding it completely from our view! Now as he continued to part his buttocks it reappeared, finally freeing itself and flopping carelessly into its rightful spot between his slender legs.

"I don't believe it," I said. "I saw it, but I don't believe it." I turned to Ian, who was applauding and cheering mightily. "Can you do that?" I said.

"Only when eet's inside me," Nicole snapped, her eyes flashing. "Ze rest of ze time eet just sticks out."

"Climb it, Nicole," Ian said bitterly.

"I would love to, *mon cher*," she said, "but I am afraid eet would break."

"Quiet, you two," Laslow said. "He's coming to the best part."

We turned our attention back to the platform, where the diminutive Hindu was tying a thick rope around the end of his cock.

"What's he going to do?" I said. "Take it out for a walk?"

No one answered me. I looked back at the platform to see the Hindu tie the other end of the rope to a large rock that was lying at his feet. I have no way of telling how much that rock weighed, but it must have been at least fifty pounds, if not more. Once the rope was secure, the Hindu shut his eyes again, trying, I suppose, to deepen his trance. The crowd grew silent, breathless.

Finally the little man opened his eyes again and began to slowly, carefully coil his dick as he had during the first trick. The difference, of course, was that this time there was a fifty-pound weight attached to it. He raised his arms in the air, and a set of hitherto secret muscles literally popped out of his belly, his groin, and the insides of his thighs. I kept my eyes glued on the rock as the rope went taut with his straining. For a moment he seemed to have been stopped—I took a quick mental photograph of the straining rope, the coiled cock, the elaborate filigree of muscles—then slowly, almost imperceptibly at first, the rock began to move.

"Unbelievable," I muttered.

"Ungodly," said Ian.

Within a few seconds the little man had lifted the rock a full foot off the ground, his cock acting like a pulley. He held it there for a moment or two, and then let it fall with a mighty yell. The rock thunked loudly onto the platform, the man bowed to the audience (which was too dumbfounded even to applaud), then slipped on his loincloth and simply disappeared into the crowd. In an instant he was swallowed up by the seething mass of humanity, leaving us to wonder if we were only suffering from some sort of collective hallucination.

We pushed our way through the crowd to a place where we could move more freely, then stopped to reconnoiter.

"That was fantastic," Ian said. "What's next?"

"Perhaps Christina can balance a basket of fruit on one of her cute leetle teets," Nicole said.

I bristled, of course. The woman was obviously spoiling for a fight. "Perhaps you can show me how," I said. "Or are you afraid your sands might shift?"

She started for me with her fingernails pointed straight at my eyes. I braced myself for the attack. But before she could reach me Ian stepped in between us and held the furious Nicole by the shoulders.

"Hold it!" he commanded, squeezing her until she finally stopped struggling. "Just hold it! Control your bloody self, will you?"

"I've got an idea," Laslow said. I turned to look at him and saw that his eyes were shining with a curious gleam. "If these girls want to fight so badly, why not let them indulge themselves?"

Ian's face broke into a broad grin. "The Polo Club," he said.

"Exactly," said Laslow. He turned to me. "Are you game?" he said.

I shrugged. "Ask Miss Femme Fatale," I said. "She's the one who wants to fight."

"Nicole?" Laslow said.

Again she gave me one of her murderous glances. *"Pourquoi pas?"* she said, her eyes shining.

"Fine with me," I said.

We started walking, moving as briskly as we could, considering the crowd. I had no idea where we were going, and was not in the least sure I wanted to go through with this, especially considering that I might need this woman's help in the morning. But my instincts told me that primitive and silly as all this might be, I could not back down. I had the feeling that I was being put through some sort of obscure initiation, and if I passed, if I acquitted myself well against this amazon, my path to Paul's "boss" would be that much straighter.

In a few more minutes we arrived at the Polo Club, which I now remembered from one of my earlier visits.

It was an ornately elegant building on the waterfront, one of those legacies from the heyday of British colonialism, where colonels and governors could drink their Pimm's cups and for a few hours each day unshoulder the terrible load of the white man's burden.

The doorman bowed immediately when he saw Ian and Laslow, and we entered a teak-paneled hallway studded with brass lanterns. The club was still impeccably English, replete with massive crystal chandeliers, a quietly bustling casino, and British naval officers in gleaming dress uniforms. We bypassed the casino, walking down a maze of corridors until we came to a set of particularly imposing double doors guarded by a fully armed soldier.

The mention of Ian's name got us through the door. Once inside, I could not have been more surprised by the sight that greeted us. In the center of an enormous, brightly lit room, there was a boxing ring, surrounded by a screaming crowd of well-dressed men and women. In the center of the ring two Malay women, entirely nude, were engaged in a vicious kick-boxing match, while a Chinese referee circled them, ostensibly to keep them from killing one another but actually just trying to stay out of the way.

As we moved closer the shorter of the two women landed a monumental kick to the other's chin, and she went down like a sack of cement. The referee counted her out, then held up the winner's hand as a chorus of cheers and boos washed over them. An excited buzz of chatter from the crowd followed, and everywhere one could see money, large stacks of it, changing hands.

Now Ian pushed his way through to ringside and caught the attention of the referee. They talked for a moment, then the Oriental nodded. He went back to the center of the ring and picked up a microphone.

"Radies and genrmen," he announced. "We now gon have speciar tleat. Two white girls gon fight."

He meant Nicole and me, of course. Since there was absolutely nothing I could do to get out of it, I shrugged, walked through the wildly cheering crowd, and climbed into the ring. Nicole was right behind me. She went to the opposite corner and immediately began to strip, shedding her lamé evening dress in one practiced motion.

The crowd gasped as the dress fell away from her, and I had to agree with them—the woman had an incredible body. She was big, of course, but her proportions were absolutely perfect, her mountainous breasts giving way to a cinch of a waist, then flaring out into a pair of the most magnificent hips I had ever seen. Standing there naked in the bright ring lights, she truly looked like a goddess, like some enormous Athena recalled from the grip of legend and revived in all her glory to do battle with the mortals.

Now it was my turn. I took my sweet time, taking off my clothes one item after another. When I was finally naked, the crowd applauded appreciatively, but somewhat politely compared to the spontaneous and thunderous applause they had given Nicole. I think it was the first time in my life that I have ever suffered by comparison to another woman, and if I do say so myself, I handled it rather well.

The referee called us into the middle of the ring. "You gon box?" he asked. "Kick-box, or lessle?"

"Wrestle," I said, and Nicole nodded her agreement. If I had my choice, I figured I'd much rather be crushed than battered.

"Okay," the referee said. "Go!"

He stepped out from between us and we immediately began to stalk one another, bent at the waist like two savages, arms extended, circling and measuring one another as the crowd egged us on. I was wary and cautious, quietly confident but at the same time duly respectful of her size and obvious strength. But while one part of my brain was coldly calculating the strategy of the wrestling match, another part of me was experiencing a quite different range of emotions. The sight of Nicole's outlandishly gorgeous body poised for action, the sounds and smell of the crowd-beast, the heat of the lights were all combining to charge my sexual batteries with a uniquely powerful erotic energy; and I found myself looking forward to the moment when we would touch, when we would lock our bodies together in the combat that is only one step removed from the quieter clinching of the love-couch.

Just as I thought it, it happened: Nicole lunged at me, attempting to clasp me in a crushing bear hug. I ducked down instantly under her extended arms, grabbed her firmly around the knees and flung her over my back, a Tai Kwan Do move I had learned from Claudio Gallardo. Nicole hit the canvas belly down, making a huge smacking sound, the mounds of her ample buttocks carving a curved swath in the air, her back already heaving with exertion.

I lost no time in employing the small advantage I had gained. I jumped on her, spreading myself full length along her back, bringing my arms up underneath hers and pulling her torso up off the mat. As I did so I threw one knee over her other side so that I was sitting on top of her back and straddling her at the same time.

The feeling of my breasts crushed against the small of her back, of my stirring and naked cunny rubbing along the sweat-streaked skin just above her flaring buttocks, was nearly overpowering, and I almost loosened my grip on her shoulders. Instead I leaned in close to her, my head buried in her hair, my lips grazing her neck.

"Is this what you had in mind, darling?" I whispered. "Feels rather good, don't you think?"

Instead of answering she let out a savage growl, at the same time throwing her lower body up into the air with such great force that I practically flew over her shoulders. As I hit the mat I did a quick somersault and came up on my feet—luckily so, for Nicole was already advancing on me, a wild grin on her face.

"So," she hissed as she came forward, "ze leetle girl knows how to fight, eh? Good . . . good . . ."

She kept coming at me, still hunched over like a maddened gorilla. I put one hand on the top of her head as a sort of early-warning system against her next lunge, but it didn't work the way I had planned. She ducked under my hand and this time succeeded in grabbing me around the waist. In the same move she reached down and swept my feet out from under me. I landed on my back on the canvas, and in a flash I felt the full brunt of her weight come crashing down on me.

She lay stretched across me for a time, pinning me to the mat. In that position I was absolutely helpless against her superior size. I struggled the best I could, thrusting my hips up at her, bucking and heaving like a madwoman, wriggling about and trying to slide out from underneath her. All these movements were frankly sexual, and the feel of her powerful muscles, the searing contact of breast against breast, thigh rubbing along moistened thigh were arousing me more and more with each passing second.

"Nicole . . ." I gasped out as she squeezed the breath from me. "Nicole, what is this? . . . You're turning me on . . . so much . . ."

"Ah," she said. "You are catching on . . . finally . . ."

Now I understood. Nicole had perpetrated the whole thing, had staged our earlier unpleasantness knowing that it would end up here in the ring. She must have done it many times before, and Ian and Laslow must have had a hand in it. Evidently she needed a bit of violence to activate her sexual juices, so she picked fights with anyone new who attracted her, just as she had done with me.

With the real purpose of our wrestling match now understood, we began to work together to make full use of the situation. Nicole still lay sprawled on top of me, her full weight pressing down on me. Now she inserted her knee between my widespread legs so that as I bucked up and down—supposedly trying to free myself— my already dripping cunt rubbed deliciously against the top of her thigh, making me groan in what must have seemed like excruciating pain but which was actually pure erotic pleasure.

I couldn't keep that up for too long, of course, or I would have had an orgasm on the spot. Realizing this, Nicole withdrew her leg and weakened her grip on me just long enough so that I could get an arm around her and roll her over on the mat. As I did so I managed to run a fingernail over the tip of one of her nipples, at the same time cupping her other breast just briefly in my free hand.

"Mmm . . ." she whispered. "Oui, ma chérie . . . now you understand, no?"

"I understand, darling," I said. "But how do we get out of this?"

"Do not worry," she replied. "We still have plentee of time . . ."

Now, in the guise of trying to roll her over on her

back so that I could pin her, I hooked one arm under her shoulder and placed the other between her well-muscled thighs. In that position my hand crept up under her buttocks, which were sufficiently hidden from the crowd's view so that I could wedge a finger in between her ass-cheeks. At the same time I lifted up and applied pressure, which brought my wrist into contact with the outer lips of her pussy. Instantly she wedged herself against me, simultaneously skewering her anus down onto my finger and pushing her cunt against the rigid bone of my wrist. We went on as long as we dared with this phony struggle, while all the time Nicole was whispering passionately in my ear.

"Oui, ma petite . . . oui . . . yes . . . touch me there . . . harder . . . harder . . . let me feel you, chérie . . . more . . . oh yes, give me more . . ."

"They're going to catch on, Nicole . . ." I whispered. "We've got to change position."

Without saying another word she rolled out from under me, jumping instantly to her feet. I followed suit, and once again we stood face to face in the center of the ring. This time she moved quickly. Coming in under me, she picked me up and lifted me onto her shoulders, stretching me out horizontally so that the two of us formed a human "t." Her left arm lay across my breasts, pushing them delightfully in and rubbing across the hardened little nipples, which spiked out enthusiastically in response. Her other hand was holding me between the legs so that the base of her thumb penetrated my pussy-lips and lodged marvelously against the elongated little cord of my clitty.

Now she began to turn slowly around, as if displaying me to the audience like some hard-won trophy of the hun. Actually, of course, she was disguising her own movements, the subtle caressing of her arm across my smooth breasts, the quick and almost unnoticeable little rubbings against my eager pussy. Faster and faster she spun, turning the room into a kaleidoscope of light and sound as the audience's roar blended with the pounding of my own blood in my ears. I was fantastically excited by this time, mashing my breasts against her arm and grinding my dampened cunny as hard as I could against the base of her thumb. The combination of this whirling, spinning sensation and the delightful electricity of my arousal was overwhelming me, driving me nearly mad with lust.

"*Yes . . . oh my God, yes . . .*" I moaned at her. "*Nicole . . . Nicole . . . you're killing me . . . oh God, darling . . . I love it . . . I love your touch . . . my pussy's on fire for you, Nicole . . .*"

"*Hush, amour . . .*" she whispered. "*Soon . . . very soon, my love . . .*"

She continued to spin me around, all the time zeroing in even more delightfully on my breasts, my nipples, my hungry cunt. After a few more spins I heard her whisper:

"*Brace yourself, chérie . . . I'm going to throw you . . . one . . . two . . .*"

At the count of *three* she suddenly picked me up over her head, hesitated for a moment, then flung me up in the air as if I were a football. Thanks to her warning I managed to make the fall convincing enough for the audience without actually hurting myself—again I found myself issuing a silent thanks to Claudio Gallardo and his training. As soon as I landed, Nicole fell across me again, rolling me quickly over onto my back. I looked up into her face, which was flushed with exertion and sexual excitement. A strange, enticing smile was playing about her lips.

"Maintenant, ma chérie . . ." she whispered. *"We are going to end this . . . now!"*

"Yes, Nicole . . ." I answered. *"Hurry, darling . . . I want you . . . I want to make love . . ."*

She leaned forward and grabbed my arms, all the time grinding her lust-slickened pussy against my abdomen. My own vagina was feeling exposed and achingly empty by comparison. Finally, as she continued to hold my arms down, the Chinese referee came over, leaned over close to us, and counted: "One . . . two . . . three . . . out!"

It was over. Nicole leapt to her feet as the referee raised her arm, which she brandished in triumph as the crowd howled its approval. After a few moments I stood up too. Someone threw each of us a silk robe, which rubbed delectably against my still-hardened nipples when I put it on.

As I climbed through the ropes I looked over at Nicole, who herself was peering intently at Ian. A nod and an eye signal later, we were both following Ian and Laslow through the crowd. I could feel my pussy still issuing the cream of my arousal, and the insides of my thighs rubbed moistly, maddeningly together as we walked. I was sure that Ian and Laslow were leading us to some place private, for this whole thing had obviously been arranged as a sort of warm-up for me and Nicole, to raise our longing to a fever pitch so as to have us both ripe and ready for the orgiastic party to follow.

Well, it certainly had worked on me. I was nearly out of my mind with longing—for Nicole, for Ian, for the strangely exciting Laslow. It was as if my insides were some sort of sexual time bomb, and Nicole had lit the fuse which was now burning inexorably toward explosion. I could have cared less where we were going—in my current state of arousal, in fact, I wouldn't have minded putting on a public foursome for the Polo Club crowd. All I knew was that I had to feel hands roaming over my body, igniting the thousand fires of my yearning. I wanted to feel Nicole's breasts against the smoothness of my skin, feel the hard flesh of Ian's and Laslow's cocks penetrating me, stirring me, filling me to overflowing with their strident sexuality.

To put it simply, I wanted to be fucked—immediately, if not sooner!

I followed behind Ian, who led us through a short hallway to what appeared to be a little-used elevator. There was no call-button on the door, but only a lock. Naturally, Ian had the key. In a moment or so the elevator door opened and we stepped inside.

"Now," Ian said, his eyes gleaming mischievously. "Time for the victory party."

"A toast to the victor!" Laslow said as the elevator door closed in front of us. He reached into Nicole's robe, pulled out one of her mammoth breasts, and raised it as high as it could stretch, making it look for all the world like a championship trophy filled with champagne. He then wrapped his lips around the nipple in a passionate kiss, sucking at it like a drunk on a bottle of muscatel, while Nicole squirmed with obvious delight.

"And to the vanquished!" Ian proclaimed. He picked me up and raised me high above his head, so that my own head was practically touching the ceiling. My robe parted and flared open as he did so, leaving the little triangle of my mound of Venus pointing directly at his lips. He pressed his face against me, burying himself, mustache and all, in the forest of my pubic hair, nibbling at the base of my overwrought vagina and inhaling deeply.

"Ah!" he exclaimed. "The smell of sport . . . the odor of battle!"

He grinned up at me, then deposited me gently back down on the floor. Just then the elevator door opened to admit us to a lavish suite, which must have been reserved only for the most important of VIPs. I had no way of knowing whether Ian qualified for that distinction or whether he simply had good connections inside the Polo Club, but I suspected the former. This in turn made me even more hopeful that he was the connection I was looking for.

But, frankly, at the moment I was not thinking much about my mission, such as it was. My blood had been stirred by the lush wrestling match with Nicole and by Ian's teasing foreplay in the elevator, and for the moment my only interest was in recreation and sexual release. And if I had had any doubts about whether or not this whole setup had been prearranged, they were now dispelled. The room had evidently been prepared with great care, for buckets of champagne were dotted discreetly about, and what amounted to a banquet of exotic food had been placed on a long table. Rose-filled vases were everywhere, and the whole room smelled deliciously of ginger-scented incense.

"A late addition to the club," Ian said when he saw me surveying the room. "Built under the personal—and private—specifications of Sir Anthony Whitcomb. Sir Tony was known to enjoy a little romp every now and again."

"Fuck Sir Tonee," Nicole said. "He eez dead, we are alive." She immediately stripped off her robe and walked over to one of the champagne buckets. In a few seconds she had the cork popping out and laughed madly as she poured the overflowing bubbly into her mouth. Then she looked at me.

"Come over here, *ma petite*," she said. "I want to congratulate you."

I walked over to her, shedding my robe as I went. Whatever she had in mind, I knew it would not call for clothing. Ian and Laslow followed me, and when I was standing in front of Nicole they drew close, forming a tight triangle around me.

"Zees is how zey do eet *en Amerique,* no?" Nicole said. "Ze bazeball players?" So saying, she poured the rest of the bottle of champagne over my head, leaving me sputtering and spitting in my suddenly chilled confusion.

But I didn't stay cold for long. Immediately Ian and Laslow both dropped to their knees and began to kiss and lick the cold champagne from my body. They each took one leg, mouthing their way up, slurping the dripping wine noisily and all the time stimulating my already fevered skin with the divine softness of their lips. At the same time Nicole bent over and began to apply the same treatment to my breasts, nuzzling them, softly sucking the wine from the surface, and incidentally rolling her tongue in marvelous little circles around the erect cherries of my nipples.

"Mmm . . ." I heard myself sigh. "*How delightful . . . keep it up, darlings . . .*"

Up and up Ian and Laslow went, their mouths like clinging barnacles on my excited flesh. Up and up, their practiced hands massaging the firm muscles of my calves as they planted their wet, sucking kisses on my trembling thighs. Up and ever up they went, teasing me unmercifully as all the while Nicole continued to work at my supple breasts, kneading the sensitive little nipples into an almost impossible hardness as I groaned and began to respond by moving my hips in well-oiled, erotic little circles.

"*That's it, love,*" I heard Ian say approvingly. "*Feel us . . . we're going to make love to you . . . all . . . night . . . long . . .*"

"Yes . . ." I cried. *"Yes . . . oh, that feels marvelous . . . so good . . . kiss me . . . touch me . . . don't stop . . . please don't stop . . ."*

"No, chérie . . ." Nicole whispered. *"No one eez stopping . . . ah, you are so beautiful . . . so beautiful . . . I love ze way you feel . . ."*

By now the two men had reached the tops of my thighs, their heads nearly colliding as they met at the "v" of my pussy. At that point Laslow quickly slid around behind me and began to nuzzle me just below the buttocks, leaving Ian to attend to the front part of my churning vagina. At almost exactly the same moment I felt both their tongues snake out, Ian's parting my tingling outer labia to run maddeningly along the length of my love-cord, while Laslow's began to explore delicately at the creamy mouth of my cunt.

Now Nicole sat down on top of Ian's shoulders and began to kiss me with great passion around the eyes, nose, and mouth, her lips grazing softly over my face while her hands rubbed and kneaded at my breasts. The three-way stimulation was almost more than I could handle—I could feel my knees go weak as I submitted myself wholeheartedly to the stroking of their tongues, their lips, their gentle fingers.

"Oh . . ." I groaned out. *"Oh, yes . . . that's just marvelous . . . yes . . . yes . . . lick my pussy, you two . . . kiss me, Nicole . . . rub my breasts . . . oh God, yes . . ."*

Responding to my heartfelt cries, Ian's tongue now began to work at me in earnest, the tip of it sliding back and forth along the full length of my aroused clitty as the honey from my vagina lubricated its way. The stirring sensations were radiating out from my pussy and screaming along the channels of my nervous system, building up a wonderful yet frustrating pressure in my steaming body which threatened to blow me apart. At the same time I felt Laslow's tongue snake into my hungry cunt from behind, parting the inner lips to flick and thrust at the welcoming walls inside, stirring its silken way into me until I thought I would lose all semblance of control. For her part, Nicole had pasted her mouth to one of my breasts like a sucker-fish to the belly of a whale, and now she rolled her tongue around it, taking occasional little nips with her teeth as well.

I could hardly keep from screaming. *"Yes . . ."* I urged them. *"Yes . . . use your tongues . . . use your mouth . . . eat me . . . suck me . . . bite me, Nicole . . . yes, darlings . . . oh, you're so good, all of you . . . I'm going to come soon . . . don't stop . . . don't stop . . ."*

I went on like that for what seemed like a very long time, babbling and mewling out my pleasure as they continued to work on me. My titillated senses could feel them all at once, but I would also distinguish the sensations one from another:

Ian's slinky tongue running up and down along my palpitating clitty, rubbing it, teasing it, caressing it, making it stand at attention . . .

Laslow's tongue, broadened like a spade inside me, lapping at the velvet, aching walls of my yearning cunt . . .

Nicole, my lovely giantess, her supple mouth fastened to one of my nipples while her educated fingers rolled and tweaked at the other . . .

They were timing their movements in unison now, each long stroke of Ian's tongue answered by a powerful thrust of Ian's, while Nicole's marvelous teasing of my nipples acted as a heady counterpoint. It was all I could do to remain on my feet, trembling like an aspen tree, my head thrown back, my eyes closed and my mouth open in a soundless scream. It was as if my entire body had become one raw nerve ending, one thoroughly stimulated sensory receptor, while my mind had shut off completely, allowing me to lose myself in this concert of desire.

"Yes . . . yes . . ." I groaned. "I'm going to come . . . I'm going to come . . . faster . . . harder . . . lick me . . . suck me . . . oh God, I'm going to come . . ."

With that, Ian buried his mouth even deeper into me, grabbing my clitty between his clenching lips and sucking at it with furious strength. Laslow added one finger, then another to the tongue that had worked its way up into my burning cunt, filling me delightfully and stirring madly at the yielding walls of my pussy. Nicole massaged my breasts with her powerful hands, squeezing them brutally until the pain melded with the other sensations screaming through my body to become pure, raw pleasure.

"Yes . . . yes . . . yes . . ." I panted. "Oh God, yes . . ."

A few seconds later I screamed out my orgasm, yelling out my release as the sensational climax surged through me. My pussy poured out its juices over the slaving faces of Ian and Laslow, whose tongues lapped up the copious oils greedily, like thirsty dogs at a desert water hole. I don't know how long my orgasm lasted in real time, but to me it felt like two days short of forever, and I basked in the delicious feeling, using their three bodies as support, until it finally faded and I grew calm again.

"Well!" I said just before I opened my eyes. "That was just magnificent. I wonder what I would have gotten if I had won."

I expected to hear a chorus of answering chuckles, or

at least some sort of droll comment from Nicole. But no one said a word. When I opened my eyes I saw why: The three of them had suddenly adjourned to the bed, leaving me alone to recover myself while they continued the party. Already they were rolling about the enormous fourposter, a mass of interlocked human flesh, giggling and tittering and wrestling like a bunch of kittens in a sandbox.

Still exhausted from their marvelous attentions, I was content merely to stand at the foot of the bed and watch—for the moment, at any rate. I have always found sex to be a fascinating spectator sport, and here, with these three major leaguers, I was being regaled with what amounted to a World Series and Super Bowl all wrapped into one.

But they would not let me remain a silent spectator for long. "Christina!" Nicole yelled after they broke from one of their three-way clinches. "Tell us what to do! Geeve us ordairs!"

The idea appealed to me greatly. Although I had once played a game somewhat similar to this with a past National Security Adviser and his mistress, I had never had such an obviously talented group at my disposal.

"All right," I said. "We'll start with something simple. A warmup."

"*Warm*up?" Ian cried. "Do we look like we're cold, for God's sake?"

"Insubordination!" I snapped, getting instantly into the spirit of the game. "For that I sentence you to stand and watch while Laslow fucks Nicole . . . in the back door!"

Ian's eyes went wide in mock horror. "Oh no!" he cried. "Anything but that!"

"All right then, quiet!" I ordered. "Keep your comments to yourself and do what I say!"

"Yes, commander," he said, trying to hide a slight grin. "Sorry."

"That's better," I said. "Now as I said, we'll start with a warmup. Nicole, jack them off. Both of them at the same time."

"Avec plaisir," she said, smiling broadly. The two men knelt in front of her on the bed, their enormous cocks pointed at her like a pair of cannon. She reached out and encircled first one, then the other with slender, grasping fingers, and began immediately to pump up and down on them with long, perfectly measured strokes.

"That's good, love," Ian murmured.

"Keep it up, Nicole," said Laslow, who was now rocking his hips back and forth in counterpoint to Nicole's languid stroking.

"All right!" I barked. "That's good! Now suck them, Nicole! First one, then the other. Keep your hands on them, too.

Nicole responded instantly, engulfing the head of Laslow's cock while she maintained a steady hand rhythm on Ian's. She worked her cheeks in and out several times as Laslow groaned with pleasure, then shifted to take Ian's enormous instrument in her mouth while she continued to pump her hand up and down on Laslow's. Both men now had their eyes closed and were moaning audibly, while Ian had his hands tangled in Nicole's lush blond hair. She went on like that for a few minutes, her head bobbing furiously as it switched back and forth from one massive cock to the other, her hands now flying along the two hardened shafts.

As for me, the sight of the two naked men being attended so expertly by Nicole was tantamount to putting a key in my sexual ignition and turning it. Almost unconsciously I found my one hand trailing down to cup and massage my breast, while the other reached between my legs to begin diddling at my reviving clitoris. The touch of my own hands, though not nearly as stimulating as the triple ministrations of my friends had been, was still more than adequate, and my eager pussy began once again to pour out the creamy juices that signaled my readiness.

"That's good . . ." I crooned as I continued to stroke myself, my eyes glued to the absorbing action on the bed. *"Keep it up, Nicole . . . good . . . good . . ."*

"What about me?" Nicole cried. "Zeez two, zey are getting everysing!"

"Equal rights," I said. "Absolutely." I thought for a moment, then hit on an idea. "Laslow," I said, "lie down on your back."

The smuggler reluctantly disengaged himself from Nicole's warm mouth and stretched himself out on the bed, his glistening cock standing up like a flagpole.

"Now, Nicole," I said, "sit down on him backwards. That way you can suck Ian's cock at the same time."

Nicole complied gladly. She arranged herself so that her buttocks were pointed toward Laslow's reclining head, then plunged her massive hips down on him, taking his cock into her with one long, smooth stroke. The sight of Laslow's gleaming prick disappearing inch by sweet inch into the tight confines of Nicole's clasping pussy nearly undid me, and I immediately sunk two fingers as deep as I could into my own vagina. When she closed her mouth over the head of Ian's penis, I had no choice but to add a third finger to the two which were already stirring in my moistened cunny.

"That's it, Nicole . . ." I heard Laslow whisper as the gorgeous amazon began to pump her hips up and down, her buttocks slapping softly against his abdomen. *"That's it . . . fuck me, Nicole . . . fuck me . . ."*

"Suck my cock, love," Ian was saying. "*That's right . . . just like that . . . I love to feel your mouth on me . . . just like that . . .*"

On and on she went, bucking up and down like a madwoman over Laslow's splayed-out body, at the same time plunging her mouth down over Ian's splendid cock. She was swaying like a seesaw—every time her hips rose to the top of her stroke she sunk her mouth down full length over Ian's penis, and every time she skewered her pussy down over Laslow's shaft, her mouth withdrew until just the head of Ian's prick was still buried inside. It was a tantalizing sight, and I spread my own legs farther, working my fingers with increasing fury in the warm insides of my vagina.

"All right," I said, laboring over the words and panting with exertion. "Let's change the tune. Ian, lie down next to Laslow. As close to him as you can get."

Ian did not look particularly happy to remove his cock from Nicole's oral embrace, but he complied, lying down on the bed and scooting over until he and Laslow were side by side.

"Good," I said. "Now Nicole, get up. Spread your legs so you're straddling both of them."

She pulled herself up off of Laslow's cock, causing him to groan at the sudden absence. Catching on immediately, she arranged her long legs so that she was effectively straddling both men—only a girl as tall as she could have done it, especially considering Ian's massive girth—and poised herself above them, her breasts heaving, a wicked grin playing about her mouth.

"Now, *fuck* them!" I commanded. "One at a time . . . back and forth . . . start slowly . . ."

She followed my orders like a loyal soldier, sinking herself down first on Laslow, then on Ian, moving slowly back and forth from one to the other, her hips rising and falling in perfect rhythm, without missing a stroke, as the two men groaned alternately.

"*Zees eez marvelous . . .*" Nicole groaned. "*Marvelous . . . like having two cocks at once . . .*"

"I'm glad you're enjoying it, darling," I said. "It may be marvelous for you, but I'm getting a bit lonely over here, you know?"

"The price of power," Ian said, grinning.

"Lonely at the top," Laslow agreed.

"Don't leesten to zees *fou,*" Nicole said. "Come ovair here and join me."

"Darling," I said, "that sounds like a marvelous suggestion."

Without further hesitation I walked over and climbed up on the bed. Nicole moved over for me, concentrating her efforts on Laslow and leaving Ian free for me. I immediately straddled him, taking his cock in my hand and pointing the head directly at my aching pussy.

"So," he said, that same insouciant grin still lighting his face. "We meet at last."

"That's right, darling," I said. "But don't forget, I'm still giving the orders here. And I order you to lie perfectly still."

"Yes, madame," he said, giving me a mock salute. "Your servant."

I kept myself poised above him, my knees on either side of his hips, my legs splayed wide. I kept a firm grip on his cock, now lowering myself sufficiently so that just the head of it came in contact with the damp flesh of my outer pussy-lips. I now started to move my hips in tiny spirals, so that the head of his cock rubbed madly against the elongated cord of my throbbing little clitty, sending divine little rushes of pleasure shooting through my body.

"Damn it!" Ian said. "You're driving me batty! Come down on me, will you?"

"All things come to he who waits," I said.

"Is that so?" he said. "Well, look at *them*. They're not doing any bloody waiting."

He was right. Next to us Nicole was thundering up and down, her firmly muscled buttocks slamming into Laslow's groin as he bucked madly up to meet her. His cock was appearing and disappearing at one-second intervals. It was covered with the shining cream of Nicole's desire and glimmered in the soft light.

The sight was too much for me. I had been driven half-mad by simply watching them in the first place, and now, with Ian's cock set at the ready to bury itself in my burning pussy, I could control myself no longer.

"All right, darling," I said. "Get ready, because here I come! And I want to feel that prick of yours all the way inside me!"

"Come on, then," Ian groaned. "I'll fill you up, all right."

With no further ado I began to skewer myself down onto Ian's magnificent shaft, screwing down on him in tight little circles, feeling the proud flesh of his cock ripple along the moistened walls of my vagina. Once I was fully down on him and my pussy had become accustomed to his girth, I began to rise and fall on him, thrusting myself down over him with ever-increasing strength and speed. Soon I was matching Nicole stroke for stroke, powering myself up and down the full length of Ian's marvelous cock, feeling it ripple and glide against the muscles of my yearning cunt.

"Move . . . move . . . move . . ." Ian chanted. *"That's it, lass . . . fuck me . . . move that sweet little twat of yours . . . move . . . move . . ."*

"Oh yes, darling . . ." I cried in response, punctu-

ating each downward thrust with another moan. *"Yes
. . . oh, it's so hard inside me . . . I love it . . . yes
. . . yes . . . it's so good . . ."*

Beside us Nicole and Laslow were driving at each
other as hard as they could, grunting and sweating and
thrashing on the slick satin sheets, Nicole's pussy fairly
vibrating in its haste and desire. Like Ian and myself,
they egged one another on with sharp little cries of
pleasure, with crazy, insensible words and passionate
endearments, spurring themselves toward the climax
that would ultimately quiet them both.

Soon I heard Nicole yelling out her orgasm and at
almost precisely the same moment Laslow grunted out
his own. I was grinding up and down on Ian with
greater and greater fervor, mashing my pussy down
onto the hard muscle of his groin, squealing like an
animal with the combination of pleasure and frustration.

Finally I leaned forward until I was on all fours, with
Ian underneath me. He raised his hips up in the air and
crashed into me with all his strength, again and again,
making me howl with desire.

"Yes . . . yes . . . yes . . ." I chanted. *"Oh, I'm
going to come . . . fuck me . . . fuck me . . ."*

"I'll fuck you, love . . ." he grunted out. *"I'll fuck
you . . . you feel this?"*

He reached back as far as he could coiling his hips
and then unleashing them in a pile-driving thrust into
my grateful pussy.

"Oh, yes . . ." I sobbed. *"Again . . . again . . .
keep fucking me, darling . . ."*

"Like this?" Again he withdrew from me almost
entirely, then slammed forward with all his strength.

*"Oh yes . . . that's it . . . that's it . . . again . . .
again . . . fuck me again . . . don't stop . . . don't
ever stop . . ."*

With his next stroke my orgasm exploded inside me, and I thrust myself back against him as hard as I could. He rose up to meet me, his groin now glued to the plane of my throbbing pussy, his hips rocking up against me like a runaway bulldozer, his cock spewing its own oily load into my receptive little quim. It seemed to me that we froze in that position, our genitalia fused together in the furnace of orgasm as waves of pure and powerful sensations washed over us.

When it was over I collapsed on top of him, my breasts crushed against his massive chest, my body weak with satisfaction.

CHAPTER ELEVEN

I awoke the next morning to the gentle but ominous sound of a door clicking shut. When I managed to pry my eyes open and look up, I saw that I was alone in the suite. The three of them—Laslow, Ian, and Nicole—had all disappeared, leaving me in essence no wiser, no further along the trail than I had been when I met Laslow in Thailand.

"Damn!" I said to myself. The realization that I was actually about to lose ground in my search was a great motivator, and in an instant I was out of bed, fully awake and alert. I rushed over to the window and looked down in the street, just in time to see a taxi dart away from the curb and blend into the traffic along the Pengkalan Weld. Luckily, I was able to get the name of the cab company and the number of the taxi before it disappeared from view.

Knowing that the cab was my only hope, I quickly called the company and sweet-talked the dispatcher into giving me the cab's destination. As I suspected, it was headed directly for the airport.

I made myself presentable in about thirty seconds flat, raced out into the street, and hailed another cab.

Twenty minutes later I was deposited at the airport—no ticket, no luggage, nothing but the sinking feeling that if I did not find the passenger of that cab Paul might well be lost to me forever.

Somehow the gods, or fate, or whoever controls such things was smiling on me that morning, for when I stepped inside the international terminal, the first thing I saw was Laslow standing at the head of a long ticket line for Singapore Airlines. I thought fast. Although all three of them had been in an equal hurry to escape me, it appeared that only Laslow was worried enough about me to leave the country altogether. My hunch—and I had no choice but to act on it—was that he himself was the one who had personal contact with Paul's "owner," and that he had placed Ian and Nicole Stenneck in my path simply to divert and distract me. In any case, even if I were wrong Ian and Nicole were nowhere to be seen, whereas at least I had Laslow where I could manage to keep an eye on him.

Still, it was going to be very important to me to get on the same plane with him without being seen. I waited until he bought his ticket, then hid myself in the crowd and followed him to his gate: Gate 31, a Singapore Airlines flight to Honolulu. Dashing back to the counter, I bought myself a first-class ticket on the same flight, knowing that on transoceanic flights first-class passengers boarded last, and that Laslow, preferring to remain as inconspicuous as possible, was probably flying coach.

I must have been right, because I was able to get on the plane and into my seat without being seen. Now all I had to worry about was pulling off the same trick when we deplaned.

The flight passed uneventfully, and the next thing I knew we were landing in Honolulu. I remained in my seat until all the coach passengers had deplaned, then exited, quickly spotting Laslow, and following him to the Aloha Airlines counter. A fast glance at the departures board showed me that their next plane was going to Maui, but that it would not leave for another forty-five-minutes.

On a hunch, I rushed over to the Hawaiian Airlines counter. Sure enough, they had a plane leaving for Maui in fifteen minutes. I bought a ticket, ran to the gate, and got there just in time to board. A half hour later I was on the ground in Maui, jingling the keys of a freshly rented Thunderbird, waiting for Laslow to show up.

A few minutes later the Aloha plane touched down. I kept a surreptitious eye on Laslow as he deplaned, following him to the passenger loading area. When a Rolls limo picked him up at the curb, I raced to my car and managed to get out of the lot in time to follow them, sure now that I was drawing within reach of the end of the trail.

The Rolls pulled out onto the highway and headed east, toward Hana and the lush, rainy side of the island. After three hours of driving along the waterfall-studded, cliff-rimmed highway—one of the most luxuriantly beautiful in the world—the Rolls pulled off on an unmarked dirt road that plunged mysteriously back into the deep jungle.

I parked and waited for a few minutes, then turned into the road myself. The Rolls had disappeared, but after a few twists and hairpin turns I came upon a sign that said:

WAIANAPANAPA RANCH

NO ADMITTANCE

TWENTY-FOUR HOUR ELECTRONIC SURVEILLANCE.

A few feet further up the road stood a twelve-foot chain link fence, its gate bristling with shiny boxes and bright little electric eyes.

Immediately my heart began to pound in my chest. This was it! I knew it! Somewhere behind that fence lived the man I was seeking, the man who had captured Paul so thoroughly and in the bargain had brought about such drastic changes in my own life. Now, I knew, it was only a matter of time.

I planned my approach carefully. First, I drove back down the dirt road to the highway, continuing on until I reached Hana, that tiny jewel of a town on the far eastern end of the island. There I bought a change of clothes, a painter's smock, some oils and an easel. After a quick lunch I got back in my car and headed back down the road toward the Waianapanapa Ranch.

I parked my car on the highway and walked back up the dirt road to the gate, knowing that from that point forward my every move was being monitored. I made a great show of staring at the gate, marching back and forth in front of it as though supremely frustrated, then shrugging and finally setting up my easel on the road itself.

I went about mixing my colors, concentrating on the emerald greens and chartreuses that predominated in this lush jungle setting, and for a few moments I was perfectly happy, perfectly at ease with myself. I had found no time to paint since I had embarked on this search of mine, and now I realized how much I missed it, how vital it was to my stability and peace of mind. With the first broad stroke of brush on canvas everything seemed to fall away from me, all the frantic scurrying and frustrating doubt of the quest, and as the first tree began to take shape on my canvas I felt in some strange way that I had come home.

As I expected, this happiness lasted only briefly, but it was so absorbing that I was not aware that I had company until I heard a voice behind me.

"Excuse me, miss," the voice said. "I'm going to have to ask you to come with me."

"Oh?" I said without turning around. "Why?"

"Let's not have a debate," the voice said. "Just come."

I put my brush down with exaggerated slowness, then turned to look at my captors. There were three of them, all huge, of course, and all men, but one of them had a face I found naggingly familiar. Even though I could not quite place him, I knew that I had met him somewhere, sometime, perhaps even in the course of my quest for Paul's boss.

"All right," I said, offering my hand daintily to the one I thought I knew, "let's go."

The Rolls was waiting on the other side of the gate, which now opened by remote control to admit us. We got in, turned around, and headed up the road. As we drove through the parting foliage, I tried to picture in my mind the man who I was finally about to meet, the man whose machinations had brought me so far and put me through so much. Yet try as I might, I could not conjure up an ogre or a monster.

A few minutes later my thoughts were interrupted when the Rolls glided through another gate, which clanged emphatically shut behind us. Now the scenery changed. Instead of driving through a choking jungle, we were now evidently on the grounds of a plantation, with pineapple fields sloping gently down the mountain to the left of us and an immense grove of papaya trees climbing the hill to the right. We drove through this agricultural splendor for another few minutes before the

Rolls turned off on a smaller road and passed through yet another gate.

When we finally came to a stop, it was at the apex of a long semicircular driveway. To say there was a house on the other side of the driveway would be something like saying that the Hope Diamond is a shiny rock, for this thing was truly magnificent—all hardwood and glass, with lean lines softened by the surrounding jungle, which seemed to be caressing it, inviting it to stay. A series of huge terraces climbed the house in gentle steps, and even from where I was standing I could tell that the view they afforded—of the massive Pacific, including the very tip of Kauai—would have satisfied the gods themselves. The house smelled wonderfully of money and power, but the rare thing about it was that it also emitted the unmistakable fragrance of sound taste.

"My," I said. "Quite a shack."

"We like it," my chief captor said.

I was quickly ushered inside, through flagstone hallways paneled in gleaming rosewood, past wonderfully designed atria in which the jungle had been allowed to grow unmolested, past an indoor waterfall that splashed peacefully into a rock-studded pool, past an enormous courtyard in which hundreds of tropical birds fluttered and sang, and finally into a huge sitting room in which the promise of spectacular views of ocean and island were fulfilled beyond my wildest expectations.

"Wait here," the errand boy said. "Someone will be with you in a minute."

I heard the door close behind me, and then I walked slowly over to the enormous window. I should have been nervous, I suppose, or happy that my search was over, or afraid for my own safety. I should also have felt closer than ever to Paul. But in fact I felt none of those things. I think that long and wonderful vista—

manicured field giving way to the chaos of jungle, which in turn plunged riotously down the mountainside toward the arms of the waiting ocean—washed all feeling away from me, leaving me with nothing but a mild, imperishable curiosity about the identity of the man I was about to meet.

Finally I heard the door open and close behind me, heard a soft voice saying, "Hello, Christina. It's nice to see you again."

At the sound of the word *again* I wheeled in my tracks, turning toward that voice which sounded so strangely familiar. When I finally turned around, it was to face that same blond Adonis who had first set me on this long and arduous road, the only man I had ever met whose first reaction to me was sheer rejection.

It was Snider, of course, Leonard Snider, the "lawyer," the gorgeous young reprobate whose advice had nearly done me in.

"So it's you," I said, feeling a bit like the astonished heroine of some B-movie. "I guess I should have known."

"Not necessarily," he said. "I did go to some trouble to keep my tracks covered, you know."

"You almost killed me," I told him, remembering how I had been abducted by Touby.

"Never intentionally," he said. "I would never have done that, not to you."

Now I *was* truly astonished. I took a long look into his eyes and found nothing there but sincerity—sincerity and something else, something deeper, something that both disturbed and excited me.

"Why not to me?" I said.

"Come out on the terrace," he said. "I want to show you something."

I nodded, somehow feeling no fear even though the rational part of my brain was bleating that he might mean to throw me over the edge. He led me outside. I saw immediately that there was an easel set up on the far end of the terrace, and I turned back to him questioningly.

"Go ahead," he said. "Take a look."

I walked down to the other end of the terrace, took the easel and turned it so that the canvas was facing me. Once I had turned it around I almost had to look again to make sure that it was not a mirror, for I was face to face . . . with myself! It was a portrait of me, a reclining nude, so faithfully rendered that I thought my eyes were playing tricks on me, yet so cleverly and insightfully done that I thought I could distinguish at least a half dozen distinct attitudes and personalities. The Christina who looked back at me from that portrait was all the Christinas I had ever been, and it would not have surprised me if it also contained a few Christinas that I was about to become. All in all the effect was thrilling, breathtaking.

"It's unbelievable," I said. "Who did it?"

"I did."

I turned back to him. "I guess this is the part," I said, "where the flabbergasted lady stammers 'Who?' 'why?' "

"That should be obvious," Snider said. "I'm in love with you."

"You have a strange way of showing it."

"I never claimed to be straightforward."

For the first time in longer than I could remember, I found myself at a loss for words. There was no doubting his sincerity, and certainly no doubt that he always held a certain attraction for me. But in his case I had the curious feeling that I could *decide* whether or not to fall in love, and knowing that made my decision for me. With Paul, there had been no element of choice, no decision to make—I had been his, almost helplessly so, from the beginning, and could not have felt otherwise. It was that lack of control, that surrender on my part, that made my love for Paul so special and unique in a life whose whole history had been one of command and self-possession. And it was that, I knew, that would someday return me to his arms.

Still, I knew that Snider's love could be extremely useful to me, and if I ever expected to wrest Paul's contract from him, this love of his could be my strongest ally. As he moved toward me, his eyes boring into mine, I realized that this was my trump card, and I had to play it to the hilt. And I also knew from experience that feeling sexy for Snyder would be no trouble at all.

Now he stood in front of me, his hands on my shoulders, a slight smile playing about his lips.

"Do you understand?" he said.

"No," I answered. "But it doesn't matter."

His hands felt as if they were on fire, burning through the cloth of my blouse and singeing the smooth skin beneath. Somehow their warmth and urgency were being transferred to me, beamed down into my flesh and injected into my bloodstream to radiate through my awakening body, warming me, arousing the first faint stirrings of desire. Now he reached for my blouse and began unbuttoning it with sure, steady hands.

I closed my eyes and leaned my head back, offering myself to him, my breath catching in my throat as my blouse fell away from me and my breasts lay exposed to the warm air and the heat of his gaze. His hands moved steadily up my belly, which shivered involuntarily with the stimulation of his touch, until finally they came to rest just under the smooth mounds of my breasts, cupping them and lifting them up toward his face. He planted a quick kiss on each of the nipples as I moaned my approval, then kissed me softly, teasingly on the lips, his tongue gently caressing the underside of each one.

"Mmm . . ." I purred. *"That feels lovely . . ."*

"Take off the rest of your clothes," he said. "But keep your eyes closed. There's something I want to do."

I did as he asked, quickly stepping out of my jeans and panties, keeping my eyes tightly shut all the while. I heard his footsteps as he walked to the other end of the terrace, then returned.

"All right," he said. "You can open your eyes."

He had brought his palette, onto which he now dabbed a series of colors, swirling each one until it reached the proper consistency. I could see that he was a master at mixing his colors, for his blues shined like cobalt, while his reds and yellows had a dusty quality that seemed to catch perfectly the spirit of the tropical heat. His green was like something I had never seen before, as if his paints had managed to capture the secret of photosynthesis itself and in so doing had turned themselves to pure chlorophyll.

"Beautiful colors," I said. "But surely you're not going to paint another portrait . . ."

"I've already painted your portrait," he said. "Now I'm going to paint *you.*"

With that he dabbed his brush in blue, then extended it until it was pointing at my breast like a softened arrow. I watched in fascination as it drew closer and closer, then smiled shyly as it touched the skin of my breast, the little hairs feeling like so many feathers as it rested there. Then the brush was moving, outlining my aureole in that mysterious, gleaming blue, making the deep brown-red of the nipple stand out in a bright and engaging contrast. At the same time, the touch of the

brush and the smooth viscosity of the paint as it spread
over my skin were like a miniature massage, sounding a
sensual alarm that now rang out insistently through my
sensitized body.

"That's nice . . ." I murmured. *"So smooth . . . I
feel like a piece of porcelain . . ."*

"Pure Dresden," he said, smiling at the metaphor.
"Let me do the other one now."

He dabbed his brush in blue again, then drew a
matching circle around the aureole of my other breast as
I shuddered with delight at the touch. Now the two
nipples stood out like the twin bull's-eyes of some
erotic target, and I quickly moved the arrows of my
fingers up to touch them, to roll and tweak them enticingly
between fingers and thumbs. The little berries responded
instantly, jutting out proudly and hardening against the
skin of my fingers.

"Here now," he said. "That's supposed to be my
job."

"Fine . . ." I said, smiling at him. *"Go ahead . . .
touch me . . . see how they want you? . . . they're all
hard, ready for you . . . go ahead . . ."*

I dropped my fingers and moved closer to him, thrusting out the nipples so that they made a silent demand to
his waiting fingers. He responded immediately, pushing
at the hardened berries with his thumbs and then letting
them pop out again, now stiffer and more alive than
ever. The maneuver was like applying two hot prods to
my already searing flesh, and I groaned out my insistent
yearning in a hoarse, throaty voice.

*"Beautiful . . . beautiful . . . oh, I love the way
you touch me . . . your fingers are so soft, so hot . . .
I love it . . ."*

Now he reached for his brush again, dipping it this
time in the hazy yellow that reminded me so much of

the color of the noontime sun. Reaching out for my breasts again, he painted two larger circles around the blue ones he had already done, an imitation of the line of the sun striking the ocean's horizon. Each new stroke of the brush on the tender skin of my breasts was like an army of tiny fingers massaging me, caressing me, rubbing me, stoking the internal flame of my desire as surely and as hotly as a bellows.

"My God . . ." I cried out. *"Your touch is incredible . . . I'm on fire . . . my breasts . . . my nipples . . . take them . . . touch them . . . oh, please . . . touch me again . . . again . . . yes . . . yes . . ."*

He took out a broader brush, smeared it with his dusty red, and in one graceful swooping motion painted another circle, this one at the base of my breast.

"Like this?" he said.

"Yes . . ." I moaned. *"Yes . . . like that . . . touch me, darling . . . paint me . . . oh God, you're driving me crazy . . ."*

Now he painted a matching red circle around the base of the other breast.

"Like this?" he said. "You like it like this? You like to have my brush touch your beautiful breasts?"

"Darling . . ." I panted. *"You know I do . . . I love it, darling . . . the only thing is . . ."*

"Yes?" he said, looking up at me in surprise. "What's wrong, Christina?"

"It's not fair . . ." I said. *"It's just not fair . . . you're having all the fun . . ."*

"What do you mean? Don't you like what I'm doing to you? You want me to stop?"

"No, darling . . . no . . . please don't stop . . but I want to paint you too . . ."

"Ah!" he said, now breaking into a broad smile.

"Of course! Here, take a brush. We can use the same palette if you don't mind."

I didn't mind. In fact, I had been hoping that he would let me use those wonderful, subtle colors of his. I took one of his brushes and dipped it in the vibrant green he had mixed, watching impatiently as he pulled his shirt off over his head.

"All of it!" I said. *"I want you to be as naked as I am, darling . . ."*

He gave me a little smile, then slipped the rest of his clothes off. His body, which I still remembered so well from that engaging little soiree on his Santa Ynez ranch, was just as gorgeous as ever, his muscles—which were masculine without being grotesquely overdeveloped— gleaming softly in the afternoon sunlight. His delightful cock was already half hard, jutting out at a perfect right angle from the rest of his body.

"How's this?" he said.

"Perfect, darling . . ." I cooed. *"God, what a magnificent body . . ."*

"It's all yours, Christina."

"Wonderful . . ." I said. *"Then let me get to work . . ."*

I started at his shoulders, painting a thin green line from the peak of them, up along the ridge of his collarbone to the base of his neck, which I then accented with a semicircle before completing the line on the other shoulder. When I was finished I leaned over, took one of his nipples in my mouth, and gave it a sharp twist with my teeth. His eyes lit up immediately.

"You like my technique, darling?" I said, nibbling up his broad chest to plant a sucking, wrenching kiss on the sensitive skin of his throat.

"Does this answer your question?" he said. He took his brush and painted a sweeping line that started between my breasts, then plunged down over my belly to softly encircle the little indented button of my navel.

"Mmm . . ." I said as the tickling motion of the brush and the smooth slickness of the paint combined to give a booster charge to my sexual batteries. *"Marvelous . . ."* I was sweating with excitement now, surveying his magnificent body with hungry eyes. *"All right, darling . . ."* I said. *"Here's a new stroke . . . see if you like this one . . ."*

I knelt down a bit, took my brush and began to draw a squiggly line, starting at his knees and moving up the insides of his thighs to the base of his testicles, which I then outlined in a few quick, bold strokes, at the same time running a carelessly contrived fingernail along the receptive skin. I noticed with some satisfaction that his cock was now fully erect, standing out at a 45-degree angle from his groin, cutting the air in front of him like a Turkish scimitar.

"Do you like that, darling?" I whispered. "Does that feel good to you?"

"You know it does . . ." he said. His eyes were literally shining now, the desire radiating out from them as if from some internal searchlight. The powerful muscles of his body, which had been relaxed, almost languorous a few moments before, were now tensed in anticipation, and I knew that we would not be able to tease each other this way much longer. Still, the body painting was such a delightfully unique interlude that I had no desire to rush it.

"Let's fill in the blanks, darling . . ." I said. "Let's take a colorbath."

"Good idea . . ." he said.

We each dipped our brushes in paint and began to go to work, each inundating the other in wild splashes of colors, as befitted our growing passion. We concen-

trated on the unpainted areas of one another's bodies—
the chests filled in with swirls of brilliant red and
yellow, the bellies in his deep, earthy greens with
borders of orange, the legs a stout blue. His brush
seemed to come alive, to acquire a will of its own, and
each graceful stroke was like a swath of pure sensation
tingling up my thighs, my breasts, my trembling belly.
In between strokes his head would dart in to take
tantalizing little licks at my nipples, then follow the
trail of his brush down, down over the vibrant flesh of
my torso, my belly and groin, until it lodged in the warm
and secret valley of my throbbing clit. Then, after one
scintillating swipe of his tongue along the length of my
erect love-cord, he would be on his feet again, transfer-
ring the fire of his arousal to his magical brush.

"Yes, darling . . ." I encouraged him. *"Don't stop
. . . touch me . . . paint me . . . oh God, lover,
you're so good . . . so good . . ."*

"Turn around, Christina," he said hoarsely.

I turned my back to him. Immediately he began to
apply his talents to my back and shoulders, and I
leaned against his brush like a cat on a scratching post,
writhing up and down, adding the natural lines of my
feline body movement to his own improvised strokes. At
the same time I began to do some self-exploration,
prodding at the swollen outer lips of my pussy with
eager fingers, parting the labia and running my fingertips lightly along the hot little ridge of my clitoris,
groaning out loud with the pure delight of the contact.

"Oh God . . ." I panted. *"I'm so hot . . . I want
you so much . . . hurry . . . hurry . . . I can't take
much more of this teasing . . . please, darling . . . I
want you to fuck me . . ."*

"Yes, Christina . . ." he gasped. *"I want you too
. . . here, finish me off . . . hurry . . ."*

I turned around again and set my brush to his back, quickly painting a series of accents along the rippling muscles, then filling in with streaks of pure color. He trembled and quivered at the touch of my brush, a combination of impatience and pure longing, his buttocks clenching and unclenching with the power of his need.

"All right, darling," I whispered finally. "I'm finished." I stood back to admire my work. "You look gorgeous," I said.

"Let's go see," he said.

He took my hand and led me back inside, to a room that was floor-to-ceiling mirrors and wall-to-wall mattresses. The sight that greeted us in the mirrors was truly awe-inspiring: Two naked savages we were, gods of the Trobriand Islands, our bodies so lush with color and swirling design that we looked ready for the sexual warpath. The room of mirrors multiplied us infinitely, spraying our dual images through planes of space so that we looked like a gaudy Adam and Eve who had somehow cloned ourselves to repopulate the earth with our own flashing bodies.

Then I felt Snider's hand on my shoulder, turning me slowly toward him. His face was flushed and gleaming, radiating the strength of his desire.

"*I want you, Christina . . .*" he said. "*Let's make a collage . . .*"

"*Oh yes, darling . . .*" I cried. "*Hold me, my love . . . I want to feel your body against me . . .*"

I fell against him, feeling his arms lock themselves around me in a sweet-strong embrace. The still wet paint on our bodies now became a slick and oozing coat that lubricated our contact like some exotic oil, allowing us to slide freely along the full length of one another's bodies as we rubbed and nuzzled like two bears in heat. As I looked over his shoulder the mirrors showed us from every possible angle: my hand trailing streaks of color across his back . . . my painted buttocks sliding up and down as I rubbed myself against him . . . his gleaming muscles undulating as if some tribe of gaily colored snakes had found a home beneath his skin . . . our fused thighs . . . our churning hips . . .

"Can you see, darling . . ." I whispered in his ear. *"Can you see how beautiful we are? . . ."*

"I always knew it . . ." he said. *"I've wanted you like this since the first time I saw you . . ."*

"Then take me, darling . . ." I sighed. *"Take me . . . make love to me . . . fuck me . . . I want you inside me, darling . . . now!"*

I put my arms on his shoulders to brace myself, then threw my legs around him and began to shimmy up his body. At the same time he put his hands beneath my buttocks and helped hoist me up, dipping down just slightly so that his cock lodged in the dripping valley of my warm crotch. I reached down with one hand to place the head of his prick at the entrance of my dilated pussy, then held myself still in that position for one long, ecstatic, frozen moment.

"You want me? . . ." I teased. *"You want to feel my pussy wrap itself around you? . . ."*

"You know I do . . ." he gasped. *"Don't tease me like this, Christina . . . come down on me . . . take my cock inside you . . . fuck me, Christina . . . fuck me . . ."*

"Like this?" I said. I wiggled my hips in two tight little circles, feeling the very tip of his cock part my pussy-lips.

"Like that . . ." he moaned. *"But more . . . more . . ."*

"Like this?" I wiggled again so that the whole head popped inside me, rubbing deliciously against the walls at the entrance to my cunt.

"More . . ." he groaned again. "More . . . I want to be deep inside you, Christina . . . deep inside . . ."

"How deep?" I said, wriggling down another inch or so. "Like this?"

"Deeper . . . goddamn it, deeper . . ."

Another inch. "Like this?"

"Christina, please . . ." He was practically begging now. "Please, no more of this . . . take me inside you, Christina . . ."

Finally I could stand it no longer. My teasing had had just as much effect on me as on him, and now my partly filled pussy was aching palpably, the little muscles along the walls beginning to ripple of thier own accord. There could be no more of this love-play—I had to have him filling me, stretching me, plunging into me, and it had to be now!

"Now!" I screamed. With one long, silken stroke I lowered myself down on him, feeling his delectable cock push its way up, up into the warm and secret confines of my eager cunt. His prick was a perfect fit, the hard flesh of it snuggling tightly against my clasping pussy walls, filling me, stirring me, igniting my grateful vagina with its heavenly friction.

"Yes, Christina . . ." he groaned. "That's it . . . I want you to feel me . . . feel me inside you . . . I want my cock buried in your sweet pussy . . ."

"Yes, darling . . ." I answered, now beginning to move my hips slowly up and down, feeling the warm flesh of his cock slide in and out of me with long and tantalizing strokes. "I'm going to fuck you, my love . . . I'm going to fuck you like this . . . nice and easy . . . slow and easy . . . you feel me, darling? . . .

you feel me around you? . . . feel my pussy sheathing your sweet cock? . . .''

"Oh God . . ." he gasped. "Yes . . . yes . . . *you feel so good, Christina . . . I love it inside you . . .''*

He now began to move inside me, his cock driving up into my creamy pussy like a piston at slow idle. I rose up and snaked down on him, timing the slithering movement of my hips so that I met him thrust for thrust. At the same time I looked over his shoulders into the mirrors that surrounded us, watching in rapt fascination as our two bodies became one multicolored, churning beast, grinding out our dance of lust, pumping and mashing ourselves against one another until we became one synchronized mass of heaving, straining muscle.

"Can you see us, darling?" I panted. *"Can you see how beautiful we are?"*

"Beautiful . . ." he repeated. *"God, but I love to fuck you . . . I love to feel your tight little pussy clinging to my cock . . . yes, Christina . . . yes . . . don't stop, my love . . . don't ever stop . . .''*

Now he began to increase the tempo, driving into me with a steady power that was setting my insides on fire. For my part, I plunged up and down on him with increasing strength, my hips undulating in frantic little circles so that his cock stirred inside me, pushing me, heating me, making my whole body quake with the fury of my passion. All around us the mirrors did their work, showing me a hundred thrashing bodies from a thousand titillating angles, a symphony of arms and legs, hips and buttocks, a concerto of vibrant, blending color, a dance of the wild, of untrammeled and unending passion.

"Darling . . ." I cried as the familiar sensations

began to build inside me. *"I'm going to come, lover . . . fuck me . . . fuck me . . . make me come . . ."*

"With me . . ." he grunted. *"Come with me . . ."* He was plowing into me with all his strength now, bucking and heaving like a maddened bull, his cock pounding into me with all the force of a jackhammer. And my body was equal to the challenge, my ass pumping up and down like a steam-driven turbine, my hips wiggling and vibrating, my pussy a blur of oscillating movement.

Then it hit me. *"Yes!"* I screamed. *"Yes! Yes! Yes! I'm coming, lover . . . oh God, I'm coming!"*

He took his hands and spread my ass-cheeks as wide as they would go, all the time hammering into me with all his strength, his groin locked against my throbbing clitty. On and on he went, his cock spewing out his creamy load in great spurts, his teeth sinking into the soft flesh of my shoulder as wave after wave of magnificent climax washed over my heaving body.

Finally it was over. He loosened his grip on me, leaving us to sink back exhausted on the satin-covered mattresses. The body paint had mixed with our own sweat, had streaked and run until we looked like a finger painter's nightmare, or one of those collages on butcher paper done by a pack of undisciplined five-year-olds. There was only one possible reaction to the sight of us lying there in a smudged, played-out heap: I laughed until my sides ached.

"What's so funny?" Snider asked when I finally calmed down somewhat.

"I can't help thinking," I said. "I've spent half a fortune trying to find you, you've spent the other half trying to keep me from finding you, and now here we are—two kids in a mud puddle . . . and . . .

I burst out laughing again.

"And what?" he said.

"We can't even afford a bath!"

I spent the next several days rolling about with Snider in what amounted to a virtual sex-fest. We took each other's bodies in every way imaginable, in every position and in most of the accessible orifices. When we grew tired of making love in his palatial home, we moved outdoors—to the papaya groves, to the black sand beaches, and one glorious afternoon to the pools formed by those unearthly waterfalls known as the Seven Veils.

Although I had no trouble whatsoever enjoying this vast erotic picnic, it was still essentially calculated on my part. I had learned long ago that the way to a man's heart is not through his stomach, but through a route that was decidedly more southerly. Even the most powerful and ruthless of men, I had discovered, could be turned into purring pussycats in the aftermath of a lush fuck. It was as if all their power, all their ambition and reach, were little more than the parrying and thrusting of an unsatisfied cock, and, once satisfied, that instrument could be put aside and the gratitude of its owner used for the purposes of she who had done the satisfying.

This, of course, is what I had had in mind all along. When, after the fourth day of our private little orgy, I felt him sufficiently tamed, I made my move. We were sitting on the terrace, looking out at the ocean and sipping a delicious guava liqueur, and somehow the combination of sun, sea, and satisfying sex seemed just right for what I hoped would be our final dialogue.

"Leonard," I said, "this really has been wonderful, you know . . ."

"This sounds like the beginning of a goodbye speech,"

he said. He didn't move a muscle, just continued staring out at the golden Pacific.

"I suppose it is," I said. "I don't want to be overly dramatic about it, but I think the time has come."

"You won't stay, then," he said.

" 'Won't' is the wrong word, darling," I said. "The right word is can't."

"Oh, come on, Christina," he said. "You can do anything you damn well please, and you know it. If you want to stay here with me, you can."

"I suppose that's true," I admitted. I could have argued, could have made up some plausible lies about being needed at *World*, but I knew he would see through them. Besides, I somehow felt I owed this man something more by way of a goodbye than a series of lame excuses. If nothing else, I at least owed him honesty.

"You'll go back to Paul, then," he said after a few moment's silence.

"I don't know," I replied. "I really don't know whether or not he wants me. I don't know whether or not he's in a *position* to want me."

Snider completely ignored this rather pointed reference to Paul's contract. "Who wouldn't want you?" he said, with just a trace of bitterness.

For some reason, in that moment my heart went out to him. I reached out and took his hand. "Thank you, darling," I said. "I mean that."

Suddenly his hand clenched mine in a grip so strong as to be painful. When I cried out, he only gripped me that much tighter.

"I could force you to stay," he said. "With no trouble at all."

"You mean you could keep me prisoner," I said, clenching my teeth against the pain of his grip. "Is that what you really want?"

"You never know," he said. Finally he released my hand. "Leave me alone for a while," he said. "I think I want this sunset to myself."

Without another word I turned and walked into the house, knowing that it would be wrong, and possibly dangerous, to crowd him at this moment. The problem, of course, was that I really had no idea where I stood. I was already his captive, in a sense, and even though I knew I could escape if I put my mind to it, I also knew that the world was not big enough to hide from him. If he were to be mean and vengeful, he could make life very difficult for me.

I walked through the house, lost in thought, until almost by chance I came upon my own bedroom. When I walked in the door, I saw a sheaf of papers lying on the bed, looking almost comically out of place in this spot where Snider and I had so recently rolled like colts. My heart skipped a beat. I went to the bed and picked up the papers, knowing without looking that I was holding Paul's contract in my hands. I trembled to realize that my search, the search that had taken me around the world and had occupied all my thoughts and feelings for so long, was finally over.

When I looked down at the sheaf of documents, I saw that there was a hand-written note clipped to the front of them. The note, of course, was from Snider.

Dear Christina, (it said)
I know this is what you've been looking for. I know also that you don't love me, although you put up a brave show (made a brave try?) at it. If nothing else, I appreciate your talent. Anyway, this thing is yours now—I was probably wrong to sign Paul to it in the first place, and almost certainly wrong to make you chase me around the world trying to

find it. I guess I thought that once I got you here I could make you forget this guy. I see now that I was wrong there too.

So take it and go back to Paul. And when you see him, by the way, tell him for me to stick with mime. The poor bastard can't act worth a damn.

Love,
Leonard

I read the note three more times, realizing as I did that Snider must have written it before our little scene on the terrace. So he had already made up his mind, and his threats on the terrace had simply been a reminder of the degree of sacrifice he felt himself to be making in letting me go. Once again, my heart went out to him.

But in an instant my heart changed direction, and went beaming out across the ocean to Paul. The message it bore, the message it had always borne, was that I was ready for him if he could prove beyond a doubt that he was ready for me. In my eagerness, I almost tore up the contract then and there. But that pleasure, I realized, should be reserved for Paul himself.

In the way of reserved pleasures, it would be the first of many. . . .

BESTSELLING FICTION FROM ARROW

All these books are available from your bookshop or newsagent or you can order them direct. Just tick the titles you want and complete the form below.

	Title	Author	Price
☐	ALBATROSS	Evelyn Anthony	£1.75
☐	1985	Anthony Burgess	£1.75
☐	THE BILLION DOLLAR KILLING	Paul Erdman	£1.75
☐	THE YEAR OF THE FRENCH	Thomas Flanagan	£2.50
☐	EMMA SPARROW	Marie Joseph	£1.75
☐	COCKPIT	Jerzy Kosinski	£1.60
☐	CITY OF THE DEAD	Herbert Lieberman	£1.75
☐	STRUMPET CITY	James Plunkett	£2.50
☐	TO GLORY WE STEER	Alexander Kent	£1.95
☐	TORPEDO RUN	Douglas Reeman	£1.95
☐	THE BEST MAN TO DIE	Ruth Rendell	£1.75
☐	SCENT OF FEAR	Margaret Yorke	£1.25
☐	2001: A SPACE ODYSSEY	Arthur C. Clarke	£1.75
☐	THE RUNNING YEARS	Claire Rayner	£2.75
☐	HESTER DARK	Emma Blair	£1.95

Postage ____

Total ____

ARROW BOOKS, BOOKSERVICE BY POST, PO BOX 29, DOUGLAS, ISLE OF MAN, BRITISH ISLES

Please enclose a cheque or postal order made out to Arrow Books Limited for the amount due including 15p per book for postage and packing for orders both within the UK and overseas.

Please print clearly

NAME ....

ADDRESS ....

....

Whilst every effort is made to keep prices down and to keep popular books in print, Arrow Books cannot guarantee that prices will be the same as those advertised here or that the books will be available.